$2

7/17

D1593962

His life was over, but maybe someone could finish the mission for him...if he could get there in time.

This is what he would miss most, he thought as he continued to drive. Those Saturday jogs with his friend. *Guess I do love her, just not in the same way.* He wondered if he should have told her the truth, but it was too late now.

The pain in his right leg from his torn Achilles ached as he pressed the gas pedal, entering the on-ramp to the freeway. He didn't have much time left so he stomped on the pedal despite the pain. It wouldn't last long.

Funny how things happen for a reason he thought. Only one year of Med School but it was long enough to recognize how injured he truly was. That whole first year was spent studying the human body and the placement of the organs. He was good at remembering the Latin word origins for their names and how they worked. He also learned how important some were versus others especially at times of injury. In his case the hole in his stomach was a death sentence. It was just a matter of time, and not that much. From what he remembered, he figured he had about thirty minutes left and it would take him twenty to get to where he was going. That was if he obeyed the speed limit.

Secret Service Agent Jack Shields has a secret...He's not really Jack Shields.

Down and out bouncer, John Ryan, finally had a good night at the track. It'll buy him some time from the various mobs he owes. Before the night is done, his luck will really change when he gets an offer he can't refuse—to be Jack Shields.

He'll need help pulling it off, especially since the bank CEOs he's supposed to be protecting are being targeted for execution. If he can't, the only question is—what will come to an end sooner, his secret or his life?

KUDOS for *Secret Service*

In Secret Service by Mark Petry, Jack Shields, a secret service agent, is dying. Unwilling to leave a personal mission unfinished, he contacts his long-lost twin brother and convinces him to switch places. So John becomes Jack and tries to assume his life, while Jack dies as John. A bit convoluted? Yeah, it is, but John pulls it off very well. At least after he learns some secrets about his brother. The story is clever and intriguing, and the author shows a good understanding of the problems inherent in trying to pass yourself off as someone else. Even someone who looks just like you. The plot has some good twists and turns that will keep you reading well into the night. ~ *Taylor Jones, Reviewer*

Secret Service by Mark Petry revolves around a down and out con man and gambler, John Ryan, who is heavily in debt to the mob. He has a good night at the track and wins enough to buy himself some time. Then his twin brother shows up with an offer he can't refuse. Keep the money and become his dying twin brother. John accepts and the fun begins, but John has no idea what he is getting into. I really enjoyed the book. The characters are charming and well developed. And even though the plot is not unique, it does have some fresh twists to it that make it seem brand new with enough surprises that the book is hard to put down. ~ *Regan Murphy, Reviewer*

ACKNOWLEDGEMENTS

I'd like to thank all the people that made this book possible. I'll do so as in the movies, by order of appearance. First I'll thank my parents who, on a modest income, were still able to send my brother and I to Germany every summer. The long flights from Texas to Germany nurtured my imagination.

Thanks to my wife and daughter for allowing me time to write and inspiring me to do it well. Thanks to my SMU creative writing instructors, Suzanne Frank and Amanda Alvarez, whose classes encouraged me to take my writing more seriously. Thanks to the brave souls who dared to read my truly rough first draft and provide much needed feedback, David Baskin, Sharla Parker, Todd Hanke and Janie Hagar.

Huge thanks to Lauri Wellington, acquisitions editor for Black Opal Books, for seeing potential in that rough draft. Thanks to Black Opal editors Cora and Faith for sparing no red ink in fixing that draft.

Thanks to Kevin Harger for turning my "HORRIBLE" (in my daughter's brutally honest opinion) stick figure art (see below) into an amazing cover. Finally *thank you* for buying Secret Service.

SECRET SERVICE

MARK PETRY

A Black Opal Books Publication

GENRE: MYSTERY-DETECTIVE/THRILLER/WOMEN'S FICTION

SECRET SERVICE
Copyright © 2015 by Mark Petry
Cover Design by Kevin Harger
All cover art copyright © 2015
All Rights Reserved
Print ISBN: 978-1-626942-51-6

First Publication: APRIL 2015

Published by Black Opal Books **http://www.blackopalbooks.com**

DEDICATION

For the two most beautiful girls in my life,
My wife Becky and our daughter Kayla

I believe that banking institutions are more dangerous to our liberties than standing armies. ~ *Thomas Jefferson*

PROLOGUE

It's just like riding a bike," he whispered to himself. It had been a while since he had last assembled a bomb. A little shaky, like someone who hadn't ridden one in a while, he steadied himself quickly as muscle memory took over. The consequences, had he not, would have been quite a bit worse than a simple scraped knee or elbow. But after all, he had been the Lance Armstrong of bomb-making at one point in his life.

"This'll fix it," he said. Admiring his work, he placed the detonator on the device and backed away, not considering the irony of his statement.

CHAPTER 1

John Ryan's heart raced faster than the horses rounding the track. He inhaled and exhaled, almost to the point of hyperventilating between each kick of dirt. They were a quarter of the way around the track and his number three, a filly named Iron Lady, was boxed in so tight by a couple of colts that she could have filed for sexual harassment. The betting magazine, rolled tightly in his hand, began to bruise his leg as he struck it at least as often and, perhaps, even harder than the jockey whipping his Lady. Normally, John wouldn't stand for a man hitting a female, but this was different by a stretch. Now that stretch was a half mile and it wasn't looking good. The bruising he would receive later would be much worse if she didn't respond.

The crowd stood as the horses rounded the first turn toward the backstretch, the sound of their hooves like rolling thunder. The lights surrounding the track shone off their sleek hides, flickering like the lightning in the distance, as their muscles flexed and stretched. He could already smell rain in the air, mixed up with the dust storm rising from the track, making its way up the outdoor stands.

"I told you to take Thunder Clap!" Charlie yelled, slapping John on the shoulder as the colt he'd bet on took the lead.

"It isn't over yet, Charlie," John said calmly.

Charlie shook his head in disapproval. "You should've listened to me."

"Do I ever?"

"Guess not," Charlie replied.

As the horses raced down the backstretch, the two colts boxing in Iron Lady began to separate as Thunder Clap accelerated.

The other colt couldn't keep up, leaving enough space for Iron Lady to slip into second.

"Told you it wasn't over yet!" John yelled as he tensed the large muscles in his arms with anticipation.

"You bet on the filly? Boy, you *are* desperate. What was she, like twenty to one?" Charlie said, almost chuckling.

"Thirty," John replied, clenching his square jaw as if it would give her the extra push she needed.

"What did you bet? Show or place?"

John kept his eyes glued on the horses, but could sense his friend's disbelief even before he said anything. "I'm head over heels for her."

"To win? You are nuts. Sorry, man. She ain't catching Thunder! Literally!" Charlie boasted as his horse pulled farther ahead.

"Literally? Don't use words you can't even spell, Charlie."

Charlie chuckled. "Then I'd be a mute."

"Can you even spell *mute*?"

"Come on, man. Don't get mad just because you picked the wrong horse. Let me help you pick out the next race."

"There won't be a next race for me." John's thigh throbbed from the repeated abuse of the magazine, the sound lost to the roar of the crowd as Iron Lady began to make her move.

"You blew your whole wad on that bitch?" Charlie yelled, turning from the race to look at John in shock.

"She's not a dog, Charlie."

"Still, you blew your money on a female."

John smiled. His horse was hanging close to the leader as they entered the last turn. "Wouldn't be the first time I did that, now would it?"

Over the public address system, the announcer sounded even more excited than the fans. "Iron Lady's coming on strong going into the final turn, but will she catch Thunder Clap?"

"She ain't gonna catch him," Charlie scoffed, turning his attention back to the track. "I can't believe you put your last two hundred on her."

Thoughts materialized in John's head at an elevated level, as they normally did when someone was facing death, in very creative and disturbing ways. Perhaps they'd take him for a swim with a new pair of cement shoes. Maybe do lunch at the slaughterhouse. Certainly would be fitting to end his life amongst the animals he had so much in common with. All he'd ever done was make others fat off his losses.

Thirty years old and what had. he ever accomplished? Odd jobs that changed more frequently than the foster homes he'd grown up in. That was about it. His latest job as a bouncer at an *urban club*, where most nights he was the only white guy there, certainly wasn't anything to boast about.

No, the slaughterhouse would be an insult to the cows. At least they were worth something, even dead. They'd probably just put a bullet in his head and throw him in a dumpster.

The real question wasn't how, but by whom since *they* could be any of the four different mobs he owed money to. Like people shifting debts from one credit card to another, chasing the best rate, John had borrowed money from one group to temporarily appease another while gambling the rest. Either way, the outcome was always the same. He just ended up owing more money to more people.

But instead of just jacking up their rates like banks did,

the guys he borrowed from jacked up the borrowers.

Yeah, probably a bullet to the head, he thought. As he pictured the gun going off, he actually heard the crowd gasped in horror—just as if someone had really been shot.

"Oh, shit!" Charlie yelled.

John snapped out of his daze to see a cloud of dust rising from the track. A horse was down, but which one?

Thunder Clap had just collapsed onto it. It was obvious to race fans what had just happened even if Charlie was in denial about it. This was no boxing match where the fighter would get back up after falling down from the weight of a punch. This looked like a snapped front leg, a death sentence for a horse—in this case, Thunder Clap. For John it was a last minute call from the governor, a pardon from execution.

The announcer yelled, "Iron Lady finishes first after Thunder Clap tumbles late!"

"Son of a Bitch!" Charlie yelled, throwing his ticket down on the ground.

"That's my bitch!" If it hadn't been for Thunder Clap's tragic accident, the filly wouldn't have won, and John didn't feel right about doing a victory dance.

Charlie looked up at him slowly then his face brightened. "Wait a minute. You said thirty to one…and you put two hundred on her! That's like four grand or something!"

John nodded. "Six, my friend."

"Six thousand?" Charlie yelled.

"Hey, don't go advertising it to everyone. This isn't exactly the safest place to broadcast your winnings" John said, squinting at him like a teacher would with a bad student.

"Listen to you. Haven't even collected your winnings yet and you're already talking like you're rich." Charlie shook his head. "Let's go get your dough, you lucky bastard," Charlie said, punching John in the shoulder.

"Luck had nothing to do with it. She was going to win anyway."

"No way."

"She was due for a win. She's gotten better with every race she's run," John explained.

"How do you know? You haven't looked at that magazine once since we got here," Charlie said doubtfully.

John tilted his head and arched an eyebrow at him, as if to say *really*.

"Oh yeah, photographic memory. Ironic how I always forget you have that, huh?"

"It is. Sorry you weren't as lucky tonight."

"Hey, I'm still up eighty bucks," Charlie said after he checked the tickets in his pocket.

"That's better than losing eighty."

"Yeah. Let's get our money and go celebrate," Charlie said, turning to head toward the cashier windows.

Charlie watched jealously as the cute cashier slowly counted out John's six thousand, seemingly not in any hurry to let him leave her window. He could tell John didn't even pick up on her flirting.

While John stared at the bills being laid out in front of him, she kept trying to gaze into his eyes.

The same girl just handed Charlie his cash, without even counting it. As he turned to walk away, he counted out his eighty bucks, taking almost as long, while John waited with a funny stare.

"Really, Charlie? And you work at a check cashing place? When you get robbed, are the crooks that patient with you?"

"I don't count it for them, I just hand it to them quick."

"I have a hard time picturing you doing anything quick, Charlie," John said with a nod toward Charlie's right leg.

"Hey, you know my knee never got right again after football in high school."

"Yeah, I know. Good thing they don't treat high school football players like horses or you would've been put down a long time ago. Besides, you were slow before you blew out your knee," John said, laughing as he stuck the money in his pocket.

"Screw you, John."

"I'm just kidding around. Chill, man."

"You chill. You've been working at that black club too long. You're starting to sound like them."

"Racist much, Charlie?"

"I'm just saying, the lingo's rubbing off on you."

"I just hope nothing else from that place rubs off on me."

Charlie sighed and shuffled toward the exit. "I'm just still a little upset about my horse. You know, they're probably getting ready to put him down."

"How about a moment of silence? Would that make you feel better?" John said, only half sarcastic, as they began down the stairs to the exit.

Charlie stared pointedly at the lump of cash in John's front pocket. "You know, a nice steak might do the trick. How about we hit Ruth's Chris on the way home?"

"Sure" John said as he put on his sports coat.

As they headed to John's El Camino, Charlie looked over at him, concerned, as if the old beat-up car had reminded him of John's situation. "Is that gonna be enough?" Charlie asked, stopping in his tracks.

John headed around the back of the car, getting the keys out of his pocket, and looked at him as he opened the door. "How hungry are you?"

"You know what I mean. I know you're in deep with the Italians. Or was it the Chinese?"

"Both. Don't worry, Charlie. It'll buy me some time. Now, get in the car. I'm hungry."

They both climbed in, closing their doors at the same time, the loud metal-on-metal thud in stereo. John looked at Charlie as he put the key in the ignition. "Besides, you forgot about the Mexicans and the Serbs."

"Then, let's just go eat a good old American steak," Charlie said, habitually reaching back for a shoulder belt that wasn't there since this model predated should belts.

"Good idea." John started the engine and a big puff of smoke billowed from the old exhaust pipe.

CHAPTER 2

Jack Shields hadn't worked on the protection side of the Secret Service for two years, but he still hung out with the guys that did. Financial fraud and counterfeiting investigation was his job now, but he still had access to their schedules. He knew that Chris Lopez and Neal Sykes would be working the plush empty house he was about to break into. They were among the huge group of new hires brought in a year earlier after the South America hooker scandal. They'd be a lot less likely to catch him breaking in.

Jack parked his black Lincoln in the alley around the corner. The car was just nice enough that it wouldn't stand out too much in this high end neighborhood. He hummed "Marina Del Ray" to himself as he walked slowly down the alley. As he turned the corner to make his way toward the large house, he pulled the ski mask over his face. Then he shook his head, disappointed, when he spotted his colleagues' car. They had made the ultimate rookie mistake of parking their equally dark car directly under a street lamp. It lit them up like a spotlight on the host of a late night variety show.

As he crept along the side of the car, being careful so they wouldn't see him, he realized that he wasn't going to have to try that hard. They were playing their usual dice game to keep themselves occupied. Jack had made the mistake of playing with them one time and lost enough money to know that gambling wasn't his thing. He could tell, from Sykes's smile and Lopez's frown, who was having the better luck. That was a good sign. Knowing how stubborn Lopez was, he'd keep playing till he either won his money back or lost all he had on him. That same stubbornness was what led to his nickname, Tres Lopez, since he lost three hundred the first time he played.

"Hang in there, Tres," Jack whispered to himself as he jumped the wall into the backyard.

After turning off the power to the house at the main power switch on the transformer, he climbed behind a bush and knelt below one of the bedroom windows. Then he pulled out his handy little pocket computer and hacked into the house's security system, shutting it down and disabling the emergency backup system.

"Oww," he said quietly as one of the bush's thorns stabbed his shoulder in self-defense. Lopez wasn't the only stubborn one tonight. It would take more than a few thorns from a rose bush to stop him.

He stood up for a second then, placing his foot on the offending branch, knelt back down. As the branch crunched under his foot, the fresh scent of roses wafted up from the crushed pedals. Jack lined up the blade of the glass cutter horizontally from the left side of the window just as the first few drops of rain began to fall. As he shifted his body to angle the blade downward, a branch swung free from behind him, striking him in the back of his neck. Rubbing his neck, he turned and cut off the branch with the blade then went back to work as the rain picked up.

Luck wasn't on his side so far tonight. He wondered what else could go wrong as he cut a parallel lower horizontal line across the window. As he looked up from the line he'd just cut, he had his answer. A pair of eyes were staring back at him through the glass.

CHAPTER 3

Thanks for the ride," Charlie said as John parked the El Camino in front of Charlie's place. John put the car in park but it kept rumbling as if gasping for air, choking on the cheap fuel from the station around the block. "I always liked this car. Listen to it purr," Charlie said as it continued to clear its throat. "Can you leave it to me?" he asked, stroking the dash as if putting suntan lotion on a hot blonde's leg.

"I told you I've got enough here," John said, patting his pocket, "to get me through till next month."

"Well, just in case." Charlie scribbled something on a napkin with a pen he found in the glove compartment. "Here. Put this in your pocket," he said as John read it.

"I'm no lawyer, Charlie, but I don't think that's gonna work. Anyway, you better get inside before you sister starts worrying about you." John looked at the worn wiper blades as they shrieked back and forth against the window like the shower scene from *Psycho*.

"Oh, she's at work," Charlie said, turning to him.

"At work? Where's she working these days?"

"I think Fifth and Vine," Charlie said as he turned to the door and bunched up his jacket at his neck before getting out in the rain.

John frowned. "Really, man? I thought she quit."

"Just like you quit gambling? Look, we all have our bad habits," Charlie said, turning back to him.

"Yeah? And what's yours, Charlie?"

"Hanging out with people that wanna get themselves killed." Charlie opened the door, got out, and slammed it shut behind him.

As he ran around the front of the car to the sidewalk, John rolled down the window, ignoring the downpour. "Hey, it's not like I want to," he yelled as Charlie jogged the best he could with his bad knee to the front door.

Without turning, Charlie yelled back, "Semantics, Johnny. Semantics." He lifted a hand to wave back at him.

"I know you can't spell *that!*" John said as he put the car in drive.

Before he could drive off, Charlie turned on the front porch and yelled, "Don't wreck my car, John!"

John responded with a one finger wave.

"I'm gonna miss him," Charlie said as he turned back to go inside.

ᜒᜓᜒᜓ

"I thought he said Fifth and Vine," John said as he turned the car around to go up Fifth again. The radio was playing "Computer Love," one of his favorite classics, as he slowly cruised back up the street. *Like a pimp looking for his ho,* he thought.

It was difficult to see out the front, since the windshield was fogging up from the humidity, even with the window rolled halfway down. The rain had slowed to the point that he had to turn the wipers off before the worn out blades began to cut into the glass. His car didn't predate intermittent wipers but they weren't standard that model year either. *Sure could use them on a night like this though.*

Like any other Saturday night, the street was crowded,

but he knew Kristin would stand out. At least he hoped she would. Normally, a car doubling back up the road would get the working girls excited, but not one that sloshed water in the bed like a sinking row boat. Part of him wondered if she had recognized his car and gone the other way.

As he reached the corner where Fifth met Vine again and slowed to a stop, someone seemed to recognize the car and walked up to him. Even with his photographic memory he didn't recognize her.

"Hey, John," said a five-foot-ten—with the five inch heels—anorexic blonde, leaning up against the car, her arms so shot up she looked like she had a rash.

"Hey," he said with a smile. "I bet you say that to all the johns."

She laughed, revealing a smile full of bad teeth. "Well, it's a common name out here."

"Yeah, I guess so."

"You really gonna act like you don't recognize me?" she said, leaning in closer, her arms barely strong enough to brace even her light frame against the side of the car.

Her voice did ring a bell, though the meth diet plan had taken its toll. She had lost a good forty pounds she couldn't afford to lose and at least three teeth, along with any hint of the innocent looking twenty-five-year-old he had met at a bar a year earlier. The only thing recognizable was that sweet South Carolina accent, although made a little sour now by her bad breath.

"Hey, Tracy. How are you?" he said, immediately feeling guilty for asking given her situation. Her smile let him know she didn't see it that way. Drug addicts saw things with tunnel vision, always looking for that next high. The drugs blurred the lines of vision, along with morality. She probably thought she looked better without the weight, not like a sluttily-dressed skeleton from a high school science class.

"I'm fine," she said as she backed away and walked around to the other side of the car.

Power locks, John thought as he considered yet another thing lacking on this car that he could have used tonight.

Tracy opened the door and sat down, closing it behind her. "So, how are you? It's been a while," she said, looking at him. "You never called me."

Before he could stutter out an answer, she laughed, cackling like one of the witches from OZ. The east or west, whichever one it was that didn't get crushed by the house, although considering how flat she looked, she could have been that one, too.

"I'm just fucking with you, John. That *is* your name, isn't it?"

"Yeah. I'm surprised you remembered, since it was only one night."

"Yeah, but that was one fucking long night of fucking, huh, John? Good fucking, right?" she said, moving closer while putting a bony hand on his leg. She tried to seduce him with her eyes, which worked as effectively as Medusa, turning his body as rigid as stone. "You were lucky I didn't charge you. That kind of action normally gets me at least two hundred dollars."

John didn't want to ask what qualified as normal in her life these days.

"You know what, Tracy? You're right. I owe you. How about I give you that two hundred, plus interest?" he said as he dug into his front pocket, separating three bills from the roll. "Here's three hundred." He took her hand off his leg and laid the money on her palm.

"Three hundred?" she said, staring at the bills. "Boy, for that you can do anal. Is that what you want, John?" she said, looking back at him.

"No, that's okay."

"Oral?" she asked as her eyes moved to his crotch. She started leaning in and John restrained himself from rudely backing away. He didn't want his dick in either orifice, not sure which would be worse.

"No, Tracy." He grabbed both her shoulders, stopping

her from going down, yet trying not to break her fragile bones as his large hands almost touched fingers across her narrow upper back.

"You gotta want something to be out here this time of night. I saw you come back down the street a second time. You ain't gonna find another lay like me out here, John. Definitely no white girl. Is that what you're into? Black bitches? You know racial profiling is illegal, John," she said with a laugh.

It sounded so silly the way she said it—gangsta rapper mixed with that southern accent. Although the racist part fit better than OJ's glove.

"No. No black bitches," he said.

"Good. I was gonna warn you. Half of them are guys anyway," she said matter-of-factly.

He ignored her comment. "I'm looking for someone actually."

"What? Asian girls? They're all in the massage parlors."

"Not what, but who. Her name is Kristin."

She leaned back as if thinking took too much energy. "Doesn't sound familiar. Is that her real name? 'Cause you know, ain't no one uses their real name out here. What does she look like?"

"Pretty. She's young, eighteen, with blonde hair and blue eyes."

"Say no more. Young and pretty like that, she ain't working this avenue."

"Where would she be?" he asked.

"All the new meat works up on High Line."

"That's where the good-looking girls work?" he said thoughtfully. Then he froze as he realized even in her drugged-out state she'd still probably be cognitive enough to be insulted by that comment. He gave her an apologetic look. "Sorry, Tracy."

"Hey, don't sweat it. I'm pretty, compared to the girls out here. Just like real estate, John. It's all about location and, hell, compared to these girls I'm like freaking Angelina Jolie."

Well, as skinny as her I suppose, John thought.

"Is she really that pretty?"

"Yeah, she really is."

"Then she's probably working for Ron."

"Her pimp?"

"On High Line, they have 'managers,'" she said, smiling that toothless smile.

"Right. Manager. How will I find this Ron?" John said.

"He usually has his girls meet their clients at the bar on the corner of High Line and Main."

"What's he look like?"

"You'll know him when you see him."

"Thanks, Tracy," he said and handed her another hundred.

"No. Thank you, John," she said, leaning in to give him a kiss on the cheek while he struggled not to grimace.

"Why don't you take the night off," he suggested as she got out of his car.

"Hell yeah! I'm gonna go get high." Without another word, she slammed the door and sauntered off down the street.

John felt like he might have just killed her with the amount of drugs she could buy for four hundred. *No good deed*, he thought as he started the car and headed north.

An old Eazy-E song came on the radio. *Cruisin down the street in my six four...*

He smiled as he began to hum along.

CHAPTER 4

The staring contest between Jack and the mastiff was at a standstill. Neither had blinked. Dammit! He couldn't just sit there all night and the increasing rain wasn't making things any more comfortable. At some point something would have to change, but at least for now he had some time to think.

That time was cut short by the sound of two car doors slamming shut. It seemed Sykes and Lopez were taking a break from their dice game to go make their rounds. By the tilt of the dog's head, Jack suspected he had heard the doors slam as well. As the dog turned completely around, Jack felt his luck had finally improved. As the dog got up and ran toward the other side of the house, Jack sighed in relief but only long enough to catch his breath.

Then he heard the backyard gate creak open. He stayed still, watching the beam of a flashlight shine from around the corner of the house, scanning the backyard, while it bounced up and down with each step of the one holding it. The walkie-talkie on Sykes' hip crackled as loud as nearby thunder.

Jack just held steady behind the bush, then a voice called out on Sykes's walkie-talkie.

"Sykes? Where are you?" Lopez asked.

"I'm in the backyard," Sykes answered. His beam was scanning along the ground again but he remained where he was.

"I can't believe they've got us checking in on his dog," Lopez called out.

"Yeah. Well, rookie, what did you expect your first year on the job? President Protection? Where are you anyway?" Sykes asked.

"I'm inside."

Now Jack knew why the dog had run off. He finished the last few inches of his cut in the glass, figuring the rain and walkie-talkie static were more than enough to cover the noise of the glass cutter scraping along the window.

"Hey, Skyes? Do you know where the dog food is?"

"It's gotta be in the pantry."

"Well, it's not. I already checked and I didn't see it. Oh, and by the way, the power's out."

"Good thing I brought a flashlight. Hold on. I'm coming," Sykes said.

As he was about to put his walkie-talkie back on his belt, Lopez crackled back, "Hurry up. This dog's looking at me like I'm a chimichanga."

"Beef or chicken," Sykes asked, quickly lifting the walkie-talkie back up to his mouth.

"Just hurry up."

"Definitely not beef," Sykes muttered, his chuckle matching Jack's around the corner.

Jack caught the now loose piece of glass as it fell outward, just as the backyard gate slammed shut. He'd have to move quickly and quietly, but not necessarily in that order, now that he had a dog plus two secret service agents to contend with inside the house.

CHAPTER 5

John turned onto High Line and slowed to about five miles an hour. He was a little concerned about being pulled over, not for his slow speed but for driving such an unsightly vehicle on this side of town. The old American car really stood out amongst the German, Japanese, and the occasional Italian cars that lined this street. Although a public street, John felt like an intruder who had accidentally turned down someone's private drive.

The street was lined with stores he'd never set foot in. Neiman Marcus and Gucci, among others, all snuggled up in a neat row. Always a season ahead, the mannequins were already wearing sweaters, scarves, and leather gloves. The rain had dissipated but so had the number of people out at eleven-thirty at night on this side of town.

This wasn't the kind of street where working girls hawked their wares out in the open. He began to wonder if trusting a meth head was a wise move. *Dumb question.*

Just as he reached Main, though, he saw a man he figured had to be Ron. He was easy to spot, after all. Standing outside a club was a white male, about six feet, five inches tall. He was wearing white pants and a matching coat, flanked by two girls dressed to impress—one blonde, one brunette. The man would have caught a blind man's eye in that outfit. If John had any doubt at all, it was alleviated when the man turned toward him. "Ron," John said to himself with a smile as he read the diamond-encrusted belt buckle.

John pulled into a parking spot along the curb, turned off the ignition, and got out, stepping in a puddle of water. The engine rumbled to a stop, as if asking when he'd be back. He slammed the door, getting Ron's attention.

"Hey, Ron," he said, walking toward the pimp.

"Do I know you, man?" Ron said with a kind of shimmy as he steered his two female companions to face John.

"No, you don't know me," John said. He stood his ground, as if preparing for anything. Working as a bouncer, not to mention jumping from one rough foster home to another, had ingrained in him some hard-to-break habits. The first of which was to always be ready to kick ass or else get your ass kicked. He preferred the former.

The girls, sensing his confidence matched with his good looks, immediately went into competition mode for this potential john. They each tried to catch his eye with their body and flirtatious glances, all while keeping one eye on the other to see how aggressive they should be. Neither John nor Ron noticed, as they were locked in a testosterone-induced staring contest with each other.

"But you know me, huh, friend?" Ron said, taking a step closer to John. Now only a foot in front of him, Ron looked down at him, since he had three inches on John, as if that would help to intimidate him.

"No, I don't know you and I'm not your friend," John said gruffly.

"Hey, man. No need to be rude." Ron relaxed his stance ever-so-slightly, sensing the lack of give on John's end. "So how do you know my name, then? Did someone recommend me to you?"

"Your name's on your belt buckle, asshole," John said, gesturing with a nod toward Ron's waist. "But yeah, someone did recommend you to me," John finished, while glaring. Then he noticed the two women at his side and glanced at the blonde to see if she was Kristin. She wasn't.

"You like blondes?" Ron said, following John's gaze. "This is Amy. Say hi, Amy. Don't be shy." He put his right arm behind her back and nudged her forward, as if shielding himself from John.

"Nice to meet you. I'm Amy," she cooed, offering her hand as if she was a British Royal.

"Hi, Amy." John took her hand by her fingers and gave it a quick shake. "You're very pretty, but I'm not interested. I'm looking for someone else."

Ron beamed, his confidence coming back since he smelled a customer, or in other words money. "What's your type, man? Maybe Jill here is more your flavor? If not, I got many more. Just call me fucking Baskin Robbins, 'cause I got all thirty-one flavors, man."

"I'm looking for Kristin," John said calmly, trying to ease the tension a little since he needed something from him.

"I ain't got a Kristin working for me."

"Maybe she's not using her real name."

"You're new to this, huh, friend? None of these girls use their real names. Do they, Amy?"

"Fuck no," she said, laughing. The harshness of her tone was in stark contrast with her soft beauty, reminding John what they did for a living. You could take the girl out of the trailer park but you couldn't take the trailer park out of the girl, no matter how nicely you dressed them up.

He smiled as he thought of a comment Charlie had made once about these types of girls. *'Only two ways out of the park for those poor girls. Hooking or tornado.'* The statement was always followed by, *'God knows what's going on in those trailer parks. That's why he blows through so often.'* It always made John wish a tornado had blown him out of the psychological hell he'd grown up with.

"Are these the only two girls you got working for you tonight?" John said, causing both girls to look offended.

"No, but these are the only two available. You can have one for a thousand or both for twenty five hundred," Ron told him, making it sound like a bargain.

"Where are your other girls?" John asked.

"Already with clients, man. Sorry, but you got here kinda late. You're lucky I still have this beautiful inventory here." Ron glanced from side to side, raising and lowering his hands before each girl as if he were a model on the *Price Is Right* showing off a new car.

"You know what? I'm gonna go inside and have a drink first, think it over," John said as he turned to walk into the club.

"Well, I ain't gonna hold them for you. I ain't Wal-Mart. I don't do lay away." His voice became a little firmer as he realized John wasn't going to turn and come back. As John pulled the door open to the club, he heard Ron mutter, "Asshole," no doubt trying to show his girls he was still boss.

As the door slowly closed behind him, softly rubbing over the thick red carpet, John made his way down a narrow hallway to another door. The hallway walls were lined with portraits, all of which were of Washington's most powerful, past and present. A state senator here, a former Secretary of State there, but John didn't really care. A club was a club and this one, just like the one he worked at on the other side of town, served the same purpose. It was a place for crooks and thieves to satisfy their thirst, among other urges. The difference was he'd felt more comfortable at the one he worked at.

He took a breath as he reached the door and slowly opened it, not sure what he would find. He'd barely started to scan the interior before someone greeted him.

"Can I help you, sir?" said a large man. At six feet four, he seemed as wide as he was tall, his massive frame stuffed into a tuxedo. Nicest dressed bouncer John had ever seen.

From experience, he interpreted the man's politely offered question as really meaning *What the fuck are you do-ing here*?

"Just came to get a drink," John said, glancing calmly around the room while curling his right hand into a fist. *Old habits...*

"We're full tonight." The bouncer stepped over to the right, blocking John's view of the half empty bar behind him. This guy wasn't to be trifled with, despite the nice clothes. A kindred spirit, John could tell he was trained in the fine art of giving a beat down when needed. It was in the eyes, he always told people. A steady glare, with a few blinks, were the giveaway. If someone felt comfortable enough to blink, closing their eyes even for that brief moment, then you could probably relax. So far, that wasn't the case.

"Look, I'm meeting someone here," John said uncon-vincingly.

The bouncer firmed his stance, like a cement truck pouring a foundation. "Who are you meeting, sir?"

"Ah...That guy," John said, pointing to one of the more recent looking photos on the wall.

"Senator Carlson?"

"Yeah, Carlson. He's a fishing buddy of mine."

"Well, you must have gotten your dates wrong, sir. Senator Carlson is out of the country right now on a foreign trip to India." Although his tone remained polite, his smile had turned sarcastic.

As John turned back from the photo to look directly at this walking contradiction of boarish politeness, he realized bullshit wasn't going to work. But the man also hadn't giv-en John a reason to resort to his old habits...yet. He'd have to speak the language understood at any club, no matter how run down or sophisticated. He unclenched his fist, reached into his pocket, and pulled out a hundred dollar bill. "One drink. Okay?" he asked as he folded it long ways, waving it briefly in the bouncer's face before slipping it into the front pocket of his tuxedo.

This was turning into one expensive evening.

The large man sighed. "Okay. One drink, sir."

He moved aside like the moon moving from in front of the Sun during a solar eclipse. The light of the club almost blinded John as he saw a whole different kind of place than he had ever been in before. No chairs were knocked over or discarded bottles lying on the floor. The music wasn't heavy and riotous, or loud enough to drown out all conversation. The air wasn't permeated with the usual stench of stale beer and cigarettes. The place silently screamed one thing— class. He felt uncomfortably out of place as he sat at the bar, already beginning his search around the room for Kristin. He knew even the hundred dollars he gave his new friend wouldn't last long. He couldn't blame the guy. He probably made six figures working in a place like this. Even though John was thirsty from the humidity outside, he'd sip his one drink slowly.

"What can I get you?" said the bartender, causing John to turn. The guy gave him a nod, like a secret handshake to one of his own.

"Miller Lite. Thanks," John said, nodding back.

"Sure."

As he turned to get a bottle and glass, John began scanning the room. Mostly older men in suits, accompanied by much younger women in skimpy cocktail dresses. The room was so full of smoke and the rich scent of expensive cigars and liquor, he felt like it was coating his body. All the men had the same expression of carefree laughter on their faces. *And why wouldn't they?* They were winning at life. They'd all figured out the game. He was in Washington, DC, after all, where everything was about having power and knowing how to use it, while taking advantage of the fools around the rest of the country. And they were good at that. There were two places to get rich using other people's money—Wall Street and Washington. *Fitting how they both start with the letter W, since we just had a president nicknamed W for eight years.*

As he finished scanning the center of the room, John noticed curtains hung along the edges, their width and heaviness perfect for concealing small booths or rooms.

"Here you go, sir," the bartender said as he placed a tall glass on a small napkin on the mahogany wood between them and began pouring the bottle of beer. John turned, shifting in the leather seat and placing his feet on the ledge that ran the length of the bar. Even the furnishings were nicer than any in his apartment.

"Thanks," John said. He took the cold glass and brought it to his mouth, the froth coating his upper lip. Suddenly thirsty, he gulped down a few swallows before catching the well-dressed bouncer watching him out of the corner of his eye. Remembering he'd get the boot the moment he'd swallowed the last drop, he slowed to a sip. *Funny how a nice glass can make cheap beer taste better,* he thought as he licked his lip.

He turned back to survey the room, focusing on the curtains again. He noticed the music this time as he took another small sip, teasing his palate. Slow Jazz, not his thing but in this place it fit. It was coming from speakers concealed in the ceiling, not some obnoxiously large juke box in the corner that only took coins. He found it strange to just sit in a club and not be on edge, ready to break up the next fight. A fight in this place probably just ended with a comment like "You'll be hearing from my lawyer."

Before he could get too comfortable, thinking he'd used up all his luck at the track and that Kristin probably wasn't behind one of the sets of curtains, he saw one of them move.

A man, about six-foot-four and dressed in an expensive suit, pushed one of them aside. Then he saw her.

CHAPTER 6

Jack had been in this house before so he knew the layout. The kitchen, where his two fellow agents would be feeding the dog, was down the hall at the other end of the house. He pushed the drapes out of the way and maneuvered himself through the hole he'd cut in the window. As he stood up, he looked down and noticed the mud he had tracked onto the hard wood floors. He wasn't too concerned about leaving prints though, as he'd bought a pair of cheap tennis shoes for just this occasion, the tread indistinguishable from the thousands of other pairs sold annually. Jack slowly made his way through the guest room toward the door.

Sykes and Lopez made no attempt at stealth, so Jack could hear their conversation as he made his way quietly through the house.

"You know you gotta clean that up, right?" Sykes asked.

In the kitchen, he would be leaning against the marble-topped island, watching Lopez pour a large bag of Purina dog food.

Lopez had probably overfilled the bowl, spilling some on the floor, as he hurried to get out of the way of the impatient mastiff.

"Why? That dog's just gonna eat it anyway," Lopez answered.

The huge dog made a growling noise as he ate.

"Good point," Sykes said, his voice filled with awe.

"I still can't believe we're here," Lopez said.

"What? In the vice president's house?"

"No, dog sitting. Four years of college and one year in the agency and I'm back to doing the same thing I did in high school," Lopez grumbled.

"You know what they call that, Lopez?"

"Yeah, a waste of time."

"No, full circle. Come to think of it, I guess I've come full circle, too."

"You had to dog sit when you were a kid, too?"

"Shit, no," Sykes said, sounding disgusted. "But, growing up, I spent some time in other people's homes uninvited and some had dogs. So, yeah, guess I'm full circle, too."

"Don't tell me stuff like that," Lopez snarled.

"Hey, I got three words for you. Statue of limitations."

"I think its statute, not statue, and that wouldn't matter to the agency if they ever found out."

"All right, then I got four more words for you—keep your mouth shut," Sykes said, laughing.

"Si, senior," Lopez said. Jack heard the smile in his voice.

"Grassy Ass," Sykes replied, clearly butchering the Spanish on purpose.

Jack could hear their laughter coming from down the hall. He'd have to go in that direction to get to the office. As he made his way down the hall, he reminded himself to grab some obviously valuable items besides the one thing he was looking for. He had to make this look like a typical robbery, since they'd find the cut power wires and window soon enough.

Although, a burglary at the vice president's home would be anything but typical. Jack felt bad for his fellow agents since they'd probably find themselves without a job after Vice President Cullen Roberts found out they had let someone break in on their watch.

Jack had witnessed Cullen Roberts's short temper first hand right here only a month ago. Jack and his partner had come to discuss some of their findings while investigating potential wire fraud within some of the biggest banks in the country.

Roberts had seemed on edge from the moment they got there. Jack remembered finding it odd that he had asked his housekeeper to keep the dog out of the study during their meeting—a silly request, considering that the mastiff likely outweighed the frail sixty-year-old woman by a good fifty pounds.

As Jack had predicted, five minutes into their meeting the dog came running into the room, knocking Roberts over as it leapt on him. An impressive feat since Roberts was no small man. At six-four and two-hundred-twenty pounds, he was a hard man to move. Especially considering that Roberts had made a name for himself at The University of Alabama as a linebacker. During those days, he was a man hated by all of the South, except for Alabama, as his team dominated the SEC conference. Funny how three decades later, all of the South supported this same man, cheering when he was selected as the vice presidential candidate by moderate republican Andrew Hastings from New York. Hastings needed the South to win the presidency and Roberts delivered. He had also delivered in the vice presidential debate. He showed that he could knock someone down verbally just as easily as on the football field. He had a talent for really tearing into an opponent while still being likable, the way only a true Southerner could.

But that day, a month ago, Jack learned that Roberts' likability was only camera deep. Jack saw a look on Roberts's face that no camera had ever captured before. Even at the age of fifty-two, Roberts exuded powerful strength. He picked the huge dog up by its neck and threw it across the room.

The beast slammed into the wall, yelping as it fell to the ground.

Jack was tempted to do the same to Roberts, but he worried it wouldn't just cost him his job but his partner's as well, not to mention earn Jack an extended vacation at the FCI in Cumberland. He figured their presence probably kept Roberts from doing the same to his housekeeper. Instead, Roberts simply knocked her over with two simple words.

"You're fired!"

After the poor woman solemnly left the study, Roberts continued the meeting as though nothing had happened.

Before Jack could make his escape, Roberts stopped him, asking if Jack could find someone to watch his dog while he was away, just until he could replace the housekeeper. Jack knew the perfect candidates.

Following Roberts to his desk for a pen, Jack wrote down Lopez and Sykes's names on a notepad while Roberts went back to discuss something with his partner. When Jack opened the desk drawer to put the pen back, his mouth dropped open in shock. He recovered quickly, glancing at Roberts to ensure the seemingly affable man's attention was still on his partner as he silently closed the drawer. It was what he'd seen in the drawer that he was after now, and it was just a few more steps down the hall.

CHAPTER 7

John leaned forward on the bar stool, trying to get a better view of the people behind the curtain with Kristin before it swung closed, but his view was suddenly obstructed. A well-dressed man got up from a table in front of him and walked toward the bar. He was wearing an expensive suit, complete with tie. *Is he the manager of this place?* As the man approached, John expected him to ask how he slipped past his gatekeeper.

"Hey, man. How are you?" the man whispered strangely while leaning in a little too close. John almost gagged at the strong scent of cologne.

"All right, I guess," was all John could muster. Interesting how this was the second person he'd met in this club to use such casual language. Was this guy a pimp like Ron?

"You don't look all right," the man said, looking him over and gesturing with his drink toward John's bruised eye.

John took the comment to mean "You look out of place here." Sensing a fight, he clenched his fist at his side.

The man leaned in even more and whispered, almost seductively, "I've seen you look a lot better."

"What?" John said, leaning away.

"Don't get me wrong. You still look great. I'm just saying."

"How about you stop *saying* anything? You've obvi-ously got me mixed up with someone else," John said, clenching his fist again. "I've never met you before in my life."

"Well, I'm not surprised you don't remember me. You were pretty wasted that night," the man said, undeterred. With a laugh, he took a drink of the amber liquid in his glass. Clearly, he'd had a few tonight already. "So, tech-nic—aly, y—you're right," he slurred. "I never did get your name that night. I'm Adam, by the way." He extended his hand, closing the small space between them.

He's just a drunk, John told himself. *Don't let it get to you.* He relaxed a little and took the man's hand. This wasn't the first time John had caught the eye of another man. He'd seen them look his way before, but none had ev-er been so forward. Was it just the guy's drunkenness or had something about John changed, giving his admirer the as-sumption he was willing to follow through? He'd heard ru-mors that such behavior was a little more accepted on this side of town, but it only made John want to get Kristin that much quicker and get out of there.

"Look, Adam. I really don't know you and even if we have met before I don't feel like catching up, so why don't you head back to your friends over there and enjoy your evening with them?"

The man backed away a bit and stared at John then down at his drink. "Maybe I've had too many of these. You must forgive me. Let me buy you a drink as an apology."

"Maybe next time," John said. While politely pushing him away, he saw the curtain for the booth behind them be-ing shoved to the side again.

"Okay. Well, here's my number," Adam said, putting a note in John's front pocket. "Just give me a call some time if you wanna *catch up*. Can I at least get your name?"

His attention focused on the booth in the back, John didn't fully grasp the gesture. He simply said, "Sure, it's Charlie," then stood up from his chair. "Have a nice evening, Adam." He didn't spare Adam another glance as his eyes were trained on the gentleman with a crew cut and suit leaving Kristin's booth. The man headed toward the far side of the bar then went down the hall to the bathroom. *Time to find out who these guys are.* He put his half-finished beer down on the bar behind him.

"I'll be back," he said to the bartender before heading across the room to the hallway.

As he entered the bathroom, the man was already standing at the urinal in midstream, rocking back and forth as if spelling his name in the snow. John immediately walked over to the sink and began washing his hands. As he glanced over, he noticed the man's large biceps stretching the fabric of his coat, as if a blood pressure cuff was squeezing his arm.

"Slow night, huh?" John said, looking at himself in the mirror as he ran lukewarm water over his hands.

"Excuse me?" the man replied, surprised, leaning back to look around a support beam. His thick neck seemed to hinder his range of motion.

"Not a lot of women here tonight," John said as he turned the water off and headed over to where a stack of hand towels laid neatly folded.

The man flushed and zipped up, heading to the sink. "I hadn't really noticed."

"Oh, yeah, I saw that hot blonde you were with. Guess there's no need to look around. At least you found a nice one to hang out with."

"Well, not me," he said as he turned on the water to the sink. "I'm working, so she's not mine. But the two guys I'm working for are gonna get lucky with her." He looked over at John in the mirror. "I hope the other guy ended up looking worse," he said, pointing toward his own eye as a reference to John's bruised one.

John tossed the hand towel into the wicker basket on the floor next to the sink and smiled. "Ran into a door."

"Must've been some mean door."

"So, your two guys only found one girl. That's too bad. See? It is a slow night."

"Actually, they like it that way, like doing 'em at the same time," the man said as he turned the water off. He stood looking at John for a moment then down at the towels next to him.

"Oh. Here you go," John said, handing him a towel from the stack.

"You know the worst part?" the man asked as he worked his large hands into the towel.

"It gets worse than that?"

"Yeah. They pay me extra to watch."

"The girls don't mind?"

"I don't think they care if the girls do or not, and frankly, I don't either." He tossed the towel, missing the wicker basket. "And even if they do mind, I usually give them a little something extra in their drink. Just like tonight."

John picked up the towel and discreetly wrapped it around his clenched fist.

As the man walked past John to the door, he said, "I just hope they let me have the leftovers. This girl is hot." He turned with a smile.

"You dropped this," John said, slamming his towel covered fist into the man's jaw. The force sent tremors up his arm, even as the muffled sound of the punch echoed in the bathroom. The man collapsed on the floor at his feet, knocked out by the punch. John would have broken a couple of knuckles had it not been for the towel, but as it was, he only broke the man's jaw.

"Shit!" John muttered, uncurling the towel from his hand and flexing his aching fingers. He eyed the man then glanced around the bathroom. No, trying to drag him into a stall wasn't going to be worth the trouble. He laid the towel on the man's bloodied face then hurried from the room. As he went down the hall, back to the main room, he tried to keep his gait casual. Coming down the hall toward him was an older gentleman who, luckily for John, was slowed as much by alcohol as his age. Still, John probably only had a minute, maybe two, before the unconscious man in the bathroom was reported to security.

The curtain flew out of the way with a swish as John looked down at the two older gentlemen sitting at the table with Kristin. They both looked up at John in surprise, but his attention was on the barely conscious woman between them.

"Excuse me, gentleman. My name is Evan Richards and I work for the club. I wanted to inform you that we are familiar with your guest. We have seen her here before," John said with authority.

"Yeah? So what?" the man to John's right slurred, clearly annoyed by the interruption.

"Well, I hate to inform you but this girl is underage."

"Ha, ha. Is that all?" the other man said. "I'll have to concur with my associate and say, 'So what.'" He raised his glass to tap it clumsily against the glass of the other gentleman, as if making a toast, spilling about a hundred dollars' worth of the thousand-dollar bottle of Champaign.

As John thought of what to do next, he glanced back toward the bar, seeing the old man from earlier talking to the bartender at the end of the bar. He was clearly excited about something.

"I'm afraid I'll have to escort the lady out, gentleman," John said, leaning over to his right to grab Kristin.

"I don't think so." The man on the left stood up. "You see, Richards, that girl right there cost me almost as much as this bottle of Champaign," he said, pointing toward Kristin. "So why don't you go back to busing tables or whatever the hell you do around here and leave us alone."

"Yeah, you should get back to work," the other man said, standing and blocking Kristin behind him, "while you still have a job."

From the corner of his eye, John saw the bartender motioning the bouncer over. It was time to stop talking. He shoved the man in front of Kristin out of his way and, in one fluid motion, quickly threw Kristin over his shoulder, straightening as he turned to face the other man. This stopped the bouncer in his tracks before reaching the bartender as he turned his attention back toward John.

"Sorry, guys. Time for her to go," John said, turning back toward the door, Kristin's long blonde hair hitting one of the men in the face as he swung around.

"You're not going anywhere, son," the other man said, putting a hand on John's free shoulder turning him back around.

John froze. In all his time growing up, in and out of foster homes at the rate of two per year, with all the bad language he was exposed to, the names he was called at such a young age, there was one word that offended him more than any other. *Son.*

John lifted his foot and planted in squarely in the man's chest, launching him backward as if he had fallen out of a plane. As quickly as the man flew backward, crashing into the wall, John realized it had been a mistake to admire his work. When he turned back to leave, he found himself staring at the large bouncer, standing between him and the exit. John had a feeling that money wasn't going to get the brute to let him pass this time.

CHAPTER 8

Jack had stood in the same spot in the hall long enough for a puddle to collect from his rain-soaked clothes. He actually worried about how it would warp the finish of the hand-scraped hardwoods before realizing that he was being ridiculous.

As the study was with in view of the kitchen, he could only wait impatiently in that spot as he listened to their conversation.

"I thought you filled up his bowl," Sykes said.

"I did," Lopez said.

"Man, that dog can eat."

"And fast," Lopez added.

"Well, fill it up again," Sykes ordered.

"I can't," Lopez said.

"What do you mean you can't?"

"The bag's empty."

"Well, go get another one."

"Why don't you?" Lopez asked.

"Because I'm guessing those are forty pound bags."

"Yeah, but I thought you worked out all the time."

"I do, that's the problem. I think I pulled a muscle. Doctor said to take it easy for a couple of weeks," Sykes told him.

"That's why I don't work out. You just end up getting hurt trying to stay healthy," Lopez said. "Do you know where he keeps the extra food?"

"Dog's got a room at the end of the hall. I bet it's in there."

"All right, I'll go get it. You keep Fido company. Let me borrow that flashlight," Lopez said and the beam of the flashlight turned toward the hall.

Jack started working his way back to the guest room.

"Wait a minute," Sykes snapped at Lopez.

"What? You don't want me to leave you with the dog? Figure he likes soul food more than Mexican?" Lopez laughed loud enough Jack could hurry back to the guest room without worrying about stepping quietly.

"The light."

"What light?"

"Outside. The street lamp is still on."

"So."

"Well, I figured the storm knocked the power out, but that would affect the whole block, and that light's still on," he said

"You're right," Lopez said.

"You go feed the dog. I got another flashlight in the car. I'm gonna go check the circuit breaker in the back of the house. The rain looks like it's died down anyway."

"You sure this isn't just so you don't have to be by yourself with the dog?" Lopez said.

"Just go get another bag, and don't spill it this time, Sykes ordered. "I don't want Roberts up my ass 'cause you messed up his kitchen. I gotta feelin' that guy ain't as nice as he acts."

"They never are," Lopez muttered to himself.

The light warned Jack that he was coming.

As Lopez passed the guest room and went into the room next door, Jack hurried out then down the hall to the study. Once there, he took out the battery sized flashlight from his pocket, shining it on the desk. Immediately, he found what he was searching for, although he still couldn't believe what he was looking at. He had only caught a brief glance of the picture in the desk during his visit to the house a month earlier. Now, he was almost as surprised seeing it a second time.

He picked it up and held it in his hand, staring in disbelief. He must have been staring longer than he thought, for he heard Lopez's heavy footsteps, weighted down with an extra forty pounds, coming back down the hall. Jack turned off the flashlight and laid the picture on the desk. Then he took a photo with his phone, figuring it was worth the risk of the flash going off. Even if Lopez saw the flash of light, he'd probably figure it was lightning.

Mission accomplished, it was time to go. With Sykes in the backyard and Lopez at the other end of the house, carrying the dog food, Jack couldn't time it any better. He checked his mask and was getting ready to run when he heard the crackle of the Lopez's walkie-talkie which he'd left in the kitchen.

"Lopez! Looks like someone turned the damn power off at the main transformer back here! Keep an eye out. I'm gonna look around out here."

Then everything lit up like the Fourth of July.

Lopez dropped the bag of dog food just as Jack began to sprint for the door. His sneakers still wet, Jack slipped and fell across the room, landing in the kitchen face to face with the large mastiff. This time there was no glass between them.

CHAPTER 9

See? Just one drink," John said with a grin, shrugging his free shoulder.

The smile wasn't returned.

"How about you put the lady down," the well-dressed bouncer ordered, curling both hands into fists.

"I can't do that. I gotta get this girl home."

"Look, I don't care about the girl, but I can't let you just walk out after what you just did to the senator. I'll need to escort you out," he said, looking toward the two men John had rescued Kristin from.

"Senator? One of them was a senator?" John asked.

"Yeah, the one with your footprint on his shirt."

"No shit? Which senator?" John said, glancing back.

"Senator Kyle Johnson."

"Oh, well—I didn't vote for him."

"I didn't either but he's a good client here and I can't just let you leave."

John eyed him for a moment realizing the guy was really protecting his job more than anything. "I understand. They need a show or the natives will get restless. Let me just put her down and get her taken care of and then you can do what you gotta do."

"Make it quick," the bouncer barked.

John walked between a few tables and one of Kristin's limp arms knocked over someone's glass. The bouncer just grimaced.

"Adam! Hey, I gotta favor to ask," John said as if they were old college buddies.

Adam looked up from his conversation with someone at his table. "Ah, sure, Charlie."

"I want you to take my friend here home right now."

"Right now?"

"Yeah, right now," John said, glancing over to see Senator Johnson beginning to stand up.

"All right, sure. Where to?" Adam grabbed a pen then flipped over the receipt he had just gotten back from the waitress.

"I tell you what." John plopped her down in the open chair next to Adam. "Why don't you take her to Denny's first to get some food in her and she'll tell you how to get her home," he said, realizing he didn't have time to write the address down. He handed Adam a hundred.

"No, Charlie. Keep you money," Adam said shook his head, handing it back. "How about you give me your number instead?" he asked, taking his phone out to type it in. "That way I can at least text you to let you know she made it home okay."

"Sure." *Pretty slick*, John thought as he gave him Charlie's phone number.

"By the way, I'm more of an IHOP guy," Adam said with a smile.

John just stared at him, confused, wondering if that was some kind of code between gay guys for which position they prefer.

"I'll bet you are. I'm sure she won't be picky." John gestured to Kristin, her head resting on the table. "Can you get her out of here now?" He put a hand on her head then leaned in and whispered in her ear. "I'll see you later, Kristin." He wondered if she'd even hear or remember later. Then he straightened, fixed his sports coat, and headed back to the bouncer. Adam picked her up with both arms and walked past John toward the exit.

The senator was clearly enraged and had already reached the bouncer. John considered slipping out the door while the bouncer's attention was on the senator. But being a bouncer himself, he figured the man probably had really good peripheral vision in order to keep an eye on such a large place. As John tried to sneak past him, the bouncer turned and placed one of his palms squarely on John's chest before looking away from the senator.

"I thought you wanted me to leave," John said.

"The senator here says you took something from him."

"Oh, really? What did he tell you I took?" John said, looking past the bouncer to the red-faced older man.

"He took my wallet!" the old senator yelled, his voice hoarse from years of smoking.

John looked at the bouncer. "Are you kidding me?"

"Well?"

"Well what? I didn't take his wallet."

"Check his pockets," the senator said as the bouncer lowered his hand from John's chest and gave him a quizzical look.

"Go ahead." John raised both his arms at his sides.

The bouncer checked his pants pockets, finding only the key to his El Camino. Then as he handed it back to John, he leaned in and reached into the pocket of John's sports coat. He gripped the roll of hundreds from the track, showing it to John as he took it out.

"Now who's taking something that isn't theirs? Clearly that's not a wallet," John said, tipping his head toward the bundle, the rubber band printed with the track's logo. "If you notice the ticket wrapped around that wad of bills, you'll see that I got that money from the track tonight—"

"He probably dumped my wallet in the trash in the bathroom," the senator insisted. The comment reminded him of what he had done in the bathroom and was wondering if his time was running out.

As the bouncer placed the money back in John's coat, he leaned over and whispered quickly, "I'm keeping two hundred for my trouble." John just nodded. "Senator, I think this has all been a misunderstanding," the bouncer said. "Why don't we go back to your table and see if we can find your wallet? Perhaps it fell out when you fell on the floor. I'll see about getting your bottle comped for this evening as well."

The senator, no doubt figuring that the bottle cost more than the girl and he was coming out ahead on the deal, nodded. He could just get another girl from Ron on the way out. "All right. Fine," he said and they both turned to walk back to the booth.

John breathed a sigh of relief, relaxing a bit as he turned toward the exit. Money always did the trick. Maybe his lucky streak was still on from the track earlier.

As he checked his coat again, ensuring his bundle of cash was still there, he heard someone yell, "That guy!"

His lucky streak had just run out. He turned, both fists clenched this time.

CHAPTER 10

The dog stood its ground, staring at Jack. He wasn't sure what his next move would be but he'd have to decide quickly. Then he heard a noise that piqued the dog's interest even more than him—the sound of the bag of dog food crashing to the ground as Lopez simultaneously reached for his gun and walkie-talkie.

"Sykes! There's someone in the house!" Lopez yelled as the dog charged toward him. "Shit!" He drew his nine millimeter, aiming directly at the dog, and pulled the trigger. Nothing.

Rookie, Jack thought. *That dog's damn lucky Lopez forgot the safety was on.*

The dog slid to a stop in the fallen and now ripped open food bag on the floor and began scarfing it down with enormous mouthfuls.

"Lopez! What did you say?" Sykes's voice crackled through Lopez's walkie-talkie.

As Jack stood and began making his way to the door, Lopez struggled to step over the dog blocking the entire hallway. "Someone's in the house! Go around to the front," Lopez said with a hurried breath as he followed Jack, gun drawn.

Jack was in good shape, primarily due to the fact that

he liked to jog. But there was a difference between jogging and jumping up into a sprint. Unless you were Usain Bolt at the Olympics. Anyone who had watched the Games knew it was all about the push off and how fast you could get out of the blocks.

Jack jumped up to sprint out of the house and pushed off his right leg, there was a loud *POP.* The torn Achilles caused him to stumble He fell back to the floor in front of the door.

At first, Jack thought there'd been a shot. Apparently, Lopez must have thought the same as he ducked down, covering his head with his arms.

Jack took advantage of the man's fear, forcing himself back to his feet and out the front door. Although slowed by the burning pain in his right calf, adrenaline fueled his senses and he managed to hobble-jog out onto the street before Sykes turned the corner of the house.

On the front porch, Sykes pushed the door aside with his left hand, while holding his gun in his right. Just as he cleared the door out of the way Lopez ran into him and they fell to the ground, both dropping their guns.

"Shit, Lopez!"

"He's right there!" Lopez yelled, picking up his dropped gun.

Jack was just turning the corner to the alley where he had parked his car. Even though he felt like he was sprinting, his heart racing from the rush of adrenaline, he knew it was really only a grandma's pace. Slow enough for Lopez to take three shots.

For all the rookie mistakes Lopez kept making, one thing he was excellent at was his aim. The one place he always won his bets at was the shooting range. He leveled three shots at the man running from Vice President Roberts' home. The three blasts from the gun lit up the street outside Roberts's home like lightning, the thunderous clap of each shot echoing off the houses lining either side of the street.

All three shots found their mark, one in the back of

Jack's already injured leg, one in his shoulder, but the worst of all hit his lower back. Tres Lopez had lived up to his nickname.

CHAPTER 11

Emotions were contagious. People saw someone laugh and they couldn't help but join in most of the time, without even knowing the cause. Seeing a child cry, it was a cold heart that didn't feel sympathy. Even anger could spread, given the environment, and John knew better than anyone that a bar was ground zero. It was a rare night for him that a scuffle didn't turn into an all-out brawl as quickly as a flame thrower brought fire to a drought-stricken forest.

While a part of him would find it entertaining to see such a swanky joint reduced to chaos, he'd prefer to just beat a hasty retreat. But that decision was in the bouncer's hands now. John turned to see the man he decked in the bathroom was awake and was now trying to explain to the bartender what happened. He figured the man's busted jaw would allow him some time before the message made its way to the bouncer standing in his way. Then he glanced back at the bouncer. In that split second, he realized that simply pointing at John while holding his bloody jaw was all that was needed.

It happened fast. The right cross coming at his chin was just as quick. He managed to duck underneath the large brick-like hand hurtling toward him. John felt the force of the punch as a breeze on his cheek as he turned his head sideways, watching the swing go past as if in slow motion.

John was used to taking a punch or two, but given the option he'd prefer not to, especially when delivered by someone so large and obviously well-trained. His usual opponents were amateurs, guys with too much alcohol in their system and something to prove. Even the debt collectors occasionally sent to his house to collect weren't typically this size. The mobs usually got their enforcers on the cheap. Why pay a lot of money when, in this bad economy, it was easy to find guys willing to rough someone up for cheap? Besides, it gave those unemployed fellas a chance to vent their frustration at the same time. Odds were they weren't going to collect the full amount owed, so why cut into that amount paying someone to collect it. Just like with any other financial institution, mobs were no different. It was all about margins.

As he straightened, still watching the guy from the bathroom head his way, John felt the full force of the bouncer's left hand hitting him in the side of his head. John staggered to the side a bit as he shook his head then turned back toward the source of the blow. Had it been the bouncer's dominate right that landed the blow, he probably wouldn't have been standing at all. As he tried to shake the cobwebs from his head, he saw the bouncer winding up his next punch, with his right this time.

Shit. This is going to suck, he thought as the beefy arm started its rotation. The fist locked onto his jaw like a missile launched with a guidance system.

Seemingly oblivious of the bouncer, another man wrapped both arms around John's torso and leaned back, lifting him off the floor.

The bouncer's fist missed its target at the last second.

"Thanks for the lift, buddy," John muttered. Taking advantage of the unintended help of a second bouncer thinking he was helping. John lifted both feet together just as the first bouncer was beginning to catch his balance from the missed punch. Then, with all his might, John kicked the bouncer in the chest so hard that it knocked both John and the guy holding him backward. The back of the first bouncer's head crashed into a support beam, knocking him out. He fell to the ground with a loud thud.

Crashing through a table and hitting the ground didn't do anything to loosen the grip the man had around John. No matter. This was the easy part—easy for him. John leaned his head forward and, with the force of someone experiencing whiplash, he slung it back, smashing into the man's nose. As intended, the man let go of John and instantly covered his face with both hands as John rolled off of him. In the time it took for John to stand up, the man's face and the floor around him were covered in blood as he writhed around in pain.

Poor guy. Hope they're paying him well. Maybe on this side of town, bouncers might even get medical benefits. He was going to need them.

John quickly focused his attention again to the first bouncer, his body automatically prepping for another assault. But seeing him lying there, unconscious on the floor, John relaxed slightly and walked toward him. He studied the man a moment then bent down and reached into his coat pocket, taking back the three hundred dollars the bouncer had gotten from John earlier.

"Consider this a refund," John said, pocketing the bills. He straightened and left the club, rubbing the right side of his face. It had been a long night and all he wanted to do was sleep. The pavement outside glistened, puddles forming in the imperfections. It must have poured while John was in the club, but now it was barely drizzling. A small pool had collected in the bed of John's El Camino. He went around and, still a bit delirious from the blow to his head, he didn't think to step back as he opened the tail gate to let the water rush out. It soaked his shoes before he slammed the gate shut with a thud.

Shit. What next? John sat down in the driver's seat and

turned the key in the ignition. *Maybe this pile of scrap won't start and I'll be stranded here.*

But luck was still on his side, at least a little of it anyway.

As John pulled up in front of his house, brakes squeaking from the rain, he noticed a car that he didn't recognize parked on the other side of the street. Most of his neighbors didn't even have a car, and anyone visiting them wouldn't have such a nice one. This was a new Lincoln, probably less than two years old.

As John slammed his car door and began heading across the lawn to his front porch, out of the corner of his eye he saw the door of the Lincoln opening. Remaining vigilant as he made it to his front door, he saw the driver go around the front of the car to the passenger side. As the man bent down, John quickly did the same, picking up the key from under the mat. He unlocked the door then shoved it open, all the while watching the man struggle with something. When the man straightened, he was holding something in his arms.

Kristin was still passed out as Adam came up the walk to John's door.

"What the hell are you doing here, Adam?" John demanded.

"Hey, Charlie. I've been waiting for you. I brought your sister home," Adam said as he shifted his weight from his right foot to his left, struggling to hold her up.

"Sister?"

"Yeah." Adam gave him a puzzled look. "She said she lived with her brother, Charlie, and gave me this address. She's still pretty out of it so maybe I heard her wrong. Did I not get that right?"

"Well, part right. I thought I told you to take her to Denny's to get some food in her so she'd sober up first," John said, looking at her seemingly lifeless body.

"You did, but remember I said I was an IHOP guy."

"So, what happened?"

"Look, man, I got my own kids to feed and I gotta get home to my wife."

"You're married?"

"Hey, everyone's got secrets. Right, Charlie?" Adam drew out the name, making John wonder if the man was onto him.

"I guess."

"Look, can I just put her down somewhere inside. This girl's light but she ain't that light, and I gotta get home."

"Sure. Come on in," John said as he turned back toward the open doorway. He flipped on a lamp in the corner of the room, revealing a sparsely decorated place furnished with mismatched curbside finds in fashion a decade previous. A green love seat, a brown La-Z-Boy recliner, and a thirteen inch TV that still had rabbit ears.

John made his way to the small kitchen area on the right side of the room as Adam reluctantly walked in. He seemed hesitant to touch anything and even continued to hold Kristin as though not trusting any surface to be clean enough to lay her down.

"What is this? An Amazon distribution center?" Adam said, noting the multiple large stacks of books filling up half of the living room.

"I read a lot," was all John said. One of the perks—or curses, depending at how you looked at it—to a photographic memory was it turned you into a speed reader.

"I'd say," Adam said, clearly struggling to keep Kristin from falling out of his arms.

"Take her into the bedroom and just plop her on the bed."

John smiled, knowing Adam would have to touch something in the process of completing the task. He grabbed a beer from the fridge then stood at the end of the hall to watch.

Adam recoiled a little as he used the back of his coat to push open the bedroom door and took Kristin inside.

John heard a thud as he dropped her on the bed then a

few claps, as though he was dusting any germs he might
have picked up from his hands.

"You can tuck her in yourself," Adam said as he came
out of the bedroom.

"Sure. You want a beer?" John asked as he took off his
coat and laid it on the kitchen counter.

"No, I really gotta go."

"You're a good guy, Adam. Thanks for the help. Now
get home to that family of yours."

"Thanks, Charlie." Then, before John knew what was
happening, he gave John a hug.

John just stood there, uncomfortably, waiting to be released. He'd rather get punched in the face than get a hug.
At least that was something he was used to and could understand.

"Uh, goodnight, Adam," John said, awkwardly patting
him on the shoulder.

As Adam backed away, he looked at him strangely and
said, "I guess it wasn't you after all."

"Guess not."

"Well, then, nice to meet you, Charlie." Then he left,
closing the front door behind him.

John went into the bedroom and stared for a minute at
Kristin. It wasn't the first time she'd been on his bed, but
this time she was actually asleep. She obviously hadn't told
Charlie about the night they'd spent together, or he and
John wouldn't still be friends. It was just one time, a year
earlier.

They were both drunk, that silly excuse that made even
the worst things okay if you were good at rationalizing, and
John was one of the best.

He looked at her lying there. A year had passed since
that night, yet she looked even younger to him now. It made
him feel bad and good at the same time.

He got the blanket from the closet and folded it over
her, then he pushed her hair from her face as he lifted her
head onto the pillow. He looked back at her one last time

before turning out the light and shutting the door to the bedroom.

John kicked off his still-soaked shoes and socks before turning on the TV and plopping down on the love seat. Without a lot of options, he settled on an old episode of *Cheers* from before Woody Harrelson joined the cast.

As he lay there, he took the wad of bills out of his pocket and laid it on the milk crate beside to the love seat, next to his already empty bottle of beer. He sat there, wondering how he should divide it up between his debtors to gain him the most time and which one he should pay first. His train of thought was derailed by the pounding on the door.

CHAPTER 12

The wipers rubbed across dry windshield. Jack left them running, as oblivious to them as he'd been to the two stop signs he ran leaving the vice president's neighborhood. Not that he would have stopped for them if he had seen them. He was thinking about the three bullets that hit him. One in particular.

The ones that had passed through his shoulder and his leg—it was still there—were the ones causing the pain he could now begin to feel. Those two didn't concern him. Pain, after all, meant he was still alive. It was the painless wound in his gut that was the problem. The bullet had passed from his back out his front side. He knew from the exit wound that this was the one that mattered.

Jack had spent a year at Harvard Medical School before dropping out to pursue another career path. He was confused at twenty three and convinced himself that he would be content following the same career route as his girlfriend. He'd followed Sara Ferguson to DC, where she joined the FBI, and he eventually the Secret Service. Not that different of paths, compared to other ways their paths would part soon after college. The breakup had been rough, mostly on Sara, since it was Jack's idea.

They had dated for two years after meeting at Boston

College. He was pre-med and she Criminal Justice. After graduating, she moved to DC to join the FBI while he entered Med School at Harvard. Jack was also entering a time in his life where he was confused about a lot of things. He thought at first it was the stress of school and being separated from Sara that brought on the changes he was experiencing. He thought dropping out of school and moving to DC to be closer to her would help get him back on track. He didn't want to smother her by following her dream into the FBI, but the stories of what she was learning, the parts she could actually share, intrigued him. He decided to join the Secret Service after learning that it wasn't just a glorified bodyguard job. He always liked finance so, when he learned that bulk of what the Secret Service investigated had to do with finance, he decided it was for him. He moved to DC, after starting with the agency, and immediately began to feel fulfilled, with his career choice if not personally. When Sara left to attend the FBI academy in Quantico Virginia, Jack felt that was the time to break it off. She was still in Virginia at the time he called to tell her. She seemed more upset by his denial to let her come back to DC to talk things through than the actual break up.

He wasn't clear why, which kept her from ever completely getting closure. Jack thought not telling her would make it easier on her. He realized later he was just making it easier on himself. He was still embarrassed about what he was realizing about himself. He offered to stay in touch, but the tables had turned and pride had her jumping at the chance to even to the score and make a denial of her own. It probably hadn't made her feel any better after she hung up the phone. They didn't talk again for three years.

With both of them living in DC and in government law enforcement, it seemed statistically plausible they would see each other again at some point. Like two lotto balls dropping down from the same machine and landing next to each other, it happened on a return flight from New York. He was seated in an aisle seat as she boarded the plane. His eyes met hers. Where he expected to see anger in those green eyes, he got the exact opposite. Her whole face lit up like the glow of a child's birthday candle. It made him feel like one again as she came down the aisle. His smile was as big as the seven forty seven she had just boarded.

Three years of separation were reconnected in that short twenty three minute flight from JFK to Reagan airport in DC. They somehow covered almost as much history between them as if from the two presidential terms for which the airports were named. When they landed, they agreed to stay in touch and remain friends from that point on. There was easiness in the air between them now that hadn't been there before. Perhaps due to the fact they had each found someone that made them happy. They saw each other once a week, finding a common interest in jogging around the park. They laughed at how they had never literally run into each other when they realized they both jogged Rock Creek Park. They both ran there every Saturday, but she at eight and he at nine. Unlike congress these days, they decided to compromise and always meet at eight thirty. Unless one of them was out of town on assignment, which was quite often, that's where they'd be every Saturday. They shared about work, but never personal stuff. Somehow they each knew they couldn't go there.

This is what he would miss most, he thought as he continued to drive. Those Saturday jogs with his friend. *Guess I do love her, just not in the same way.* He wondered if he should have told her the truth, but it was too late now.

The pain in his right leg from his torn Achilles ached as he pressed the gas pedal, entering the on-ramp to the freeway. He didn't have much time left so he stomped on the pedal despite the pain. It wouldn't last long. Funny how things happen for a reason he thought. Only one year of Med School but it was long enough to recognize how injured he truly was. That whole first year was spent studying the human body and the placement of the organs. He was good at remembering the Latin word origins for their names and how they worked. He also learned how important some were versus others especially at times of injury. In his case the hole in his stomach was a death sentence. It was just a matter of time, and not that much. From what he remembered, he figured he had about thirty minutes left and it would take him twenty to get to where he was going. That was if he obeyed the speed limit.

CHAPTER 13

The knock on the door was more of a demand than a request. The door vibrated as if crying uncle to the force of the beating. It was just after midnight and the knocking reminded John of when Cinderella's luck had run out at the ball. Perhaps his luck had run out at the same time. He grabbed the stack of bills in front of him as he got up. He put half in his front pocket. Looking quickly around the sparsely decorated room, he ended up just dropping the rest behind the love seat.

"Come on, John, don't make us break down the door," a very deep and all too familiar voice yelled from outside.

"Hold on a second," John said as he went to check on Kristin.

She hadn't budged. He closed the bedroom door and headed to the front door.

Knock, Knock—the door flew open before the third knock.

"What do you want, Billy?" John said, addressing the six-foot-five, three-hundred-pound man in a sports coat standing a few feet behind two average-sized men.

"What do you think we want, John?" Billy said, smiling with his crooked teeth. "Heard you had a good night at the track."

This was serious. Billy rarely needed back up and to-night he brought two guys with him. John had figured word about his winnings would spread quickly, but they usually would wait till the next day to come collect. The bad econ-omy had hit everyone hard and, just like the banks, the mobs were low on capital liquidity. Mobs were not unlike any other business, it was all about cash flow, and if you didn't have the cash, blood would flow. And, not unlike the bankruptcy proceedings around the country, it was all about being the first debtor in line.

John wondered how accurate their source had been. "It was okay, I guess," he threw out, as if begging a response, shrugging his shoulders and tilting his head so that the street light shone on his face.

"Shit, man! Did the Italians already get to you?" Billy said, walking up next to the other two men while gesturing to John's bruised face.

John just rubbed his chin while he nodded, realizing his luck had not run out at midnight, after all.

"Yeah. Sorry, Billy I was planning on coming to see you guys first tomorrow morning, but they got to me first."

"Sure you were, John. So why'd they sock you then?" Billy asked.

"You know how those Italians are," John said.

"Yeah, but I heard you won over six large at the track tonight."

"So?"

"So I also know you only owed those guys four just liked you owe us."

"What the hell? You guys share all that info? Are you going to do like all the banks and start merging, too?"

"Serbs and Italians? I don't think so, John. Besides, that'd be more like a hostile takeover not a merger any-way," Billy said, surprising John with his knowledge on the topic. "So what happened? Did you lie about the money?"

"I might have fibbed a little before they checked for themselves," John said with a smile.

"Well, either way, you should still have some left over," Billy said, putting a hand on each man's shoulder in front of him as if a signal to proceed.

"Would you believe me if I told you they took it all?"

"Don't be offended if I don't." Billy leaned down, his face only a few inches from John's.

"Whoa, your breath is offensive enough." John scrunched up his face. "You know flossing could help with that."

"Fuck you, John. How about I make it so that you never need to floss again, just put your teeth in some bleach at night?" Billy asked, clearly done with the small talk.

"I don't think they soak dentures in bleach if that's what you meant," John said.

"Whatever, John. Grab him guys," Billy ordered.

Each man grabbed an arm then waited further instruction from Billy.

"Really, Billy, three on one? I've never seen you need help with your collections. Although, I do have to say I'm glad someone's hiring. But seriously, what gives?" John asked, unfazed by the actions of the two men holding him.

"I'm forty now, John. I can't risk guys running away on me anymore. My knees aren't what they used to be and I've been eating a little too well," Billy said putting both hands on his protruding belly. "These guys protect me from giving myself a heart attack trying to catch the guys dumb enough to try and run."

"Well, we wouldn't want that, would we, Billy? Who would Len send to do his collections, his son?"

"Ha, that snot nosed cheat? Half of what he would collect wouldn't get back to his dad."

"Really? You should tell him."

"I don't think so, John. I may be getting old physically, but not mentally. That's his only kid and he's already grooming that punk to take over."

"Guess you're never too old to learn to kiss someone else's butt."

Whoosh was the sound John heard as Billy's fist blew a breeze between the two guys holding him right into John's gut. He lurched forward, his head down. The only thing stopping him from falling down completely were the two men now struggling to hold him up.

"Any other smart comments, John?"

"Uh—cuh—cuh," John coughed. "Sure just give me a second to catch my breath."

"You do that while I check your pockets." Billy went through his right pocket then his left, finding the bundle of cash, and pulled it out. He smiled at the two men as he held up the wad of bills made small by his large hand.

"Looks like the Italians didn't take it all after all, John," he said, patting him on the back of his still downward facing head. He then turned away from the three of them and took a few steps as he began to count the money. John raised his head to watch him as he counted. He could tell when he was done by the way Billy tilted his head. "Something's not right here," Billy said raising his head but not yet turning.

The two men still holding his arms, John prepared himself as Billy turned.

"There's three thousand here," Billy said and gave John a questioning look.

"Yeah, so? I already told you the Italians got their take first," John said just as confused as the two men whose faces reflected the same.

"You won six tonight, right?"

"Yeah, lucky me."

"And you owed Angelo four."

"What's your point?"

"My point, John, is why didn't they take the four you owed them and just three? Why would they do that?"

"Those guys didn't seem too bright, Billy. Maybe they couldn't count that high," John said with a smile, looking at the two guys, who returned the smile.

"I've got another theory. Maybe you've been lying to

me this whole time. Maybe it was the Chinese that came by first and got the three you owed them."

"Maybe you're right, but even though sometimes I can't tell you guys from the Italians, I can usually tell when they come calling."

"That's kinda racist, John."

"I didn't mean it that way. They tend to use their feet and not their fists when they collect."

"That's true, but I also have another theory that neither of them came by and you still have all the money."

Before Billy finished stating his theorems, step-by-step like a geometry teacher, John's body tensed as he had a good theory of his own as to what Billy was planning to do next.

It wasn't the rest of the money that John was concerned with protecting. John knew Billy well enough to know the girl wouldn't interest him, but he also wouldn't care to stop the other two guys from taking their rewards of a job well done out on her. So far this whole exchange had been just business and that was ok, but it was about to become quite personal.

"I bet you have the rest of your winnings inside," Billy said.

The two guys had a good grip on John as Big Billy began to approach. One thing John had learned through all his bar-room brawls as a bouncer was that there was a difference between holding someone and holding someone up. Especially when you're not expecting to do the latter.

In the time it took Billy to take his first step back up the sidewalk toward the door, John lifted both of his legs up off the ground. At two hundred pounds, it was a little much for the two smaller men. They fell into each other, dropping John to the floor. The guy on the right had let go of John's arm as he also fell over. The guy on the left was still holding on to John's arm as the both landed on the ground. A quick right to his jaw from John quickly solved that problem as the man went limp from the punch. John followed the momentum of his own punch, using it to roll over and stand up before the other guy could find his feet. As the man rose, it seemed a silly endeavor. As soon as he stood upright, John leveled a punch to his nose, immediately knocking the man back down. John turned quickly back up the sidewalk to prepare for the real challenge.

He was thrown by what he saw. Billy was just standing there with an amused look on his face.

"Really, John?" Billy said with a smile looking at each of his downed men.

"Really," John said back, catching his breath, a little slumped over but still with a look of "You'll be next" in his eye.

"All right, John, how about you bring the rest in the morning?" Billy said, still smiling.

"Sure, Billy, I'll bring it by first thing."

"Come on, boys. Looks like John's got company," Billy said. He winked at John then looked up at the sky. "Besides, it looks like it might start raining again and I don't want to get my suit wet."

John helped lift up the guy he'd hit in the jaw. "Sorry, man."

"It's okay," the amiable gangster replied.

The other guy rejected John's help, shaking him off while still holding his nose with both hands as he rose to his feet. He stumbled along, still woozy from the blow. John gave him a shrug as he backed out his way. The two men followed Billy back to his Hummer.

"See you tomorrow, John." Billy said as he walked around the car and got in the driver's side while the two others climbed into the back.

John had already gone inside and closed his front door before the three car doors slammed shut. He hurried back to the bedroom to check on Kristin. She was still asleep but lying sideways on the bed. From his one night with her, he remembered how she moved like a decathlete in her sleep. Apparently, she was still in training. As he finished straightening her out and pulling the covers back over her, there was another desperate knock at the door.

Billy had either changed his mind or the Italians were next in line. Either way, John's luck had definitely run out at midnight. When he opened the door, what he saw hit him in the gut harder than Billy had.

CHAPTER 14

The cell phone vibrated on the nightstand as Sara lay in bed. At first she thought it was just the rumbling of the far off thunder, the remnants of the storm that had just passed. She had been woken an hour earlier by a louder thunder clap, as the storm passed over her apartment, and she was unsuccessful in trying to fall back asleep. She noted the time on the cable box across the room and wondered who was texting her at eleven forty five at night. In her days in college she had gotten her share of late-night booty calls. But that was almost a decade ago. It wasn't that Sara was any less attractive now than when she was in college. If anything, with her obsessive need to work out, her body was in better shape now at age twenty nine. She also was just as obsessive with her forty-five-plus sun screen so her face hadn't aged much either.

She was fortunate to not need the sun to have that oft-desired brown skin, thanks to her Italian dad and German mom. She kidded with her friends that the real benefit was not that it was year round but that it was all around. No risk of photos of her sunbathing topless like Duchess Kate Middleton. She wasn't in the mood to check her phone. She just lay there, staring at the ceiling.

She turned over her iPhone so it stopped lighting up the

room like a night lite. She sat up, glancing over briefly at the other side of the bed, reminded that she had it to herself. It had been a long time and now she was realizing for the first time the expansiveness of the California King. Sara had just broken up with her boyfriend of exactly one year on Monday. They hadn't lived together, although with as often as he'd stayed over, they might as well have. The problem was that, even though she could kick Todd Lofton out of her apartment, she couldn't kick him out of her life. He wasn't just her boyfriend, he was her boss. She wasn't mad at herself in hindsight for falling for someone at work. That's how many people met. In intense work environments, it was natural for people to form strong emotional bonds. On a scale of one to ten, the FBI qualified as an eleven when it came to intense work environments. What she *was* mad about was what he did, and even more so *who* he did.

Sara didn't just lose her boyfriend that week. She also lost the person that normally would have been the first person to console her on this kind of situation, her best friend, Cynthia.

Cynthia was a fellow analyst who had joined the FBI training program the same time as Sara. They quickly bonded, even though they were quite opposite in personality as well as looks. Sara was tan and a bit taller than average at five foot seven. Cynthia, at five-foot-three, had an almost porcelain-like whiteness to her skin with dark eyes and long black hair. While attractive was the word most often used to describe Sara, the best Cynthia could ever conjure from people was cute. But her boisterous personality and almost cackle of a laugh more than made up for it. She got her share of attention, even while hanging out with Sara. She was a good friend, at least Sara had thought so until Monday night. She was the kind of friend who had always listened intently when Sara would talk about her relationship issues with Todd. In hindsight, it seemed perhaps that she was collecting intel just like she did at work.

Todd's constant flirting with the other analysts at work

was something that took her a while to get used to. Sara knew she was attractive and Todd had often told her that her confidence was the reason he made the choice to commit. This didn't mean she didn't have the same insecurities as any other woman. She caught the more than occasional lingering glances he made as women walked by. What she thought of as cute at the beginning started to concern her after a while. She looked inward at what she had done to drive him to someone else. Maybe he picked up on her lost confidence and that was the hook that had worn and let him loose.

Sara spent a large part of the rest of the week thinking back nostalgically to her time with Jack in college. Not that it helped ease her pain. She should have known better, since it was Jack who had told her while in med school what the word actually meant. He had said it originated from a med student in the seventeen hundreds referring to pain brought on by being homesick. Nostos meaning returning home and algos pain. A medical condition, he had said. Well, that was what it felt like. But some people liked to feel pain since it was better than nothing. For her it was like her penance for allowing Todd's lack of discipline to change who she was.

Perhaps she had been spoiled while dating Jack in college. He never once looked at another coed while they dated. Even when she noticed an attractive one across the room at dinner and pointed over at them, he wouldn't even turn his head out of curiosity to look. Todd, on the other hand, never needed a spotter and didn't fear being caught with a lingering eye. He always said it was part of being a man.

If this had been the only issue, she would have been okay, but what really wore her down was when Todd would blur the line between boyfriend and boss. He did it often and left her spiraling down the rabbit hole of a weakening self-esteem. It was especially hard when he did it at work. It was on those days that she needed Cynthia to go with her to happy hour, listen to her problems, and make her laugh. Cynthia knew about all of Sara's insecurities and issues with Todd. On those nights of talking about Todd, Cynthia had done a lot more than kindle the flames of doubt that Sara had about him. Cynthia was more like a refueling truck backing up and turning that small spark of frustration, like a flick of a lighter, into a full blown towering inferno. Cynthia acted as if she hated Todd, complaining about him as a boss not a boyfriend. She never showed any attraction to the man, quite the opposite. But, just like in grade school, wasn't that how it always started?

It all happened on Monday. Sara thought it was cute that day when she mentioned how it was a special day for them and he clearly had no clue. He would just furrow those dark eyebrows, pinch those hazel eyes with curiosity, and smile with those perfectly paid for teeth of his. Most men couldn't even remember a birthday or the day they were married so she hadn't really expected him to remember the anniversary of their first date. Of course, he had an even better excuse. There was much dispute as to when that actual first date was. There had been many happy hours before what she considered their first date. Many of those nights had them wondering off from the rest of the office to go sit at a table by themselves. Any one of those could have been considered dates. For her, Monday was the anniversary of their first solo date. She had a surprise planned for him that night. It began by telling him that she wasn't feeling well and needed a good night's sleep. He had asked if he could come over and she had said no. She kidded at how it was his fault, anyway, since the assignment he had given her to finish before the next day would have her working late. She pretended to look angry but that came off like a kitten trying to look like a lion as she scrunched up her face. He just patted her on her head and laughed as he walked off. He wouldn't be walking away later with what she had planned, she thought and smiled as she looked down at the large Leaning Tower of Pisa stack of files on her desk.

She considered that now as she lay in bed, how she got stuck in her office most of that day working on those files he had her analyze. Was that on purpose so he had more time to talk and plan with someone else in the office. Was he trying to make it so that she *would* work late and guarantee she'd be too tired to meet up that night at her place or his? It seemed plausible now. What never seemed plausible was how much he took her for granted at her job. Sara was really good at it. The stack that any other analyst would spend after hours finishing she had done by four-thirty. Of course, being a government position, anything after four is considered after hours. But at least she wouldn't be there till six or seven.

Although she was good at her job, it didn't mean she was without stress. For Sara, the best release of that stress was exercise. She changed into her jogging outfit when she got home and ran a quick two miles, three less than her usual five. She barely broke a sweat as she ran slower than normal to save her energy. She would burn more calories later that night.

Sara draped the towel around herself as she got out of the shower, smelling of spring flowers. She walked toward the bag that she had placed on her bed when she got home. She had made one stop on the way from work, a gift for Todd she mused. She picked up the bag and read the name aloud.

"Victoria's Secret, huh?" she asked as she pulled the small purple two piece outfit out of the bag. "Oh, Victoria, you wouldn't last long at the FBI trying to keep secrets, since I think everyone in the world knows what your clothes are for." She laid the towel on the side of the bed, put the outfit on, and walked over to a full length mirror in the corner of her bedroom. The satin fit snuggly, accentuating the curves that didn't really need it. She picked purple because Todd had told her when she wore a dress of the same color that he liked how it brought out her green eyes. She admired her tan body in the mirror as she turned from side to side, one hand on her thigh, the other on her flat belly.

"Damn, I look hot!" she said, turning to see her backside. "I'd better get a thank you card for this gift." She laughed as she went to finish getting dressed. Not normally one for perfume, she took the small bottle the girl at the store had recommended from the bag. She sprayed enough to douse the smell of flowers, replacing it with a scent not so innocent.

ᴇᴏᴇᴏ

Sara was still smiling as she turned her generic black GM car onto the block toward Todd's home. Just about all the employees at the agency had one. After the Bailout, all government agency employees were strongly encouraged to purchase one. But, just like a lot of things in government, when it came to the people actually running things it was still "Do as I say not as I do." Todd drove a seven series BMW.

Her heart raced with anticipation when she saw his car parked in front of his large castle-like house. As she drove slowly up the gravelly road, the sound of tires crackled like a bowl of Rice Krispies. And just like a child, she couldn't wait to poor on the sugar and get a big spoonful. Of course, she did regret one thing as her car crept up the driveway. That she didn't eat first. She knew once she walked in, eating would be the last thing on either of their minds.

"Oh well, breakfast in the morning will just taste that much better," she said as she reached the circular part of the driveway. The large oak trees on the massive estate his parents had left him when they decided to move to New York had blocked her view of the other side of the driveway until she reached the area in front of the home. She didn't notice the other car parked on the other side of Todd's at first. It was another GM, same as hers, black as well, of course. Black was a popular color for cars in this town. For that same reason it could be anyone's. That was until she made the final curve and reached the part of the drive parallel to the entry of the house. At that point her headlights shone on the back of the mystery car, right on the only clue she needed. A sticker on the back bumper, and a colorful one at that. A really offensive one to the men in the FBI. It was a rainbow peace sign.

"Cynthia!" Sara said aloud as she dug her hands into the steering wheel like an archaeologist digging for a dinosaur bone. She slammed on the brakes, staring at the peace sign, thinking anything but peaceful thoughts. She immediately thought of all the *signs* she had dismissed as silly self-doubt and insecurity. They all came flooding back into her mind like the waters that had breached the levy in New Orleans during Katrina.

The times Todd commented on how Cynthia was cute in her own way. The times he had jokingly asked if they had ever hooked up, and how he wouldn't have minded if they had. Like any other woman, of course, she had thought about it. Cynthia was cute. But thinking about it and acting on it were what separated normal people from porn stars, she'd always thought. Maybe it was her conservative Southern upbringing, though she'd never share that with anyone, since conservative was a bad word in DC. It had been a while since he had commented about Cynthia. Now she knew why.

She didn't confront them that night. She was worried what she might actually do to her or him. The rage Sara was feeling inside, coupled with an empty stomach, which made most people irritable anyway, were a potentially deadly combination. Instead, she hit the gas and sped by the two cars on the large driveway, kicking up gravel and scratching the paint on both cars as the pebbles bounced off of each of them in her wake.

She tore off her dress throwing it to the floor in her bedroom. She didn't take the time to change out of her lingerie. She hurriedly put on her jogging outfit and shoes. When running to burn off the stress of work, she would normally go five miles, when angry, six or seven. Tonight she figured she'd have to go at least ten before she got it out of her system. Or at least long enough till she sweated off that stupid perfume she was wearing. She ran half a marathon that night!

It had been a rough week at work. Breaking up with her boyfriend. Ending her friendship with her best friend. That was all by noon on Tuesday. It made for a long week, made longer by the fact that her excessive running on Monday night had her too sore to run the rest of the week. At least it was Friday night. Now she had even more reason to look forward to her Saturday jog with Jack. After losing the two people she usually could talk to she needed to talk to Jack. Thinking of seeing him in the morning now that she was single again made her think of him in a way she hadn't in a while. Whereas Todd was a cut to the chase aggressive lover, which she didn't mind at all, she did long sometimes for the gentle way Jack had been with her in college. Other than not having someone to talk to this past week, she was also missing some other stimulation she had taken for granted this past year with Todd. Before she could finish opening the nightstand drawer to get the one thing she knew would satisfy that urge, she was interrupted by something else vibrating. This time she decided to go ahead and see who it was. It was two texts from Jack.

The first upset her, the second worried her. *Sorry I can't make it tomorrow*. And *Love You, Sarabell*. He hadn't called her that since they dated in college, a play on her name and people always calling her a southern bell.

Who wasn't going to let her down this week? she thought. As upset as she was that she wouldn't get to lament her week to Jack, she still was feeling those urges, now made stronger after Jack's second text.

She pulled out the one thing she figured she could always count on from her drawer. An old friend she hadn't seen in a while since she had Todd to take care of her for the last year. She lay back, readying herself as she slipped down her already moist panties. She flipped the switch to turn it on. Nothing. She shook it, still nothing.

"Et tu, Battery?" she groaned, glaring at it as she realized she truly was on her own. She put it down on the dresser next to the phone and took care of it herself.

CHAPTER 15

John didn't know this man standing in front of him, but he recognized him. The same brown skin, the same blue eyes, the same strong jaw line. Everything about this man was the same as…him. The only difference was the style of clothes. That and the lack of bruises. Although this man was actually in a lot worse shape than John. Before John could say a word, the man slumped over falling onto him.

"I don't have a lot of time. We need to talk," the man said between coughs and gasps for air.

John looked down at his arms after lifting the man upright. His arms were covered in blood. While looking down at his arms, the man stumbled past him and plopped himself down on the couch.

John closed the door slowly still in shock. He stared at this man and noted the blood dripping down on the floor, already forming a puddle around the bottom of the couch.

"Who the hell are you?" John asked.

"I'm Jack, your brother," Jack said.

"What are you talking about?" John said, still standing by the door across the room.

Jack clutched his stomach. "Isn't it obvious, John? I'm your twin brother."

"I don't have a brother."

Jack grimaced. "I can assure you that you do, although not for much longer."

"Look, I don't know who you are but—" John began but Jack cut him off.

"I'm Jack Shields."

"Okay, Jack. Look, we gotta get you to a hospital."

"No point. I'm not gonna make it. I drove here to see you. If I thought there was a chance, I would have driven myself to the hospital. Like I said I don't have a lot of time so please sit down and listen." Jack said as he rocked back and forth slightly while holding his stomach.

"I don't get it."

"Then sit down, shut up, and listen before I die," Jack said, gesturing to the chair with the arm that didn't have a bullet lodged in the shoulder.

John turned the chair to face Jack and plopped down. "Okay fine, shoot."

"Please don't say shoot," Jack said with a grin, trying not to laugh.

"So you just came here to die in my apartment," John said, looking at him and then down at the growing puddle of blood.

Jack grimaced again then looked John in the eye. "Well, not exactly, the person dying here tonight is you."

"You'd have a hard time pulling that off, Jack, even if you weren't bleeding to death."

"Let me explain why you want to die tonight instead of me. I've only got probably fifteen minutes left to convince you."

"You sound pretty sure about how much time you got. Are you a doctor?"

"Was gonna be at one point, but no I'm Secret Service," Jack said, reaching into his pocket with his good arm.

Still on edge, John readied himself. Jack pulled out his wallet and tossed it to him.

John caught it and flipped it open, revealing the Secret

Service emblem with his picture. He felt as though he were looking at his first fake ID again, seeing this picture of him with information that didn't fit. Then he looked back up at Jack.

"Well, you're doing a good job since you've kept the fact that you existed a secret from me for thirty years," John said, closing the wallet still in his right hand.

"Actually, I just found out myself six months ago."

"And you decided not to tell until you thought you were dying."

"Let me finish because I assure you, John, I am dying," Jack said with a more earnest tone, which John was finally starting to believe.

Jack coughed up some blood, John noticed, and he had seen enough movies to know that was never a good sign.

John leaned back in his chair, a little less on edge now. "Okay, go ahead. Why don't we start with the part where I'm the one dying tonight?"

Jack looked at all the stacks of books in the apartment. "It looks like you like to read. Have you ever read the Prince and the Pauper?" Jack asked him.

"Sure. Let me guess you're the Prince in this story."

"More or less, just no happy ending for me in this story."

"No, I guess not."

"But I do want you to be me," Jack said with a whisper as he ran out of breath.

"Why?"

"I think the better question, John, is why not?" he said with a look around the apartment and an implied stare back at John.

"For how long?"

"Permanently, John. Like I said, you are going to die tonight."

"Okay, back to my first question. Why would I want to do that?"

"Let's look at reasons why you don't want to be you

anymore and that might make it easier. Number one, at the rate you're going and the amount of money you owe, not to mention the people you owe it to, you'll be dead soon anyway," Jack said, trying to make himself comfortable, unsuccessfully.

"You've been checking up on me?"

Jack grunted in pain. "I have my ways."

"And your life is so much better? Looks like I'm going to outlive you. Being you doesn't look like the safe bet to me."

"When have you ever taken the safe bet? Besides, you're not really good at it," Jack said, smiling again.

"Hey, I had some luck tonight."

"Is that how your face looks on a good night?" Jack asked, gesturing to John's banged up face.

"This is nothing, I get worse at work."

"Which brings me to point number two as if number one wasn't reason enough. You work as a bouncer. How many forty year olds do you know who are still bouncers. Do you think they retire early?"

"You haven't met No Nose Bob. He's almost fifty and still going at it."

"So what's your nickname gonna be by then. Look, quit dicking around. I don't have time. I'm offering you a better life. Now just tell me yes, so I can tell you why. What do you say?"

"Okay, yes," John said. "Tell me why."

"I'm gonna keep it simple since—" He coughed. "Well, two reasons. First you got screwed when they didn't point to you."

"When who didn't point to me?"

"William and Charlotte Shields, my parents, who pointed at me instead of you at the orphanage when asked which one, since they only wanted to adopt one of us. He was a doctor and she an English professor at Georgetown."

"They retired now? You said was."

"They died in a car accident six months ago."

"Wait, you said that you learned about me six months ago. Is that related?"

"Yes, they had their will in a safe deposit box. When I went to get it out, there was an envelope in there with the will. It was a letter from the orphanage. It was written to them a few months after they adopted me. The orphanage had lost its funding and they wanted to ask my parents one more time if they had reconsidered adopting you before you got stuck in the revolving door of foster homes."

"More like a slamming door."

"Obviously, they hadn't."

"Obviously, so why wait so long to tell me."

"I didn't know the whole story. And it took me a while to find you since, like me, you don't have the same name we were both born with."

"That I do know. Our Mom's name was Jane Wilson."

"That's right. What else do you know about her?"

"Just that she died during childbirth."

"And…" Jack prodded.

"And that she was a hooker," John said reluctantly, looking down at the floor as if that would hide his shame.

"Exactly, that's the story they got from the hospital the night the orphanage came to pick us up. This is my second and more important reason for you to live my life. I want you to finish looking into what happened to our mom. You can use all the resources I have used as a Secret Service agent and my contacts in other agencies in DC to find out what really happened."

"What do you mean what really happened?"

"Who killed our mom and why?" Jack said, his whole body tensing.

"Killed her?" John demanded, sitting up in his chair and leaning forward. Then John realized that the look Jack sent him wasn't just meant to emphasize the point, but that his brother's time was almost up.

"Promise me, you'll do it, that you'll find out why and get the real bastard in our lives," Jack said as he began to shake and slump down. He held out his hand. "Promise me."

"I promise." John shook his hand. As he did, he could feel the life leaving Jack, as his hand seemed to already be turning cold.

"You wouldn't lie to a dying man, you're own brother, would you?"

"I'll do it. I just don't know how."

"Just don't tell anyone and leave here tonight. My car is outside. Just hit home on the GPS. Leave me here and they'll just think one of your debtors got tired of waiting. Then just contact my partner Richard, he's in my phone. You can tell Richard and he will help you with the rest. He knows everything about me. He'll help you be me."

"You're partner knows about me?"

Jack fell down to the floor. "Richard knows about you."

John jumped out of the chair, leaned over him, and took him by his shoulders, getting even more blood on his hands from the shoulder wound.

Jack looked up at him. "You can do this."

"I will," is all John said back.

With that, Jack closed his eyes and was gone.

CHAPTER 16

John sat there for twenty minutes before moving. The sight of his dead brother lying on the floor held him in place almost as much as the thought of what he had just committed to doing.

"Well, first things first. We gotta get you out of those clothes. I wouldn't be caught dead wearing an outfit like that, pardon the pun," he said, trying humor to get through the situation.

He needed to move quickly, after the time he had already wasted, before rigor mortis set in and made what he was about to do impossible. If getting the clothes off was basic algebra, getting one of his outfits on was AP Calculus. One thing that helped was that Jack had been in much better shape so John's clothes were much easier to get on.

John continued to joke as he pulled a pair of his jeans onto the body. "I love you, man, but brother you stink," he said as he finished struggling with the pants, a bead of sweat forming on his forehead. As he looked down on the shirtless body, he noted the exit wound from his stomach and then glanced at the blood around the floor.

"I'm surprised you didn't bleed more. If I wasn't trading places with you, I might be upset about cleaning this place up. How the hell did you even make it here?" He stood up to go get one of his few button down shirts figuring it would be a lot easier to get on. As he walked back with the shirt he noticed how in shape Jack had been compared to himself. He stared down at his own bit of a gut then back at Jack who looked to him as if he had a smirk on his face.

"Hey, don't laugh. At least I'm still alive. What did all that working out get you?" He laughed and knelt down next to him. "This is my best shirt, so no complaining."

The body had already begun to stiffen so it was a struggle getting each arm through the sleeves. After a few minutes of struggling he was able to connect the front of the shirt and button it up. He worked up more of sweat with this fight than the previous two he had earlier in the evening. He sat back up in the chair across the room wiping the sweat from his brow with his forearm as he admired his work. As he looked him over something didn't seem right.

"Bullet holes dumb ass, come on, John, the cops aren't that dumb."

He grabbed a knife from the kitchen and went to make holes in the shirt and jeans corresponding to the wounds. He guessed that the shot in the gut had gone straight through so two holes for that one.

"I really did like this shirt," he said as he cut the hole in the back and propped the body up against his leg. The other two wounds he guessed that the bullets remained in the body so just one hole each for the entry. He wondered, though, if that was the correct guess but he wasn't too concerned.

"Good thing that's supposed to be me down there. They won't go all CSI on this shooting. They'll probably look at me, I mean you, and say, 'Surprised he made it this long.' They'll just pick me up and throw me in a body bag. Case closed as soon as the bag is zipped shut."

He walked to the kitchen to grab a well-deserved beer. As he took a swig and placed the bottle on the end of the kitchen counter he saw the glimmer coming from Jack's arm. "Damn, I'm bad at this," he said as he went back toward the body, knelt down, and removed the Rolex watch from his arm.

He wiped a drop of blood from its face and put it on, noting the time at twelve thirty. He couldn't take much more time admiring it since the increasing bad stench of something akin to rotting chicken was filling the room as if it had been tear gassed by SWAT.

He went back to the kitchen to finish his beer before heading out to his new life as Jack.

He took one more swig, his back to the room, as if that would weaken the scent enough for him to finish. This tranquil moment was interrupted by a loud scream.

"John!" Kristin screamed, looking down at the body.

He dropped the bottle. As it exploded on the ground, Kristin turned and looked toward the man in the kitchen. The light was off so she couldn't recognize who it was, but she saw who she thought was John lying dead on the living room floor. She stood there frozen, somewhere between shock and fear. As John looked down at the smashed bottle on the floor he was reminded of the wallet he held in his right hand. No time like the present to begin being Jack. He cleared his throat before deepening his voice.

"Who are you?" he said in an authoritative tone as he took a step out of the kitchen, revealing himself in the light from the living room.

"Uh, I'm Kristin," she said with a stutter as she glanced no less than three times back and forth between the man addressing her and the one laying on the floor. Was it the alcohol or whatever it was that had knocked her out that was causing her to see double? she wondered.

"John?" she asked the man hopefully with a whisper.

"No, ma'am, you were right the first time. That's John over there," he said, gesturing with his left hand toward the body.

"But you look just like him," she said as she stumbled on her weakened knees, falling back into the wall.

"Why don't you sit down before you fall on the body?" he said, changing the subject.

She looked back at him after settling herself against the wall.

"Who are you then?" she asked with anger, expecting something bad and readying herself for the worst.

"Well, I'm not the guy who killed your friend there, if that's what you're thinking. He was like that when I got here."

"That doesn't answer my question."

"I'm with the agency," he said, flipping his badge at her.

"What agency?"

"Secret Service."

"What? Why would you be here? Don't you guys just protect the president?"

"Actually, we investigate all kinds of things, but mostly money laundering. You're friend here was helping us out in that matter. He was getting us some dirt on one of the mobs he owed money to," John said, almost as if convincing himself as he went along. It must have been convincing enough, since Kristin was comfortable enough to sit down in the chair and put her head between her hands.

"So what happened?"

"Like I said, he was like that when I got here." He gave her a suspicious glare to get her to look away from him.

"Don't look at me like that. I was passed out in the bedroom."

"Passed out?"

"I mean asleep."

He figured staying on the offensive was his best play. "You didn't hear the shots?"

"No. I just got up. I'm not even sure how I got here."

"Did you know the deceased?" he asked, trying to keep it formal.

"Yes I know John—knew him. He's a friend of my brother."

"What is his name?"

"Charlie."

"Charles Riley?"

"Yeah, how did you know?"

John grabbed the napkin out of his pocket that Charlie had written for him earlier and showed it to her.

"He left his car to Charlie?"

"You sound surprised."

"He would never let him drive his car," she said.

John smiled to himself inside, proud of her knowing this about him. "Well, maybe he figured after he was dead it didn't matter. Tell you what. You seem like a nice girl. Why don't you get out of here, before my backup gets here to clean up this mess?"

"I told you, I don't even know how I got here."

"Take Charlie's car. You know what?" He tore the napkin up. "Take your car. I don't think anyone's gonna come looking for it, anyway, and I won't tell Charlie if you don't," he said, holding out the car keys. "I already checked the car. The title is in the glove box. Go ahead and sign it over to yourself."

"Thanks," she said as she stood up slowly and walked over, taking the keys.

John looked away and walked toward the body. He bent down by the edge of the couch and grabbed the roll of bills behind as he picked up her purse. He stuffed the bills into it before turning to hand it to her.

"Here's your purse. Now hurry up and get outta here," he said.

As she grabbed the purse, he put his hand on top of hers and held on for a second. She looked at his hand as if recognizing the feel of it.

"You never told me your name," she said, looking up at him in the dark kitchen.

"Jack Shields."

CHAPTER 17

The black sedan was not brand new. It had a little over twenty thousand miles. For John it might as well have been driven right out of a show room.

The leather seats were more comfortable than any piece of furniture he had ever owned or even sat on. The position of the power driver seat fit his body perfectly. He noted all the other little extras—navigation system, satellite radio, sunroof, push button start. It had everything but, as he looked around before starting the car, he noticed one thing missing. He didn't see blood anywhere, which was quite surprising considering the mess Jack had made in his now old apartment. That's when he noticed the bunched up leather coat with the blood-soaked lining on the passenger-side floorboard.

"Thanks for keeping the car clean, bro," he said. He even detected the remnants of new car smell it still had. He hit the start button and the engine began to hum like a symphony, silently warming up but accompanied by a dinging of the seat belt reminder.

"Didn't have a problem bleeding all over my place," he said and strapped on the seat belt, silencing the dinging noise. "At least he kept my car clean." He adjusted the rearview and went through the preset radio stations, one through

five. The first was classic rock, then contemporary, eighties
music, another classic rock, then country. "Really, Jack. I'm
supposed to listen to country? I'll work up to that." He hit
preset number one again and it was playing some Pink
Floyd song that seemed to fit the surreal situation he was
now in.

"Okay now, where to?" He turned on the Navigation
system. Again, he went through some of the preset destinations, home, office, Sara, Richard, Lauren, and some other
names he obviously didn't recognize. "Time to go home,"
he said as he turned the dial and locked it in.

"Home. Calculating route. Destination twenty-three
miles," the sultry voice announced through the eight speakers.

The car seemed to float down the highway. His El
Camino didn't have power steering. That was something he
was going to have to get used to. A small adjustment compared to the many new things John was going to have to
learn. As nice as the car was, he figured he was in for more
of the same when he got to his new home. The first indica-
tion was the gate outside the neighborhood entrance, armed
with not a key pad but an actual person. He noted the time
on the clock in the car at one a.m.as he slowed the car to a
crawl and pulled up the guard's office.

He reached for the window roller that wasn't there,
panicking slightly as he didn't see the button on the door.
The guard stepped out of his office. John found the button
in the middle console and rolled the window down just as
the guard stood next to the car.

"Hey, Jack, long night?" the twenty–something, messy-
haired guard said.

He looked more like a member of the Foo Fighters then
your typical security guard. Kind of a waste with all the
former retirees looking for work again after their retirement
portfolios got demolished in the financial crash.

"You know me," was all John could think to respond,
smiling at the irony of it. He purposely didn't lean forward,

staying in the shadow of the car. He didn't want the guard to see his bruised face.

"Well, at least you'll get some sleep tonight, I still got six hours on this shift," the guard said, shrugging his shoulders. "At least, I'll have time to work on my novel."

"Good idea. How's that going?" he asked the guard, regretting it as soon as it left his lips. What was he thinking, extending the conversation with an open ended question? This guy clearly knew Jack. John should have kept it short and had him open the gate. Too late now. He was engaged.

"Pretty good, I just hit one hundred pages."

"So what? You're like half way done?" John said, even though he knew that most novels averaged at least three hundred pages.

"No, about a third. Any decent mystery needs to be at least three hundred pages."

"Is that so?" John asked. "Well, that's still pretty good."

"Yeah, I guess but I also hear that's where a lot of first time writers get stuck."

"Well, write five more pages tonight to prove to yourself you're not one of those."

"That's the plan. Hey, are you still okay with sitting down with me sometime to give me some good 'inside Washington' stuff to make the book sound more realistic?" the guard asked.

What inside Washington stuff? John didn't know anything about DC, definitely not enough to sit down with this kid and give him ideas for his Great American Novel. Any details he would share would risk the kid getting barred from the industry due to plagiarism. He had to think of a way to stall.

"How long did it take you to get to a hundred pages?" John asked.

"About six months."

"Okay, I tell you what. Let me know when you are at one hundred fifty. That's usually when a book starts getting into the heavy stuff," he said, like a quarterback throwing a Hail Mary.

"That makes sense."

Touchdown, John thought then he exaggerated a yawn, raising a fist to his wide open mouth.

"Let me get that gate for you. Have a good night, Jack."

"Thanks, you too," he said, thinking *I gotta get that kid's name.*

ℰℛℰℛ

John parked the car in the condo's garage downstairs. He threw the coat in a trash can in the garage and entered his new home. He turned on the lights as he walked in, tossing the keys on the counter. They bounced off the granite counter top of the island in the kitchen with a clank then scraped as they slid down the already hand scraped hardwood floors.

"Nice place you got here, Jack," he said as he admired the expansive room. The furniture was what he thought might be considered contemporary. It was a balanced mix of Ethan Allen blended with IKEA. No cardboard boxes with a TV sitting on top. His sixty-inch Sony flat screen was mounted on the wall. It seemed bigger to him than some of the movie screens he watched at the dollar movie house in his neighborhood.

He veered into the kitchen to see what kind of drinks he could find in the fridge. His mouth was dry and he was thirsty.

He saw that all the appliances were stainless steel and, when he reached the refrigerator, it had two doors—each of which was bigger than the one on his old fridge. When he opened the door on the right side, he immediately saw things in there he wasn't used to eating. Vegetables.

"Again, I ask. Where did that get you, Jack?" He bent

down to look on the bottom row. "Bingo," he said as he found some bottles of Heineken on the bottom shelf. "These are just as healthy in my book," he said.

He grabbed a bottle and, without hesitation, turned the twist off cap with his hand, not even noticing as the cap ate into one of the callouses. After swigging the beer down, he opened the pantry door to look for the trash can.

In the pantry, that was bigger than his old kitchen, he saw two options, a regular trash can and a blue one that looked like it was for recycling. He tossed the empty bottle in the trash, because that one was closer.

As he walked around the place and headed to the bedroom, he felt more comfortable, noticing the wood stained shutters were all closed. His first instinct was to be curious and look around the room, in all the closets and drawers. He was tired, though. It had been an eventful night. He knew he would have to track down Jack's partner the next day and begin being Jack. He wasn't sure about Jack's habits, at this point, but for him Saturday mornings were for sleeping in.

John stripped down to his boxers, throwing his clothes off onto the floor, making a mess of the immaculate surroundings. He plopped down on the ridiculously large bed and crawled into the luxurious five-hundred-thread-count Egyptian cotton sheets. In this kind of comfort, he figured he'd sleep more snug than King Tut. As he got himself comfortable, not a hard task, he thought this was his last night as John and, when he woke up, he would be Jack from that point on. He smiled as he closed his eyes, thinking he was okay with that.

CHAPTER 18

Sara got back at her apartment at ten a.m. She had run eight miles at a more relaxed pace. She didn't torture herself this time, physically or mentally. She felt that, beyond shedding a few pounds, she also shed some of the guilt she had been feeling during the week.

Guilt for trusting a friend she knew was selfish and being a friend to someone like that in the first place. That was the easy one, that only took the first mile. The other five were spent sweating out the guilt of not recognizing Todd for the spoiled rich kid that always got everything thing he wanted and still hadn't grown up. Now she also realized he had no intention of wanting to grow up and, for that reason, he'd always want someone younger to keep him feeling young. At mile six, she broke free. The last two miles she ran for herself. Maybe it was the endorphins kicking in but, for the first time that week, she finally felt happy. She was free from Cynthia, free from Todd, and even free from Jack. Although she still wondered where he was and why the strange text the night before.

Sara kicked off her running shoes in the kitchen while she stood at the fridge filling a large tumbler with ice and water. The ice cubes rattled in the glass as she drank while walking toward the shower, letting articles of clothing fall off of her on the way. She thought with this energy rush she was experiencing that she'd do something she hadn't done in over a year. She'd go into the office on a Saturday. Why not? She wasn't going to spend the day with Todd, definitely wouldn't be shopping with Cynthia, and her friend Jack was MIA.

Before starting the car, she checked her phone to see if Jack had texted her back from her earlier text that morning.

Nothing.

She looked at her phone as if it had insulted her, and threw it back into the middle console.

Sara drove as fast and sporadic as she jogged. She passed cars on the freeway, on the right as well as the left. She hated slow drivers in the left lane. One of the things she liked about her time in Germany, beyond the no speed limits thing on the autobahn, was that with a simple turn signal people actually moved out of your way. All she got by trying that this morning was the finger. So she passed them on the right and waved right back. Sure, Germans had tried to take over the world, but that was just because they loved following the rules. They didn't know the guy making the rules was a crazy psychopath. Had they won the war, maybe the world would be a little more organized, at least when it came to the roads. Hah, who was she kidding? Sara wasn't one for rules. She pressed the pedal and passed everyone in the far right lane. It only took her twenty minutes to get to the office, half the time as during the week. She parked her car backward in Todd's reserved spot.

In five years of working at the FBI as an analyst, her job had always been just that, analytical. In other words, boring. Funny how Todd dumping extra work on her to allow him time for his distractions actually resulted in work she found interesting for the first time in a while. What was even funnier was that it was in banking. She had now a vested interest in finding something wrong with banks. It was that institution that was the source of Todd's famously reported accumulation of wealth the past few years. Todd's great grandfather founded a bank over a hundred years ago. Its current name was First National Bank, or FNB for short, bankers loved acronyms. Now, after eight or nine mergers, that bank had grown to the third largest in the country with over a trillion dollars in assets and Todd's family still held over fifty percent of the stock. The two most recent mergers came after the financial meltdown in 2008. To say FNB benefited from downturn would be like saying the Saudis benefited from finding oil in the ground.

Todd was considered the black sheep for rebelling against the family and not joining the family business. He, being the only son, was expected to be next in line after his father to run the bank. His one sister had no problem trying to take that spot. She did follow the family and now headed up all of retail banking in the US for FNB while Todd carved his own path in law enforcement. Now, at forty two, he was assistant director at the FBI and could more than hold his head up high at the occasional dinner parties hosted at their home in New York. His dad actually toasted his son now, whereas in the years as he worked his way up, he sometimes wasn't even invited. Although a rebel, Todd wasn't stupid. He did keep a large share of his stock in the bank and also benefited by its recent rise after the two mergers. You didn't see a lot of FBI men on the Forbes richest four hundred list, but there Todd was ranked at three hundred and sixty two, just after some make-up heiress and before some Russian textile manufacturer.

Of all the secrets at the FBI, the one her coworkers always wondered about was why Todd even worked there. For Sara, the answer seemed obvious long before she even started dating him. Todd liked women and he'd figured out that what worked even better than money was power. Now he had both and only one promotion away from Director. And here she was investigating a number of banks, looking for a kink in this charmed boy's life, and she liked the idea of finding something. Maybe she'd even find something to knock the bank stocks back down like in 2009 after the crash. Never mind the millions of people who would lose value in their retirement funds if she did. It didn't matter, as long as she could knock Todd off the Forbes list.

The bank she was looking at wasn't FNB. Not even close. It was what was considered a regional bank with only about fifty billion in assets. *Only*, she mused. They were in trouble and were now on the radar of not only other banks but also the FDIC. That was one place a bank didn't want to be. It was kind of ironic. The FDIC was like the banks' best friend, with the banks telling customers their money was always safe, thanks to that famous FDIC guarantee. The thing was, after the crash, the FDIC was just like anyone else when money was tight. And that was what happened when the money started running out. Instead of being a bank's best friend, if they felt you might be going down, they came in and shut you down. They forced banks to merge, and do it quickly, so they wouldn't have to pay as much in claims. Just like a loan shark looking to collect its debts, they were circling the regionals. Now they had their sights on Nation One, and there was blood in the water.

About an hour into her research, she found something very interesting in the transactions of this bank. Interesting enough that she now had another reason to talk to Jack. She needed to show him what she found and see what he thought. He worked on this stuff more than her at the Secret Service and could verify what she was seeing. She texted him again.

I need to see you ASAP! Lunch Monday @ 11. I need meat. Ruth's Chris.

The personal stuff would have to wait. She'd have to discuss work-related things.

This was too big not to. It's not like they talked personal stuff much anyway. Jack was just another man with secrets when it came to his personal life. In a solar system full of men, it was always the ones with secrets that pulled her into their gravitational pull.

Jack was like the sun as to the size of the secret he kept

from her. The next time she would see him though, the se-cret he held would go super nova. She put the phone away and headed back home, but not before stopping for some batteries.

CHAPTER 19

The new Jack woke up slowly but realized quickly it wasn't a dream after all. He was Jack now, time to get up and get used to the idea. The comfortable sheets held him in bed like a wrestler pinning him down not ready to let go. As he sat up, he took in all the comforts of this new life that surrounded him. The nice clock on the nightstand that had a port for an iPod, oh, and central air. It was keeping the place nice and cool, a little cooler than he liked. As he got out of bed in just his boxers, his first mission was to find the thermostat. He checked the bedroom then went out into the living room as he held himself, trying to stay warm. When he was unsuccessful, he went through the kitchen on his way to the front door, figuring in would be on the wall next to the door. That was when he saw the iPad-looking thing on the island. He remembered one time when he had actually been at the Italian boss's home. The man had one of those controllers that did everything in the house. Jack went over and picked it up.

He walked into the living room and pushed a button on the screen labeled number one. The shutters began to open, letting in the light of the sun that had risen two hours prior.

"Okay, that's not it," he said as he tried button number two. The TV came on. It was on CNBC. "Great a whole

channel dedicated to rich people so they can keep an eye on
their money." He watched it for a minute. It was recap of
the week's decline in the market of over four hundred
points, something about a double dip finally hitting after
being long overdue. Lately, you could categorize this channel as horror since all it did was scare the shit out of people.
Another bank had failed, this one in Alabama, that Jack had
never heard of. A New York bank was taking it over after
the FDIC had moved in and seized control. A new civil war
was underway, this time in the banking world. Just like in
the original, the Yankees were winning.

Jack left the TV on as he turned, trying button number
three, just as he stepped below an air vent, feeling the
breeze on his already-goose-bumped body. He didn't hear it
turn off like the window units in his old neighborhood that
had a backfire to rival any old car's. The breeze just simply
stopped. He must have hit the right button. He sighed in relief as he shimmied one more time to shake off the cold.
Even if he hadn't, he was done pushing buttons. He feared
the next one might launch a nuclear missile at Russia.

"Russia, ha, are they even still our enemy anymore?
Real good, Jack, you're in the Secret Service and you don't
even know that," he said as he laid the controller back on
the island. He took in the place, again feeling very much
like Tom Hanks in *Castaway* all alone on his island by himself.

He walked over to the fridge and opened it up to find
something for breakfast. He looked through the vegetables
and vitamin drinks that either didn't interest him or he
didn't know what they were.

"Here we go," he said as he settled on a jar of pickles
and grabbed the large glass bottle with one hand, shutting
the door behind him. He took a bite of one of the kosher
dills, crunching it. It burst its sour juice like a child's water
balloon in his mouth.

"Breakfast of champions! Wow, that's sour, Jack. Oh
well, this will wake me up," he said.

He grabbed a glass and got some water from the kitchen sink. *Old habits, come on, Jack,* he thought as he saw the drink dispenser on the fridge while gulping down the glass.

Three pickles later, he put the jar back in the fridge. Time to get ready. He headed back to the bedroom, let his boxers fall down next to rest of his clothes from the night before, and went into the bathroom to shave and shower. He figured he'd spoil himself and do both.

Before he got to the bathroom, he glanced back at the pile of clothes. What would Jack do? he wondered and went back, standing nude over the pile. He felt like he'd get a ticket for littering if he left it there on the floor. He bent down and picked up the pile and went toward the closet.

The fact it even had a door was something new for Jack. He opened it to a room bigger than his old bedroom. A light came on as he entered. Apparently, a motion sensor triggered it. He saw a wicker basket at the other end about ten feet back, went over, and lifted the lid with his left elbow. He plopped the clothes in and took in the room. At least it was easy to see that he had work clothes on the right and non-work clothes on the left. Each row was full of stuff nicer than he had ever worn. Whereas the clothes on the left shouted out style and independence with wild colors, the left side was in black and white. He was literally watching the beginning of the *Wizard of Oz* play out in the two opposing rows in this large closet.

"I'm not in Kansas anymore, am I, Dorothy?" He turned from the colorful clothes back to the black and white and ran his hand across the many black ties hanging down from a rack. "What a waste. They're all the exact same. Why not just buy one?" Then it hit him. "Oh, yeah, I'm rich now. Who cares?" Then something else hit him, but this time like a punch in the gut from his visitor from the night before.

"Shit! I don't even know how to tie one of these," he said, grabbing one off the rack and stretching it between two hands while looking at it. It was like trying to solve a

Sudoku Puzzle. Actually, with his memory, he was good at those. Then he laughed out loud, realizing how silly this seemed.

"Yeah, this is my problem. Trying to pretend I'm Jack Shields, Secret Service Agent, and not knowing anything about that, not knowing who my coworkers are, or even who my friends are that I'm supposed to convince I'm him. How I'm supposed to pull that off? That hasn't concerned me. But oh, the fact I can't tie a fucking tie, really, Jack?"

He continued laughing as he hung the tie back up. "Besides, it's Saturday. I don't need to worry about that today, anyway. He walked out and toward the shower."

As he got out, he wrapped the softest towel he had ever felt around his waist and went back into the closet to pick out an outfit from the Technicolor side of the closet. This actually made him look forward to work on Monday where at least that part of being Jack would be easy.

As he got back into the living room, he saw the phone on the kitchen counter was blinking ,signaling a missed text message. He picked it up and read the two messages, both from someone named Sara.

Missed you this morning, I did 8 miles. Sent at ten a.m. The next came just before he got up at eleven. *I need to see you ASAP. Lunch Monday @ 11. I need meat. Ruth's Chris.*

As urgent as the second one sounded, it was the first text that worried him.

"I jog?" he said, still staring at that first text, even more panicked than from all the ties that he didn't know how to tie.

It was time to go see his partner and start figuring out what other things he needed to know if he was going to get ready for Monday.

CHAPTER 20

Mikal Ginsberg had always been neat. Today was no different. Perhaps he was a slave to routine, more than anything else. Lately, his routine was working at the office on Saturdays. As the CEO of First Federal Bank, the fourth largest in the country, he had been working on the merger of his bank with National Trust.

"Merger?" He laughed at mention of the word. "The Germans taking Poland wasn't called a merger and, in a lot of ways, that could have been considered even less hostile, since the Poles didn't put up much of a fight."

Mikal had been fighting with everything he had but, unfortunately, what he had was running out, money. This was a takeover in the most hostile of ways, National Trust had teamed up, in his mind, with the FDIC to take them over. Yes, the banks' best friend was at it again, stabbing another bank in the back. What changed was as simple as that old saying, "Follow the money.". Banks were running out of it and, with banks, it was all about capital ratios, how much cash they had to offset loans not getting paid back. There were a lot of loans not getting paid back and, therefore, the ratios were in trouble. The scary thing was that it wasn't just the banks that were in trouble. After the downturn and all the bank failures, the FDIC was running out too.

Insuring a single person's funds up to one hundred thousand dollars meant it didn't take long to go through a lot of your funds. It was one thing to prop up some of the smaller regionals, but not the fourth largest bank in the country with over eight hundred billion in deposits. Not only would they not have the funds to cover the claims, a failure of that magnitude had the potential to collapse the system.

In Mikal's mind, it was a self-fulfilling prophecy with the FDIC. He still felt they could sell some of their many assets and raise the capital needed to right the ship. The problem was that National Trust was turning up the heat and threatening to walk away if the FDIC didn't force his bank's hand. The FDIC had a choice to make, wait it out and see if FFB could raise the capital they needed or risk having to come up with the funds themselves if it failed. It really wasn't much of a choice, so they sent their normal warning shot over the bow. They'd issued a Cease and Desist Letter to FFB. As soon as word got out that it had been sent, insiders started referring to FFB as the financially fucked bank.

Now the clock was ticking since they had been given only sixty days to raise their capital levels. That was fifty days ago. Time was running out for Mikal and he still needed to raise another thirty billion. Everyone on Wall Street considered it a done deal and were placing bets against him. Two years prior at the start of the downturn, before anyone knew how bad it would get, National Trust had offered eight dollars a share. That was soundly rejected even while the stock hovered barely over five dollars a share at the time. NT became known as Nice Try. Now they were done being nice. With the pressure from the FDIC, it was about to gobble up FFB for less than the price of a happy meal at two dollars a share.

Mikal was not a quitter. He would fight till the end. He'd fought tougher battles in his days in the Israeli Army. He had spent the last month sitting in on *Power Lunch* on CNBC at least once a week, arguing his case. He hated the network and never really watched before, but he knew the

PR game. The only shining light in it all was that he would occasionally be interviewed by Maria Bartiromo

"What man wouldn't like talking to a beautiful woman, one that talked more about making money than spending it? Especially an old Jew like me?" he'd said with a laugh when his son had questioned him on his many appearances on the show.

Mikal was the last man standing when the rest of the board said to let it go. They were going to hold a vote on Monday to allow the sale to go through. Even with his thirty percent of the vote, he would not have the majority since the remaining members were in complete agreement, including his son, Ian, who held twenty percent. While pride of his company surviving was what drove Mikal, Ian, on the other hand, was more focused on the three billion in stock value he had lost over the last few months. He worried that the bank needed to sell before he would not even be a footnote on the next Forbes list.

Mikal had a feeling it was coming with NT. He took note of how they had offered to come in and rescue another investment firm on Wall Street the past year. They acted as if they had done the government a favor, and maybe they had. Now it was time to pay that favor back.

"I guess it's not collusion when it's the government you're colluding with," he'd told the board at the last meeting, warning them of what was coming a month after that happened. Most just took it as the ramblings of an old man. Some went so far as to think this still had to do with the fact that the NT Chairman was German. It was a plausible argument to make after Mikal had made the comment comparing NT's partnership with the government as the AXIS countries coming together in World War Two. It had come to a sad end, the board thought, but they had to leave with something, so the vote was coming on Monday.

What they didn't realize was that Mikal did find a way to raise the capital. He would just need more time. He found a buyer for the European arm of the bank. The third largest bank in Germany felt this purchase could move it to number two.

"Fucking Germans," he growled at first when they contacted him two weeks prior. He had spent every day since in his office, negotiating the price and terms of the deal and now it was close to closing. It would give them the buffer to get their capital ratios up where they needed to be. High enough so that Mikal could tell Claus Steinherz to fuck off. The fact that it was the bank that Claus used to run before taking over at National Trust that was the bank to kill the deal would just be the cherry strudel on top. The only issue was that the deal wouldn't close before Monday morning's board meeting. Mikal knew he had to come up with something big to delay the vote and he figured he had found it. He, like any CEO of a major company, had an ego. His thoughts quickly went from not just being happy about saving his own bank from a takeover, but maybe this would save all of them and turn the tide so no more ships would have to sink.

Mikal was still smiling as he closed the door to his Mercedes after sitting down. The car was just as neat as his office. He had to admit the Germans built a nice automobile. Out of habit, he adjusted the rearview mirror, even though it was usually dead silent on Saturdays. He put on his seatbelt and placed the key in the ignition. As he turned the key, he couldn't wait to see the expression on Monday from the members of his board.

The explosion rocked the entire sixty-story building, collapsing two levels of the garage.

There was nothing neat about Mikal Ginsberg's death.

CHAPTER 21

J ack pulled up to the house. The sultry female voice
from the GPS said, "Destination reached."
  He parked the car and looked at the quaint three-
bedroom brick home. It was in one of those *Leave It to Bea-
ver* kind of neighborhoods. He envisioned a wife, two kids,
and a dog. As he walked up the sidewalk to the front door,
he noticed how immaculate the grass was in the lawn. It
looked nicer than the turf at Redskins Stadium, not that he
had ever seen it in person. The side of the home was surrounded with full green bushes and with rose bushes, red
and white alternating in between. It was so Americana, he
wondered to himself *No blue*? He rang the doorbell and then
readied himself to meet Richard and his family.

  The door opened and a surprised Richard stood there,
holding the phone to his ear. He looked him up and down
and then with his free hand motioned him to come in. He
took him in with his eyes as Jack walked past him while he
closed the door. Then he passed him on his way back to the
kitchen still apparently listening to someone talk on the other end.

  Jack looked around the home for signs of the rest of the
family. He didn't find any. Clearly they were already gone,
probably at some soccer game or some other extracurricular

activity that kids were into these days. He did see a picture on the fireplace mantle of himself and Richard next to a huge blue marlin behind a boat named, *Game On*. As he turned back from the picture to take a seat in the nicely decorated and colorful room, he noted the vanilla scent coming from the candle in the center of the coffee table. It almost smelled like cookies were baking. Pickles didn't hold the appetite for long and his stomach growled a little, but he wasn't worried that Richard had heard since now he was talking on the phone.

"Look, I got you what you wanted. If you want me to go further, you know my rate and where to send the money. And I don't want bitcoins, so don't ask," Richard said to the man on the other end, shrugging his shoulders, making a "whatever" face, raising his eyebrows as he looked at Jack and smiled. Jack returned the smile and the shrug. Richard mouthed "Two more minutes," to him as he turned and went into the back bedroom down the hall.

"Of course I 'can do it.' It's just going to cost you twice my usual rate. That's high end security they have…" he said as his voice trailed off when he turned the corner out of sight into a back room.

A few minutes later, Richard hurried back out of the hallway and placed the cordless back on the receiver. Then he looked over at Jack.

"So did you lose your key?" Richard asked him.

"What?" is all Jack could muster as Richard came out of the kitchen, looking at Jack as if a doctor evaluating his patient after a procedure. Of course, he did look as if he had similar bruising as someone having a nose job. Swollen face, black eyes.

"Don't worry about it. I'll get you another one," Richard said as he sat down on the couch next to Jack, still evaluating.

Jack wondered if he would notice the difference.

"You know if you were anyone else, I would say you look like shit, but you fucking never look like shit. Hell, you even look more handsome. So what the fuck happened to you? Did you go slumming on the east side of town, or is this work related?" he said, leaning in a little too close for comfort for Jack.

"I've had a rough night," was all Jack could come up with. He'd have to do better he figured.

"I'd say." Richard leaned in still closer looking at the bruises, awkwardly close. Then it got way beyond awkward. Richard didn't stop leaning in.

"Even all banged up, like I said, still handsome," he whispered then fell into him kissing him, *on the mouth*!

Jack shoved him back and jumped up off the couch, yelling, "What the hell, man?"

"Shit, do you have amnesia from that beating you took?"

"No, what's your excuse? You just fucking kissed me."

"Uhh, yeah, that's what we do."

"No, not me," Jack said, backing away.

"Okay, now you're starting to worry me, Jack. Why don't you sit back down?"

Jack was pacing around the room in utter shock as to what just happened. Then he took Richard's advice and sat down, but not on the couch next to Richard. He sat on the opposite side of the room on a soft cushy chair that made him feel as if he was sinking into it like quicksand as his full weight settled onto it.

"Okay, first question, Do you know who I am?" Richard asked, staring at him intently like a hawk hovering over a mouse it was about to snatch.

"Yes, you're my partner," Jack said as he wiped his mouth with his sleeve.

"Well, yeah, okay, good, although you know I hate it when you call me that."

"What am I supposed to call you?"

"Well, I prefer boyfriend."

"Oh no, I didn't sign up for this."

"Sign up for what? Seriously, Jack, are you okay?"

Richard stood up and walked toward him, lifting his hand toward Jack's forehead as if to check his temperature.

Jack slapped his hand away. "Just sit down, Richard, I gotta tell you something."

Richard eased himself back onto the sofa, clearly feeling anything but at ease. "What is it, Jack?" he asked nervously.

Jack struggled to find the words. Richard clearly feared the worst—that he was about to break up with him, not realizing what he was about to hear was so much worse than that.

Then Jack collected himself and looked up at him. "I'm not Jack," he said, the words almost knocking Richard's two-hundred-pound frame off the couch in shock.

"Holy shit, you're John, aren't you?" Richard said, standing up and slowly walking toward him.

"Yes," Jack said, remembering that before he died, his brother had told him that Richard already had heard of him.

Although Richard looked tough, like a real John Wayne type, he softened quickly and physically began to shake. He lifted both hands to his face as if to hold back the next question that was about to come from his mouth, as if afraid of the answer. "So then where's Jack?"

"He's dead," Jack said solemnly.

Richard dropped to the ground in a squatting position, his large hands raised to cover his eyes, but not large enough to hold back the tears.

Jack sat there, silent for a minute, but the thought that had bubbled up in his mind had turned into a shaken can of Coke, that he had to open. "Jack was gay?" he blurted out as he stood up from the chair.

Richard, while still crying, began to actually smile and laugh still with his face in his hands. Then he lowered them and began to let out his emotions with a Santa Clause caliber chuckle. "Oh, Jack was so many things, but yeah that is one of them," he said, still laughing, then standing up.

"And you're my partner at the Secret Service?"

"Oh, god no. Crime isn't my thing, well, at least not solving them. No, computers are my thing. Besides, I'm not as good with secrets like Jack."

"What do you mean?"

Richard smiled at him, the tears slowing now as he wiped both his cheeks with the back of each hand. "Secret Service, hello."

"Oh, yeah."

"Yeah, and I have always been open with who I am, but Jack kept it quiet."

"So no one knows I'm gay?"

"No, but why do you keep saying I?"

"Because I'm Jack now," he said as he turned to go sit back down in the chair. "That's why he came to my place before he died. He wanted me to be him, live out his life, and I agreed to do it. Hell, I wasn't leaving much behind. I probably wouldn't have lasted out the year."

"Are you serious? He wants you to be him?" Richard asked, shaking his head. "Not possible."

"I know. It's fucking crazy. But, hey, I look like him, right?"

"Well, yeah. Maybe not as in good of shape," Richard said with a smile.

"Hey, I'm in better shape than him now," Jack said. He saw Richard flinch at that as if poked in the eye. "Sorry, man, I didn't mean that."

"Oh, it's all right. You actually sound like him, same personality. He would have said something just like that. I just don't see how he thought you could pull it off."

"That's where you come in. He said go see his partner, that he'd help me, I just hope I got the right 'partner,'" he said, doing quotes with his fingers.

"You did, don't worry. I know everything about Jack, things no one else does, obviously. In fact, come look at this picture." He waved him over toward the mantel where he picked up the picture of he and Jack by the boat. "This is my second favorite picture of us," he said as he held it up for John to see. He pulled a picture out from behind the first, from inside the frame. "Now, this is my favorite."

"Looks almost the same as the other one. Just that he's leaning on the boat in this one," Jack said, looking at it then up at Richard.

"Here look at both," Richard said, holding them next to each other. "See the name on the boat?

"*Game On.*" Jack said.

"Now look at this one where Jack is leaning with his hand on the O."

"Ga Men?" Jack said as he was looking at it.

"Yep, that's as close as he ever came to admitting it in public. He didn't know I kept that picture."

"So you can keep some secrets, which is good 'cause I'm gonna need you to keep this one."

"I will."

"So I've got two days for you to fill me in on everything I need to know about Jack."

"You sure you're not gay?"

"Yep. Why?"

"That sounded pretty gay. 'Fill me in.'"

"Ha, ha. I like you Richard. I can tell we're gonna get along."

"Well, we'd better. We're in for a long weekend. Lucky for you, I know quite a bit about Jack's coworkers and what he does, since that's all he ever talked about. Hope you have a good memory, 'cause I'm gonna cram your brain with about five hundred gigs of memory."

"Photographic, so yeah, I'm good. Cram away."

"Why don't we use index cards? I'll write down each person you're supposed to know on a card and put all the details I know about them. Then when you meet them at the office on Monday, you can recall the card."

"Sounds good. Let's get to work."

"Oh one more thing," Jack said as he pulled a tie from his pocket, "can you show me how to tie one of these."

"Sure," Richard said, leaning in and tying it for him,

showing him the steps, "you know I used this same trick on the first guy I liked in boarding school."

"No trick here," Jack said with a smile.

Richard backed away, admiring his work with the tie. "Okay, let's head to my office. I got pictures of all the people he knows on my computer, even some he doesn't work with that you need to know," he said as he headed down the hall with Jack following.

"On your computer?"

"Yep, that's my thing, remember? We're not off to a good start, John."

"How about we start calling me Jack now so I get used to it?"

"Good idea, Jack."

"So computers are your thing?"

"Yep that's how I helped Jack find you. You ever heard of a group called Anonymous?"

"The computer hackers?"

"Let's just say I'm a member. Now you've got a secret about me, just to keep it fair."

CHAPTER 22

Jack waked into the Secret Service Building on H Street, feeling as nervous as someone getting ready to play in the super bowl and world series combined. He felt as if the world was watching his every move. As he stepped through the front door, he knew there would be no turning back. According to his notes from Richard, identity theft was one of the key things the Secret Service was charged with investigating. Talk about letting the fox into the hen house, he thought as he walked up to the person with the machine scanning IDs. No need to say "Hi." The guy just nodded professionally to everyone that went by. Good thing it was just a metal detector he walked through and not a heart monitor. *That was easy*, he tried to convince himself as he walked to the elevators.

That moment of calm in the storm came and went with what felt like a hurricane force wind as he was shoved from behind.

"Rough weekend, Jack?" someone yelled as he caught himself halfway to the ground.

Jack looked up and recognized from one of the note cards who it was, and it made sense why he was pushed. He quickly recalled the index card for Scott Mullis.

Scott Mullis: Six feet, three inches, brown hair, blue

eyes, played linebacker in college at Notre Dame. Senior agent in the protection detail. Thirty five years old. Womanizer.

"Hey, Scott."

"The Starbucks girl says 'Hi.' No coffee today?"

"No, not today," Jack said, thinking *Damn, I hate coffee*, and realizing he'd probably have to drink some now.

"What happened to your face man? I'm gonna start calling you car-jacked." Scott said, pointing to his face with more of a laugh than a look of concern.

"Lo Jack is still good, Scott," Jack said, recalling the nickname Richard told him they all used for him. Apparently, Jack was known for his sarcasm at the agency and his comments were usually categorized as low blows, hence the obvious Lo-Jack a reference to the stolen auto recovery system. "I was playing Rugby with some guys at the park this weekend."

"Rugby?" Scott said with disdain. "I didn't know they used your face as the ball in that sport. Why don't you stick to Football next time? Or better yet, stick to just jogging with your girlfriend, Sara.

"She's not my girlfriend," he said quickly.

She was a topic of his study session that Richard took a long time with, but Jack didn't mind. He had lots of pictures of her and, in each, she was beautiful. He thought as he soaked in everything Richard had to teach about her, what a waste. Now he knew why he had broken up with her, even if she didn't. But as sad as that made him feel, he was encouraged by the fact that his brother had never told her the real reason. The thing that concerned him was these Saturday morning jogs they went on. He had a week to get in shape before Saturday. Of course, he and Richard added a twisted ankle to the rugby story to explain away his sure inability to keep up with her at least for the first Saturday.

"Man, I always thought a hit to the head would knock some sense into you with her. What a waste. You know what they say about guys that have hot girls as friends,

Jack?" Scott said as they the elevator bell dinged. The doors opened and they both got on.

"What? That all their guy friends are jealous?" Jack said as he pushed in front of him firmly to hit the button for the 8th floor.

Scott followed pushing six after Jack moved out of the way. "No, you know what I mean," he said with a shrug.

"Scott, I just turned thirty. You know what they say about guys that are still single pushing forty? What are you, like thirty eight?"

"Yeah, yeah, whatever. Just put in a good word for me, Jack, and I'll take care of the rest. That should take care of those rumors."

"I would, Scott, but I can't lie to my friends."

"That's low, Jack."

"That's what they call me."

Ding, the door opened.

"You're floor, Scott," Jack said, motioning back to the door.

Scott exited then turned as the doors began to close. "We doing lunch today?"

"Actually I have a lunch date with Sara."

A large arm landed between the doors, causing them to reopen.

"You do? Well, at least mention my name and see how she reacts."

"Well, since I know the Heimlich maneuver, I'll give it a shot."

"Funny, Jack. You learn that in Med School?"

"Actually, I leaned that working at McDonalds when I was kid."

Shit! His first slip up. John worked at McDonalds growing up. Jack's first Job was the Secret Service after college and it was well known. He was saved by the ding as the elevator door closed on Scott, who had a confused look on his face, but he walked off probably figuring he was just being his normal sarcastic self.

At least, Jack hoped that was the case.

As the elevator headed up to his floor, he considered it minus one on his first test. Anything less than an A, and he would be spending a long time in detention, even longer than he had growing up.

He avoided any other tests as he reached his office, entered the room, and closed the door. He took in the large room, with mahogany wood surrounding it as if he was in the red wood forest. He could even smell the high quality wood around the room with its wooden file cabinets on the side and large desk in front of a five by five window overlooking the city.

He glanced outside at the sun still rising over the city. He was still more used to it going in the other direction. Then he turned and looked down at the black leather chair behind the desk.

"Okay, now what?" He pulled out the chair, which rolled on small wheels, and sat down. Then he thought of Richard, "I'm a computer guy." He turned on the computer and logged in with the password that Richard provided him.

Jack spent the next three hours reading files by date to get an idea what the hell he was currently working on and what other cases he had worked in the past. It was a lot to take in, even for a speed reader with a photographic memory. Legal jargon he had never heard of. Richard told him about the case he had just closed, so the timing couldn't have been better. There was nothing pressing on his schedule at the moment so he had time to just study in his office. The only thing he had to worry about as to his schedule was his lunch date with Sara. He checked the Rolex on his wrist that was worth more than his old El Camino. He was surprised to see it was already eleven fifteen.

"Shit, I gotta go," he said as he dragged the mouse to the bottom of the screen to shut down the computer. Before he could click the button he saw a note at the bottom that said *New email message*. He clicked on it.

Agent Shields,

I enjoyed our meeting last week. I look forward to following up with you. I think I have found a way to stop the merger. If for some reason I'm unsuccessful, I may take you up on your idea. I will forward you some information you may find useful. I feel I can trust you to do the right thing with this information.

You're friend,
Mikal

Jack just shrugged his shoulders, clicked the mouse to close the email, then logged off.

It was time to meet Sara.

CHAPTER 23

The valet driver gave Jack a wink as he took his keys. It reminded him of the guy at the bar on High Line. Was this another of *his* former flings? He shook it off, really not wanting to dwell on it. He straightened the uncomfortable tie that had a choke hold on him as tight as any he had experienced in his many bar room brawls.

Jack walked through the elegant restaurant as carefully as if he were in a china shop. He might as well have been, with the fine china they used. This was a far cry from McDonalds. "Speaking of fine," he whispered to himself as he followed the hostess who directed him to his table with Sara waiting. As fine as the waitress may have been, she was soon forgotten when he reached the table. Richard had showed him many pictures of Sara and, as photogenic as she was, there wasn't one in which she wasn't beautiful. Even with all of them, not a one came close to how beautiful she was in person. He felt the tie grab tighter around his neck as his blood pressure rose when he approached her. As he reached the table, she rose and leaned in for a hug. Even in what appeared to be a conservative work ensemble of gray skirt and white shirt, they couldn't hide her curves. As she stood, her auburn hair, cut to shoulder length, danced on top of her shoulders like the ballet of the Nutcrackers. Her joy in seeing him could not be hidden behind that huge smile of hers. He noticed that in person now that her two front teeth were a bit bigger than normal, but that just made her look even sexier, drawing his attention to her mouth. Her green eyes squinted as she leaned in as if eying her target through a rifle scope. If Richard wasn't verification enough that Jack was gay than the fact that he had broken it off with this woman clearly was proof. As she hugged him, he thought on how Richard said that Jack had never told her he was gay, and all he could think was, *Thank God*. With the secret he would now have to keep from her, it made him feel a little less guilty knowing his brother had kept one almost as big from her. As he hugged her back, he couldn't tell if the pleasant scent he smelled was her perfume or her shampoo as her soft hair brushed his cheek. He knew from what Richard had told him that even though his brother broke up with her he did still love this woman, and before he took a seat he already realized that he would as well.

"You're late," she said while gracefully taking her seat and unfolding her napkin on her lap.

Looking at his watch, Jack said, "Not by much."

"That's not like you, Jack," she said with a smile.

Oh those teeth, he thought. "Sorry," was all he said, nervous now that his voice may sound different to her.

"Looks like you may have a good excuse, though. Did you get mugged on the way over here," she said with a curious glare.

"What?" he said.

"You're face. It's all jacked up, Jack," she said, laughing at her own joke.

"Funny, Sara," he said, taking his napkin and folding it on his slacks while looking down as if that would save him.

She picked up the glass of water and took a drink. "Seriously, Jack, what happened?"

"Played rugby with some guys on Saturday."

"Oh, so you skipped jogging with me to play Rugby. Well, look what that got you. I needed to talk to you, Jack, and you let me down. I call that Karma," she said, pointing to his face.

"I call it three guys trying to take away the ball."

"Well, whatever you call it, you got what you deserved."

"Yeah, well about next Saturday, I'll probably have to skip out on you another week. I twisted my ankle."

"Well, if it's as bad as your face I understand. But I don't know, Jack, skipping two weeks in a row, you might be too out of shape to keep up with me by the next week."

He thought to himself how ironic that his plan was to try and get in better shape to do just that and, after seeing her, he realized he'd need that extra week. She laughed, taking another sip of water. There was something seductive in the way she did it, holding the glass to her side as she kept her gaze on him while she swallowed. Then she really caught him off guard as he watched her take a big piece of ice, bite it with those teeth, and begin to slowly chew before swallowing again.

The sound of it crunching in her mouth raised his heart beat a notch. He was jealous of that piece of ice. "So what was so urgent that you needed to talk about?" he asked, trying to ground himself before complete lift off with his imagination.

She jumped right into the heart of the matter. "Todd and I are done."

Richard had given him enough to know this was her boss at the FBI and they were dating, and Jack didn't like him. "So he turned out to be the asshole I thought, after all."

"Yeah, and so did Cynthia," she said as she gripped her knife on the table subconsciously.

Jack noticed this and the look on her face was just as threatening. His mind raced to try and recall Cynthia and what Richard had said about her, but he couldn't remember the details. Someone she worked with, a friend perhaps. *Never mind her. She's not a main character in this story*, he thought, *focus on Todd*.

"He fucked her?" Jack said rather loudly and, by the turn of the heads in the restaurant, you could tell how many tables deep his voice had carried to. It had been at least three, one of which included a couple in the midst of ordering that had their and the waiter's attention.

"Geessh, Jack, keep it down," she said, although somewhere between put off and amused

It was hard for him to tell. She did shrug her shoulders as if ducking for cover from the embarrassing shot fired from out of his mouth like a shotgun blast from Dick Cheney.

"Sorry," he said, grabbing one of her two hands that she was holding together in front of her on the table.

This was more shocking to her than what he had just said. Jack was never a touchy feely kind of guy. It excited her and made the rest of the room disappear, and especially those that were staring at them. It was just the two of them now. He held her hand and she stared into those intense blue eyes. Even with the bruises surrounding one of them, he was still deadly handsome. Maybe even more so, now that he wasn't perfect since that's how she had always considered him, at least when it came to looks. Todd had been on the cover of a magazine as a most eligible bachelor, but the only thing keeping Jack from the cover of *People's* sexiest man was that he wasn't famous. There was something about a guy with a flaw and now, if only temporarily until it healed, he had one. She looked down at his hand holding hers, mostly out of fear that he might see the flush she felt in her face.

"It's okay, Jack. Like you said, he was an asshole. And, besides, maybe Cynthia was just being a true friend, proving it to me," she said, laughing and trying to convince herself as she tried to take her hand away from Jacks. His firm grip wouldn't let her.

"I don't know, Sara. If that's how your friends treat you, I'd hate to see you have a run in with one of your enemies."

"Oh, like your friends are so great?" she said, lifting up her free hand and gently brushing his cheek below the bruise around his eye.

Jack recoiled at the touch, not from any pain that she had caused by touching him, but quite the opposite. He let go of her hand as he backed away.

As in so many stories, the uncommunicated got misinterpreted and she backed away as well. "Thanks for coming, Jack. Are you guys busy at the office?" she said, as if taking a dead man's curve at ninety miles an hour and changing the subject, the abruptness of which signaled to him to follow her down this new highway and try to keep up.

"Today was a good day to catch up. I just finished wrapping up a big case," he said, referencing in his mind the case he had just finished reading about in his office. "What about you?"

"Not yet, but obviously it's about to be."

"Obviously?" he asked.

"Come on are you kidding me, Jack?"

"What?"

"The explosion this weekend. You didn't hear?"

"I did know about that."

"Yeah, but this morning they got through the rubble and it looks like a car bomb. How do you not know this?" she asked, leaning in and making him nervous as if she had him under a microscope realizing his cells didn't match up properly.

"No, I didn't hear. I've been in my office all morning and, remember? I was running late getting over here. So it was a car bomb? No shit?" he said.

"Jack!" she gasped "I've never heard you curse so much. Remind me not to hang out with you and your rugby friends if this is what rubs off on you," she said, although this just added to his rugged appearance that had her more attracted to him than ever. She'd be putting those new batteries to good use when she got home later that night. Unfortunately, with what was going on, it would be much later.

"So what else do you know that I obviously don't?" he said, anxiously changing the topic quickly from anything that might make her feel he was different.

"Well, how about that this wasn't like ninety three with the World Trade Center car bomb. This time the car had someone in it."

"Who?" he asked, leaning in, actually curious, her enthusiasm rubbing off on him.

"It was the CEO of the bank," she whispered sitting up and glancing around the room as she said it as if she had revealed a secret she was not sure was public knowledge yet.

"Who is that again?" he asked.

"Shut up, Jack. Someone killed Mikal Ginsberg." she said picking up her water.

She might has well have thrown the water from that glass in his face. That was the name in the email he had just opened before he left the office. He didn't want to keep another secret from this beautiful woman. Hell, at this point he didn't even want to keep the main one. He considered telling her about the email he just read from the now deceased Mikal Ginsberg but didn't know enough to maneuverer down that road. While he debated it and almost made the mistake of bringing it up, he got a signal, like a fighter saved by the bell, stopping him. It was the growl of Sara's stomach.

"Let's get you something to eat," he said with a chuckle and turned to look for the waiter.

CHAPTER 24

The CEO of National Trust, Claus Steinherz, was surprised the phone hadn't rung sooner as he went to pick up the one ringing in his office. An hour had passed since it was made public that Mikal Ginsberg had been killed in the bombing.

What was even more surprising was who called him first. He figured, when he answered, it would be someone from the Wall Street Journal or at least some other news agency calling. What the person asked was beyond shocking.

"Did you do this?" yelled Congressman Raymond Childs from New York, ranking member on House Finance Committee.

"Are you out of your mind, Raymond? Why the hell would I do something like this?" Claus yelled back in his thick German accent. He had left Deutsch Eins Bank in Germany many years before but the accent still stuck.

"Well, maybe because Mikal was holding up the merger. The merger I told you was already approved by the committee. I told you all the pieces were in place and not to meddle," Raymond said, still seething.

"I am not the cause of this, Raymond. You are on the inside so you find out what the fuck is going on and make sure this doesn't kill the deal. As you say, make sure all the pieces are in place," Claus said.

"I'll check it out," Raymond said.

"Don't just check it out. Fix it!" Claus said as he slammed down the phone with as much strength an eighty-one-year-old could muster.

CHAPTER 25

Settling quietly back into his office was out of the question for Jack after returning from lunch. The bees were buzzing around the office worse than the Africanized kind. A bomb in the heart of DC was enough to shake the whole hive and get even the queen's attention. It was high alert for all agencies, especially the Secret Service.

His team was meeting in one of the larger conference rooms. He'd gotten an email on his phone just as he was leaving the restaurant. As he got on the elevator and pushed the button, a huge Popeye-sized forearm kept the doors from closing.

"Hold on there," Jake Miller said as he pretended to push the already retreating doors to the elevator fully open, as if in some show of strength. Jack quickly flashed in his mind the notes on the index card for him: Jake Miller, ex-marine, blond hair, built like a tank, six feet, two hundred twenty pounds. Ten years with the Service. Protection side.

Jack smiled as he thought about Richard's comment. *'Probably only reason he survived the South American scandal was that no one was brave enough to fire him.'*

"No need to impress, Jake, it's just me in here," Jack said, smiling as he noticed Jake checking the elevator then getting in.

"Boy, you did get messed up, Jack," Jake said, looking at his face.

"Well—"

Jake cut him off before he could tell his story of what happened.

"Rugby, huh? Scott told me. I don't know the rules, Jack, but I don't think they are supposed to kick your head versus the ball. You sure you didn't piss someone off with that smart ass mouth of yours? I know I've wanted to do that to you a time or two," Jake said, gesturing toward the black eye with his right hand.

Running off at the mouth was one part of being Jack that he found easy. *Must be a genetic thing.*

"Jake, you're just jealous that I'm still better looking than you, even like this."

"Ha, jealous of you? Have you seen the guns?" he said, flexing his right arm in front of him.

"Oh, yeah, 'cause that's what impresses the ladies."

Jack wondered if this guy was maybe gay himself. He showed all the cliché signs of someone in the closet. Worked out a lot and was always talking about women, so as if to compensate for or repress his true feelings. He wondered if Jack had ever said anything to him about himself. He wasn't going to go there. Let Jake show his cards first, although at this point, Jake wasn't showing anything other than his shallowness. Then Jack noticed he hadn't pushed another floor. "Where you headed, Jake?"

"The big conference room. We all are."

"But you're not on Financial Fraud, you're in protection."

"Everyone's going to this meeting. It's time to circle the wagons, Kimosabe!" Jake said as he punched Jack in the shoulder.

A punch hard enough that it would have knocked over any average sized man, but Jack just stood there and didn't budge, absorbing it like a punching bag. "I don't think you got that expression right," he said.

"Whatever." With that, the doors opened and Jake stepped out to a full floor.

As Jack walked through the large room, the index cards filled his mind like a Rolodex being thumbed through quick enough to make a film.

He began to realize that although they were all mixed together—protection team and financial fraud, even some of the identity theft guys—they had self-segregated themselves into their groups. It reminded him of high school, protection guys were the jocks, identity theft the band geeks, and financial fraud the nerds. Of course, Jack didn't fit the mold, and neither did his partner, that he now saw her for the first time in person.

She was already seated and the chair left open next to her was clearly being saved for him as she waved him over.

He smiled as he recalled the index card. *Lauren Kurtz—Partner—GORGEOUS.* Even Richard agreed. Long brown hair, large blue eyes, and a sculptured face. Three years with the agency, undergrad from Yale, masters from Harvard. Recently broke up with her fiancé of two years. Beauty and brains.

She was almost perfect, except for one little crooked tooth on the top of her smile. It was just enough to make you think she was approachable when she smiled. Like a Venus fly trap pulling in its prey with that innocent smile. Richard had warned him that she was anything but sweet. Now, after her fiancé broke off the wedding, she had moved into Mike Tyson status, the one that bit off a piece of Holyfield's ear. Jack couldn't see it, though, as he approached. He just thought to himself how damn pretty she was. *Hold it together, Jack.*

"Hey, Lauren. That seat taken?" he said playfully.

"Just sit down, asshole," she said firmly but still smiling.

There it is. "What's your problem?" he asked as he sat down in the chair next to her, noticing the hint of perfume.

"I heard you had lunch with Sara," she said.

"What is this junior high?" was the best response he could come up with.

"Scott told me," she said.

"I know Scott told you. He was the only one who knew."

"Oh, was this a secret meeting?"

"How about you remind me again how this makes me an asshole?" he said, trying to stay on the offensive while also trying to get some information not provided on his index cards.

"It just does, Jack." She turned from him as if readying herself for the meeting but then she punched him in the shoulder hard with her left hand.

Unlike in the elevator when he saw the punch coming and braced himself, this was unexpected and Jack fell out of his chair onto the floor.

"I was wrong. This isn't junior high, this is grade school," he said as he rubbed his arm and climbed back into his chair.

"By the way, I like your face like that much better," she said while still looking straight ahead as the meeting was about to start.

"Of course, you do," he said, smiling at her then turning his head forward to the front of the room, but not before catching her look his way with a smile.

As the man took the podium, Jack glanced at his index card in his memory.

Roger Mansfield, Secret Service Director. Fifty eight years old, former SEAL. Thirty years with the Service. Worked his way up from protection side. Handsome in that Sean Connery kind of way. Graying dark hair. Soft spoken raspy smoker's voice. He spoke in such a formal manner that it almost came across like a British accent like Cary Grant.

According to Richard, Jack and Roger were close, so the idea was to avoid direct contact with him as long as possible till he had his act down.

Roger walked to the podium and began to address the fifty or so agents in the room.

"Good afternoon, everyone," he said in a commanding yet pleasant tone. "Obviously, you all probably have an idea why I've called this meeting. With the revelation of events just a short while ago all agencies are on high alert. The fact that this event was here in DC puts it at the highest level." He paused looking around the room, then continued. "Here's what we know. At ten forty-five a.m. Saturday morning, a bomb was detonated in the parking garage of First Federal Bank. The blast collapsed two levels of the parking garage.

"This morning search and rescue found the body of Mikal Ginsberg, CEO of the bank. It appears the bomb was attached to his car. Now, instead of a random act of terrorism, it seems to be a specific attack on the CEO of First Federal Bank. I've called this meeting with both protection division as well as financial fraud division because you will be working together on this. Not only will you be coordinating, but we will all also be partnering with the FBI. Since Nine-Eleven, there have been calls for better communication between all agencies. In this case, you will be working directly with the FBI. Obviously, if you've seen the news, nothing I've told you so far today is anything new. But what you don't know are some other details that have come out, which demand this partnership between our agencies. I didn't want to waste any time starting on this so I asked FBI Assistant Director Todd Lofton to address you directly with this new information and our plan to work together."

Todd walked out from the side of the room and shook Roger's hand.

So that's the asshole, Jack thought to himself. He noticed Lauren sit up straight and cock her head in Todd's direction, clearly finding him attractive. He did have that Harrison Ford look about him, the young cocky one that played Han Solo in *Star Wars*. Now, Jack really didn't like this guy.

"Thanks, Roger. Hello, everyone," he said to the room with a guttural deep voice, clearly playing to the crowd. It reminded him of all those female sideline reporters on ESPN that purposely spoke with their deepest voice as to not offend their audience with a *girlie* high-pitched tone. In his case, just trying to sound older. Todd cleared his throat, not used to talking this way, and continued.

"Our team has secured the site and we have found no other victims. At this point, it's still too early to determine the exact type of device and how it was detonated. However, it is clear that the blast originated from beneath Mikal Ginsberg's car. In accordance with the Homeland Security Information Sharing Act, we plan to share all information as it becomes available."

"Ahh, Bullshit—chu," Jake sneezed out loud with his fist covering his mouth, looking for a laugh, but no one was in the mood. Jake didn't take into account how quiet the room had been and that his voice would carry like an F-16, breaking the sound barrier. Not only that but how clear his failed attempt to muffle his fake sneeze would be to everyone in the room, including his boss, Roger. He easily spotted Jake in the crowd, not by his size, compared to those sitting around, him but by how red his face had become from fear and embarrassment. It glowed like a runway light for incoming planes to find. Todd clearly sensed the tension between them and did something that surprised Jack and perhaps made him hate him just a little bit less, but not much.

Todd nodded at Roger as if to say it was okay and then he continued. Then he impressed Jack even more.

"I know it does sound like bullshit, the FBI working with the Secret Service, but in this case, not only is it true, but we really do need your help. Actually a lot of people need your help. Let me explain by showing you something you haven't seen in the news."

Todd turned sideways to someone standing next to a computer that was connected to the image projection screen.

As they turned it on, Roger nodded for someone at the side of the room to dim the lights. The screen lit up at the same moment the lights went out, as if a flash of lightning had struck the building. The thunder that would follow a few seconds later was the grumbling of the crowd after he clicked to the next screen. The first screen simply had a definition of the TARP program. The Troubled Asset Relief Program, which was better known as the Bank Bailout, where twenty five of the nation's largest banks received billions of dollars to settle the financial crisis.

"Obviously, most in this room should be aware of this program. Well, when we searched Mikal's computer this morning we found an email referencing this program. This email was sent approximately one week before the explosion." Todd nodded for the person to hit the next screen, and the image lit up the room. "This was what the email said."

Tell America the Real Problem!

CHAPTER 26

If Todd didn't have their attention before, he had it now. Everyone sat up, needing to know more. He didn't disappoint.

"Here are all the names of the people who received this email." The screen showed the email addresses.

"Let me make this simple. There are thirty-six names in this email. Twenty five are the CEOs of the banks that received TARP funds. Ten are the members of the House Finance Committee that drafted TARP. And the last one is the Federal Reserve Chairman."

Todd paused, as if catching his breath, and then began again with even more passion.

"That's thirty-six people who have been directly threatened! That's why I'm here. There's no one in the world better than you at protecting people and now we have a lot of them to protect. Each one of these people listed here will have two of you assigned to stay with them until this investigation is solved and the threat is eliminated. You will also be partnered with an analyst from our agency to report back any suspicious behavior since we also can't rule out that any one of these thirty-six people could also be the suspect. The FBI is asking for your help in this." Todd paused from his passionate plea for a second and looked even more emotional than anyone expected. If anyone doubts my sincerity, I'll end on this note before I turn you back over to Roger for your assignments. Keep this in mind, one of these thirty-six people is my father."

❧❧❧

Over the next hour, everyone lined up and received their protection assignments. As each pair would enter Roger's office, they would be introduced to Todd and given a file on the person they would be protecting. They were then asked to contact their analyst and arrange a meeting before picking up their assigned person. As Jack and Lauren were called into the office, they ran into Sykes and Lopez coming out.

"What are you two rookies doing here?" Lauren asked. "Did one of the CEOs have a dog for you to watch?"

"Fuck you, Lauren," Lopez said rather loudly.

"Oh chill, Lopez, just like a little Chihuahua, always barking the loudest." She followed with a confident smile, showing no fear. "I'm just messing with you. Seriously, who did they give you?"

"We got someone who wasn't even on the email. They just wanted to keep an eye on him and make sure he's okay.

"Who?" Jack asked.

"Ian Ginsberg, Mikal's son."

"Hm, makes sense I guess. You should be safe with him. You can eat with him at the kid's table while we grownups sit in the dining room," she said with a laugh as Lopez showed his teeth as if about to growl.

Sykes grabbed him before he could bite. "Come on, Tres, let's go," he said, dragging him away.

Lauren just walked on into the office.

"Hey, guys, let me introduce you to Todd Lofton," Roger said, gesturing with his right hand in his direction.

Lauren took a step and shook his outreached hand. He

held her hand a bit too long, but she didn't mind. She knew damn well who the most eligible bachelor in town was. She gave him a subtle smile as she spoke. "Lauren Kurtz." is all she said.

Jack could tell Todd was attracted to her by the way he leaned in as he took her hand. He also could tell the attraction was mutual with the way her attention was peaked. Her eyes opened wider and seemed to dilate as she took him in, as if she literally would have right there if they were alone. *I really don't like this guy.*

"Lauren, nice to meet you," Todd said and looked into those big blue eyes.

"And this is Special Agent Jack Shields," Roger said, steering Todd's attention away from Lauren toward Jack.

Todd was still holding her hand. Then he abruptly let it go and turned fully toward Jack. "Jack Shields," he said as he shook Jack's hand twice as firmly.

"Todd," Jack said rather causally, although returning an even firmer grip, getting a glare from Lauren at the apparent lack of respect as well as from Roger.

Todd pulled his hand away with a slight struggle, as if in a grade school tug of war, while Jack stood there motionless. "As I mentioned in the meeting, you will be assigned to one of my analysts to report to during this time if you notice anything suspicious," he said, strengthening his tone—the adult version of a pissing contest.

"Two birds with one stone I guess," Lauren said rather flirtatiously.

"Yes, something like that," Todd returned, turning to her and breaking the tension between him and Jack. "I've assigned you two to one of my best. Her name is Sara Ferguson."

With the mention of the name, Lauren turned as stiff as Jack had been, while he on the other hand almost crumbled at the knees.

"Sara Ferguson," Lauren said as if spitting out a curse word.

"Yes, Sara, why? Do you know her?" Todd asked, looking a little uncomfortable.

"Yes, but I've only met her a few times. But Jack knows her pretty well," she said allowing Todd to catch his breath.

"Really, Jack? Well then, you'll work well together," Roger said with a smile, distracting Jack away from his glare at Todd and reminding him where he was and who he was supposed to be.

"Yes, they were friends in college. Sara's told me a lot about you, Jack. That's why I picked you for this assignment. She's always said great things about you," Todd said, turning back a little more calmly now as if he knew he had something on him.

"I bet," Lauren whispered under her breath, catching a quick glance from Todd.

"Says you're one of the best, and Roger here has assured me she wasn't just being biased because you used to date in college," Todd said as if upping the ante at a poker table.

Shit, what didn't she tell this guy? Jack just stood there, bluffing as if he had a strong hand. He was literally holding nothing since he didn't know enough about the relationship he supposedly had with Sara.

"You dated in college? I thought you were just friends. That's what you told me," Lauren said, forgetting for a second where they were.

"Yes, that's what she told me," Todd confirmed. "That's why I figured it would be good for you to work together since you know each other so well."

"Well, who is our guy?" Lauren said as if wanting to change the subject.

"Here." Todd grabbed a file folder from the desk, the last one he would hand out. Lauren and Jack both stepped in and reached for it at the same time, their arms touching as they each grabbed the file.

Jack took half a step back and let go of the folder so

she could open it but remained close enough to see the name and picture inside.

"Harris Lofton?!" she said loudly as if announcing a surprise Oscar winner for best actor. She looked up from the file at Jack, then turned to Roger, and finally at Todd as if looking for confirmation from any of them.

"Yes. My father," Todd said.

CHAPTER 27

Ray Childs was used to meeting with crooks. He'd been in congress for more than ten years. For Ray it had actually started farther back. Growing up in Queens, he had taken part in a number of small-time crimes. But if you judged the crime by the number of victims, then some of the laws he helped pass screwed over so many more people. Sure, he'd held up some convenience stores one summer when he was a kid but at least he never got caught. He couldn't say the same about his friend Brad. The bad part for Brad was it was never his idea. He just had a hard time saying no, especially to Ray.

Brad had looked the part that summer. He was a stocky sixteen year old who looked nineteen. He had a square jaw and those downward facing eyebrows like Michael Keaton that made him look perpetually pissed off even when he wasn't. Ray on the other hand was fifteen and looked twelve. He was more like Bobby Brady, young, round face with big cheeks and soft brown eyes.

Ray learned at a young age how to use people to get what he wanted, especially when they had something he needed. In this case, Brad had the look but he also had his dad's gun. They'd robbed five places that summer, all planned out by Ray. Brad would point the gun at the clerk, demanding the money from the register. Ray would stand watch at the door. In all five occasions, it played out the same way. The clerk would panic and say "Take the money. Don't hurt me." Each time, they would look away from Brad and see Ray looking at them by the door. His innocent face seemed to sooth them for a second and, a couple of times, the clerks even gave a look as if asking for his help. Ray really hated that look, the assumption that he was innocent just because of the way he looked. He hated not looking tough like Brad. He would just smile at the clerk and think '*What the fuck are you looking at*? *I'm not gonna help you. This was my fucking idea*! Ray would learn to use that to his advantage throughout his life and, especially now, in Congress. He was a hard guy to say no to, even while he screwed you over.

Brad had been a good partner that summer, as long as he stuck to the plan. Of course, it was not sticking to the plan that ended their run. Ray always knew to keep it simple, and for Brad, who he assumed when he met him that summer wasn't too bright, he figured he'd keep it real simple.

Just three steps.

Step one: Wait till the store was empty.

Step two: Rush in with the gun and ask for the money while Ray watched the door.

Step three: Leave Fast!

On Store number Five, Brad forget step three!

That morning when Ray rode up on the dirt bike he had borrowed, he found Brad outside his projects smoking a cigarette.

"You smoking now?" Ray said as dirt flew up from where he had just slammed the brakes in the yard.

"Yeah," was all Brad said, taking another puff of the cigarette. He was never much a conversationalist.

"You ready to go?" Ray asked.

"Sure. Let me get my bike," Brad said. And when he said "my bike" he meant one of his neighbors that he would threaten to beat up if they didn't hand it over. When you looked nineteen and your friends your age still looked like they were ten, he was a hard guy to say no to also. In that way, Brad could be quite persuasive as well. He had a number of them to pick from. They usually didn't mind, not that they would say no to him if they did, since he always brought it back. That wouldn't be the case this time and, unfortunately for Matt, today was his unlucky day.

When Brad decided on his bike, he simply pointed and said, "You!" and Matt just got off slowly, laying it down, and backed away. That was the last time he would see his bike, but sometimes good can come from a bad thing, because it the last time he would see Brad.

☙❧☙

"Someone's coming, Brad! Come on, let's go," Ray yelled as his head swung back and forth from register to outside the door as if watching a tennis match. Brad wasn't following step three.

"Give me the damn carton of cigarettes!" Brad yelled at the clerk who was trying to pull a box from the upper shelf on the wall behind the register.

"Forget the cigarettes, Brad. We gotta get the hell outta here! Now!"

"He's almost got 'em. Don't worry. We got time," Brad said, not turning from the clerk.

Those were the last words Ray heard Brad say. Ray opened the door and left as the man walking up the street reached the door. He felt bad but the humor wasn't lost on him either at those last words. He would always play it back in his mind, '*We got time*,' And then think, *No, Brad just got time*.

The guy who walked into the store as Ray left was an off-duty cop. It took him only a second to realize what was going on. Brad turned to look at Ray who wasn't there anymore and found instead a gun pointing at him for a change. *What a weird feeling*, he thought as he dropped his gun. Brad was sentenced to ten years.

A number of years after Brad got out of jail, they reconnected. It wasn't out of any sort of guilt that Ray reached out to him. He did tell Brad what he wanted to hear and that he wanted to help him. He did so by getting Brad a job. Of course, Ray had his own selfish reasons for doing it, but at the time Brad didn't realize it and was just thankful.

Brad actually learned in prison that he was pretty smart, and not as dumb as he had initially accepted he was. He just got distracted in regular school. Prison didn't have as many distractions so he could actually concentrate better. He spent the ten years learning about computers and also found he was good at math. A perfect fit to work in IT in banking.

As head of the finance committee, Ray didn't have to pull too many strings to get Brad a job. He placed him with the OCC—the Office of the Comptroller of Currency. The OCC was an arm of the US Department of Treasury, so Ray did have to pull a few more strings to get the felony conviction off of Brad's records to qualify for the position. Its main purpose was to investigate banks and evaluate their soundness. In the current financial turmoil, they were working overtime and needed to staff up big time anyway.

Brad had been with the OCC now for almost five years. He worked his way up to Senior Bank Examiner focused on Bank Information Technology. Not by coincidence he had most recently been assigned to National Trust.

He was placed there with his team to clear the way for the merger and make sure there wasn't anything that would hold it up.

At least that was what Ray told National Trust.

"What are you having?" Ray asked a hunched-over, worn-out looking Brad sitting at the bar.

"A beer," Brad said.

Same old Brad, Ray thought, as he pulled up a chair

and sat next to him in the empty bar since it was two in the afternoon.

"I'll have one too," Ray told the bartender at the other end of the bar, who grabbed a glass and started filling it up from the tap.

"What do you want, Ray?" Brad said as he took another gulp of beer.

"I need a favor," Ray said with a pleasant smile.

"Of course, you do. Let me warn you, I've got a lot of work piled up over at NT," Brad said with some spit to it.

"Hey, don't forget how you got that job, friend." Ray put his arm around Brad's shoulders, not in a friendly manner. "Did you ever think when you were in jail that you'd get out and have a job making over a hundred thousand a year?" he whispered to him then turned his head and took a big gulp from the glass the bartender just placed in front of him.

"Did you forget how I ended up in jail in the first place?" Brad said, turning to him with a stare, furrowing even farther the already down turned and fuller with age eyebrows.

"Hey you're the one who wanted those cigarettes and didn't stick to the plan."

"Whatever. I don't smoke anymore, by the way," Brad said, turning back and taking another gulp of beer. "What do you want? I gotta get back to NT."

"That's exactly what I need you do, go back to NT. Just take this with you," Ray said as he pulled out an envelope from his pocket and shoved it under Brad's right elbow.

Brad looked down and picked it up with his left hand. "What's this?"

"You're currently reviewing trade activity over there. Well, I need you to add these trades to their computer log."

Brad opened the envelope and looked inside.

"Derivatives Trades for three billion! What the hell is this?"

Ray chuckled. "It's derivatives, my friend. Don't ask me. The people who invented those fucking things don't even know what they are."

"Yeah, but don't you think someone is gonna notice when I add a trade for three billion?"

"They didn't notice the last one you did," Ray said.

"Well, that might be because they're a little distracted by the CEO getting blown up," he said as he looked forward, taking another sip, then suddenly turned to Ray as if a thought just hit him in the jaw like one of his former cell mates. "Did you do that?"

"Come on, Brad. What kind of guy do you think I am? Don't answer that, but no actually I didn't," Ray said with a smile. "I really do need your help on this. Will you do it?"

"All right. I'll put it in when I get back," Brad said, folding the envelope and putting it in his inside coat pocket.

"How about another round first?" Ray said, turning to signal the bartender anticipating Brad's answer.

"You know I can't say no to you," Brad said as he turned away and finished his glass.

Ray smiled, thinking to himself, *You never could.*

CHAPTER 28

Putting all the agents together with their assignments was made easy by the fact that all the CEOs were flying in for Mikal's funeral. The public was not made aware of the threat against them. The plan was to keep them all in town for meetings with congress. They actually had a reason to meet, albeit not a good one. They needed to discuss a potential second round of TARP. The first round settled the markets but a second looked like it would be needed after the crisis hit Europe and threatened to drag the US financial industry back down with it. Misery loved company, after all. Besides discussing the structure of this second round, they had a harder job of coming up with a way to sell it to the American people. Since they had buyer's remorse after the first round, initiating a second round of bailouts was going to be a tough sell.

"Like selling ice cubes to Eskimos," one congressman had said.

The agents were each going to pick up their person at the airport for those that were flying in. Jack had to first pick up Lauren at her apartment. She was still getting dressed in her bedroom and she yelled for Jack to come on in when he knocked on the door. Jack entered and turned to close the door behind him. As he turned back around he was greeted by a gray and white calico cat arching its back on the end of the couch. It hissed loudly at him as he walked by.

"What did you do to Tabby?" Lauren said, opening her bedroom door slightly to look out after hearing the loud hiss.

"Nothing. I guess your cat doesn't like me," he said, staring it down as if to tell it to shut up.

"Tabby loves you," she said, walking by the doorway to her room in her skirt and bra. She caught something stranger than the rare noise she heard her cat make. She saw Jack looking at her almost admiringly as she walked by. She turned quickly and walked back toward her bathroom, feeling flush all of a sudden. *What was that?* she wondered. In the two years she had been partners with Jack, he'd never showed any hint of finding her attractive. She'd tried to get his attention at first and dropped the usual hints, a fling of her hair, grabbing his arm, and over-laughing at his jokes. Sure, he complimented her from time to time but she could always tell he was just being polite. She gave up after the first three months. A girl could tell when a guy meant it. The look she'd just seen was quite meaningful. She reached for her usual work perfume, but then stopped and grabbed the bottle next to it instead. The sweeter and more enticing one she wore on the weekends.

She realized her shirt was on the other side of the room and she decided to see if maybe she had imagined what she noticed. She wouldn't leave it to chance this time. As she crossed the room in front of the open doorway, she called to him.

"Hey Jack, do you think I need a jacket?" she said as she paused in the door way. He looked up and stood there, as if dumbfounded, taking in her ample breasts in a tight black push up bra. She considered how he had seen her get dressed a few times before and it never sparked a reaction. This looked like she'd backed up a fuel truck onto a camp fire. There it was.

He bit his lip and looked away quickly, but not until after taking a full look at her. "How 'bout you start with a shirt and we'll go from there?" he said, turning and walking around to the other side of the couch to get away from the cat. The cat simply pranced down the end of the couch and stopped with a pirouette at the other end, backing on its hind legs and trying to swipe at Jack.

"Seriously, Jack, what did you do? Maybe it's your bruises that are scaring him," she said as she came out of her room, grabbed the cat, and squished it against and in between her breasts.

"He doesn't sound scared. I should be scared," he said, backing away as it was still swiping at him with one of its free paws. But not before inhaling deeply as he took her in again.

She could feel him do it and was in no hurry to go back to the room. She decided to take it up a notch. She grabbed the cat's loose paw to hold Tabby as if in a strait jacket and walked up to Jack.

"Here, why don't you pet him? Then maybe he can smell you and remember it's you," she said as she stepped close enough for Jack to get a whiff of the newly applied perfume.

He hesitated at first, his arm almost appearing to shake as he reached forward with his right hand. He was like a kid playing operation trying to hold his hand steady. He stroked the cat on top of its head as it squirmed underneath. Cats didn't like to be held. He looked at it and said to himself, *You have no idea how good you have it fellow.*

She watched as Jack's large and bruised-knuckled hand moved up and down right between her breasts. Then it happened. One of his fingers accidentally grazed her. He may as well have stuck his finger in an electrical socket, since the current was felt by both of them. He looked up at her for a second then put his hand into a fist and pulled his arm away. Lauren looked up and gave him an intense look to let there be no doubt that she felt him touch her. Then she just smiled and squeezed her cat, turned and walked back toward the bedroom. Then she stopped.

"I better leave Tabby out here to keep an eye on you." She plopped him back on the couch. The cat just sat there this time and began licking itself as if annoyed by the remnants of perfume that she had just rubbed all over him.

Lauren went back in the room. Just like with the perfume, she stopped short of grabbing the blouse she planned to wear and pulled off the hanger a form fitting sweater instead. As she pulled it over her head she sighed as if that would release the pressure building, but it wasn't building in her lungs. She had no doubt about what just happened. She was sure. What she wasn't sure of was what to do about it. She opted for the most common reaction that most normal people have in these situations. She decided to pretend like it hadn't happened and focus on the job at hand. *Oh that hand*. She allowed herself that one last bit before entering the living room.

"You ready to go?" she asked rather casually.

"Sure," he tried to say as calmly as he could, although his heart raced, full of lust.

"Oh, hold on. I still need to take my medicine," she said, walking toward the kitchen.

Watching her walk, in the skirt that fit her almost as snugly as the sweater, didn't help his heart. Perhaps he should ask for an aspirin for himself, just in case. He almost asked "What medicine?" but the way she said it Jack apparently already knew the answer and he caught himself.

She on the other hand caught him still staring at her ass as she went around the kitchen counter. She purposely arched her back and lifted a leg as she reached up for her pills in the cabinet. She could feel his eyes on her and it felt good. She better take two, instead, she thought. She took the pills and but the bottle back. She opened the refrigerator and got one of those smaller sized cans of Coke, bending over for one more grand finale of this show she was putting on.

"Coke with pills huh?"

"The fizz helps me swallow," she said, emphasizing the last word. She smiled and popped the pills into her mouth and then took a swig, finishing the whole can.

Oh my, Jack thought.

"All right let's go!" she said as she threw the can in the trash from across the kitchen. "Now, I can pay attention."

Aha, ADD medication he realized.

"Okay, after you," he said, gesturing with a slight bow.

"Okay," she said, walking in front of him.

Guess he wanted an encore performance, she thought proudly. She was pleased with herself. Later that night, she'd have to do so literally.

CHAPTER 29

Jack let Lauren drive since he wasn't sure where he would be expected to park. He figured they'd have a special spot for law enforcement agencies. Even if that had been the case, Lauren opted for one better. She simply parked by the exit to baggage claim. Before Jack even got out of the car she had already flashed her badge at the parking attendant and was heading inside.

She stopped to hold the door for him, giving him a "hurry up" look. "After you, old man."

"Thanks," he said as with a sheepish grin, walking on in ahead of her. She took the time to admire the view this time. *Not bad*, she thought to herself.

He stopped at the large screen displaying the flight arrivals. "Here it is, baggage claim three."

"All right," Lauren said and was off like a gazelle in one of those nature shows.

Jack would have to get used to keeping up with her. He started in her direction before fully turning, which caused him to bump into someone which knocked him back a step.

"Whoa there, cowboy," Jake said to Jack.

"Hey, Jake," Jack said, collecting himself as if he had run into an immovable pillar.

"Look at that, would ya?" Jake said, his head and his

eyes following Lauren's every step. "How'd you get her as your partner and I get stuck with Scott?"

"Simple, Jake, wrong department. She's FF, Financial Fraud," Jack said, joining his gaze.

Jake laughed then punched Jack in the shoulder. "I agree, FF, Fucking Fine. Maybe I should put in for transfer."

Jack was starting to think he was going to get hit more in this new job then his old one. "Stick with what you're good at, Jake."

"What's that?"

"Keeping people alive, not stalking them."

"Oh, I can be good at both trust me," Jake said then went to punch Jack again. This time Jack grabbed his fist and held it in place.

"So who are you guys here to pick up?" Jack asked him, changing the subject.

Jake grabbed a note from his coat pocket, clearly not one with the same memory skills of Jack. He took it out and looked at it. "Joseph Randall, CEO for New York National Bank."

"No shit? Well, you guys better be careful," Jack said with a look of concern.

"Oh why? Is he the next likely target?"

Jack was still used to the hours of his previous profession. He had been up most of the night studying the CEOs from the list. He decided it was time to practice getting used to drinking coffee and the caffeine he wasn't used to helped him stretch out the study session. He wanted to create a most-likely-suspect list from what he read about them. Joseph was on his short list but that wasn't why he told Jake to watch out. "Guy's a genuine asshole."

"How do you know?"

"Did some reading on him last night. There was an article in the *Post* a year ago about how none of his employees liked him."

"Former employees?"

"And current. He doesn't have a lot of friends, so don't bother trying to be his while you watch him, just watch out."

"Well, maybe he doesn't need any. With the kind of money these guys have they can rent their friends."

"Yeah, kind of like you with women," Jack said and laughed.

"Good one, Lo-Jack." Jake laughed and then looked over his shoulder. "I see Scott over there. Let me go get him. You got someone on this same flight."

"Yeah, Harris Lofton."

"Oh, shit. You got the assistant director's dad?" Jake said, looking back at him.

"Yep. Lucky us."

"And you told me to watch out. Good Luck."

"Thanks. See you at the next debrief," Jack said.

"That's what she said," Jake laughed but could see that Jack didn't get it.

"De brief, get it?" Then he hit Jack in the other shoulder and walked off.

Jack rubbed his other shoulder and went to meet up with Lauren at the baggage carousel.

"There you are. What happened to you, some bad breakfast food?" Lauren said as she turned to see Jack walking up to her.

"I didn't eat breakfast. No, I ran into Jake."

"Oh, I bet he liked that," she said with a smirk while still staring over at the exiting passengers coming into baggage claim.

"What?" Jack said, confused.

"You know he's gay, right?" she said, matter-of-fact.

"Jake?" he said, just as he turned to watch him walk over to Scott and put his arm around his shoulders. "Really?"

"Come on, all that over compensating and he obviously spends a little too much time at the gym."

"What's wrong with the gym?"

"Really, Jack?" she said just staring at him, making a silly face.

"You know some people might think I'm gay, still single at thirty," Jack said as if testing to see what she would say, trying to see if his brother had done a good job with his secret.

"You? Hah, not even close. Bisexual at best," she said, smiling at him.

"At best, huh?" he said, smiling back.

"Yeah, but I'm guessing, no. You're straight as your tie. Speaking of which, though, did you forget how to tie these things?" she said, walking over and fixing his for him.

As she did, he couldn't help but look down as if ready to dive into her large blue eyes. She grabbed the tie with both hands grazing his chest with the back of one of her hands.

She adjusted it, pretending not to notice his gaze on her. Then she looked over his shoulder. "Here they come."

They both turned and stood next to each other, looking at the exiting passengers trying to see Lofton.

"*Boom!*" A loud noise crashed behind them, vibrating the ground. They both were startled. Lauren reached for her gun while Jack, not used to carrying one, just kind of ducked his shoulders. They both turned quickly toward the noise behind them. One of the bags, a large medal one, coming from on top of the conveyor belt had hit the bottom of the carousal and bounced over the side. After realizing it was just the suitcase, they both released the nervous energy with laughter then turned back to the exiting passengers.

"There's our guy," Lauren said, walking over to greet him.

"Okay, I'll wait here."

"Mr. Lofton, I'm Lauren Kurtz," she said as she approached.

Lofton looked every bit the part of a New York bank CEO, distinguished looking, his suit not even wrinkled from the fight.

"Hello," he said, extending his hand and continuing to walk toward the carousel.

"This is my partner, Special Agent Jack Shields. We'll be escorting you back to your hotel."

"Sure, if you must, Hello Agent Shields," Lofton said with a smile.

He didn't seem anything like Sara's asshole ex, Jack thought as he shook his hand.

"I have a bag to get first," Lofton continued.

Just as he said that the conveyor stopped and a red light turned on.

"Looks like it might be a few minutes," Jack said, letting go of Lofton's hand and looking back at the dysfunctional carousel.

On the other side of the building, things couldn't have gone more smoothly. Jake and Scott found Mr. Reynolds as soon as he exited the terminal.

"I'll need to get my bag," Mr. Reynolds said after meeting the two agents.

"Wait here, I'll go grab it," Jake said as he hurried around to the other side.

As Jake walked up to the same conveyor belt that Jack and Lauren were waiting by, there was a loud buzz. The red light turned off as it started moving again.

"Look at that, it must have been waiting for me," Jake said, looking at Lauren with a smile.

She just turned her head and walked a few steps away.

"There's my bag," Mr. Lofton said, pointing at it as he began to walk toward the conveyor to pick it up.

"I'll get it for you," Jake offered since he was standing closer than Lofton and Jack. "Don't want these guns to go to waste," he said, flexing his arm before bending over to pick up the bag.

Jack turned to gage Lauren's reaction to the comment. Then there was a noise louder than any medal suitcase crashing onto the floor. The explosion knocked everyone over. It took Jack a minute to gather himself and get up.

When he did, his first thought was to check on Lauren. She'd been knocked back from the blast, but was okay. He turned to the source of the blast and saw that a beam had fallen from the ceiling and landed on top of Lofton. He was unconscious but at least he was still breathing. Jake, on the other hand, Jack couldn't find. He looked around through the rubble and then he saw his hand. Jack jumped over to clear the plaster from the ceiling off of him. There was nothing there. It was just Jake's hand, still gripping Lofton's bag.

CHAPTER 30

Jake's funeral was a couple of days after Mikal's. The CEOs were on lock down at their hotel while their assigned agents attended the funeral. FBI agents were placed there to secure the hotel so the Secret Service members could all attend the funeral. An agent's death was always a big deal. It had been a long time since the agency had had one. The fact that the killer was still out there made it even more emotional.

Although, Jack didn't know any of the people he was surrounded by that day, he felt the bond between them. Before this, he'd had a mild interest in figuring out what was going on, if for no other reason than trying to solve a real mystery like so many of the books he had read. Even though he really didn't know Jake, in the time he'd spent with him he saw how he could have been a friend. Now Jack was committed to finding the guy that did this. You didn't mess with Jack's friends and you definitely don't get away with killing them.

The FBI had shared the information they'd obtained from the explosion the day before. Jack could tell they didn't share everything.

They never do, he had thought. They told him that the bomb was in Lofton's suitcase. The trigger was in the handle. Jake's obsessive need to lift heavy objects finally did him in.

People were numb and not due to the biting cold from the early winter front blowing through Maryland. Jack sensed it as he looked around. The sadness was evident as the cold air turned their watery eyes even more red. They were all connected in this now, including Jack. Then he glanced over at Lauren. She looked intense, as well, but he couldn't quite place her emotions at the moment the casket was lowered into the ground. Maybe she was still in shock since she was there with him when it happened. As the casket went down slowly, he took hold of Lauren's hand. Her grip let him know what emotion she was feeling. Anger. Probably not the best time for his suggestion but, he thought, in a strange way, it might help to get started working on the case.

"Let's go talk to Sara," he said as he let go of her hand, thinking immediately after that maybe he should have held on a little longer just in case.

Her response surprised him. "Okay," she whispered while still looking at the grave site.

Whereas the other agents would be going back to the hotel to meet up with their assignments, Jack and Lauren had time to do other things. Their assignment, Harris Lofton, didn't need their protection. At least not while a police officer was stationed outside his hospital room where he was still in a coma.

ᘓᘓᘓ

Lauren and Jack walked up to the guard inside the FBI building, IDs in hand.

The young guard looked at each of the IDs then looked up at them with a youthful smile. "Wrong building, guys," he said with a chuckle, clearly clueless as to recent events in the city.

"We're here to see someone," Lauren said, clearly not amused.

"Name?" the guard asked with a professional tone to match Lauren's.

"Sara Ferguson," Jack said calmly, feeling for the kid just doing his job.

"Okay, let me call her line," he said, gladly taking the opportunity to turn to the phone and away from Lauren's glare.

Jack wondered if she was really that mad at the joke or if she just remembered who they were about to meet with. Jack was already regretting the idea of putting them in the same room together, especially while Lauren was clearly feeling more emotional than normal. Part of him hoped that there wouldn't be an answer on the other end of the guard's phone call.

"Ms. Ferguson, you have two guests here to see you." He reached over for the ID's on the desk in front of him. "Agents Jack Shields and Lauren Kurtz with the Secret Service." There was a brief pause, "Okay, I'll send them up She's on the eighth floor," he said, handing them their IDs back. Then he gestured with his right arm behind him toward the elevators.

"Thanks," Jack said as Lauren was already half way toward the elevators.

After the elevator doors closed and he had pressed the button, the dings of each floor going by felt like another bomb counting down. He wasn't sure how the chemistry of these two would combine to form a woman's unique kind of explosion. Richard didn't really know anything about why Lauren didn't like Sara and Jack couldn't ask her why. Couldn't ask Sara either.

He wondered as the countdown continued if his brother even knew. Ding, went the final floor and the doors opened. It reminded Jack of a bell at a boxing match.

Sara was waiting for them as the doors opened. She stood like a statue with her arms at her side, wearing a red blouse and black skirt. She only half smiled in respect to the circumstances. Of course, a half-smile on Sara would rival most women's full one.

"Hello," Sara said.

"Hello, Sara," Lauren said, as Jack stood in silent surprise that she led with politeness versus a fist to the trachea. "It's been awhile. How have you been?" she asked, extending her hand.

"Oh, I've been better," Sara said, shaking her hand.

Jack thought for sure Lauren would give her a death grip but it looked like a regular pleasant handshake. He was confused. In a town full of politicians, Jack still had a hard time watching people play politics and even now so up close and personal. Of course, he'd never had to work in an office environment. When he wanted to tell someone he didn't like him, that's exactly what he did. Nevertheless, he breathed a sigh of relief at their interaction.

"Hey Sara," he said to her.

"Hey, Jack," she said in her soft voice. "Let's head on back to my office."

"Is Todd here?" Jack asked before she stared walking, causing her to turn back.

"No, he's at the hospital with his father. I'm going to go by later this afternoon."

As she shifted her weight from one high heel to the next Jack couldn't help but glance forward at how good she looked in the skirt she was wearing. As if in a trance, he forgot where he was and more importantly who he was there with. He was quickly reminded.

"Oww," he mumbled under his breath as Lauren's fist hit him in the shoulder. He could tell now that she was left handed, since she always led with her left. He looked over at Lauren and mouthed "*What?*"

She just rolled her eyes at him and sped up to catch Sara. Of course, now he had both of them to admire. He noticed Sara smiling in the reflection of the office windows in the hall. Apparently she had seen what just happened.

When they reached Sara's office, she went to grab one of the chairs to pull it out, making more room for them to sit. She leaned over a little bit more than necessary as she did so, not needing the reflection of an office window to know that she would be noticed. She didn't care what Lauren thought. Why shouldn't she enjoy the spoils of all that jogging she did?

"Have a seat," she said as she slowly straightened herself.

Jack did notice but this time he shifted quickly, giving himself space in the doorway from Lauren. He kept an obvious eye on her this time to avoid another blow to his already bruised shoulder. Instead of a fist, she offered her palm and simply said, "After you."

Jack almost sprinted between the chairs, still not trusting Lauren. He stepped between the two chairs before Sara had even fully straightened, almost bumping into her. She turned back to grab his arm and then looked at him for a second and then at Lauren. There was nothing subtle about it. Home field advantage, she figured. So why not? She wasn't sure why she was even doing this. She and Jack weren't anything but friends, but something about the way Lauren looked at him made her competitive side come out. She smiled at her as if she'd gone up forty-love in a tennis match. "So what do you want to know about Lofton, other than his son is a jerk?" she said as she sat down at her desk.

"Nothing," Jack said overly firm, surprising even himself.

It definitely surprised Lauren, since she thought that's why they came to her since she was doing all the background work on him.

After all the studying Jack had done the past few days he knew all he needed to know about Lofton.

"You don't want to know about Lofton?" Sara asked while Lauren just looked at him, confused as well.

"No, I want to know what happened."

"What are you talking about?"

"At the airport."

"Jesus, Jack a fucking bomb went off," Sara said, shedding the innocent façade. It actually impressed Lauren for the first time. She'd always thought of her as one of those prissy spoiled little princess girls.

"I'm talking about before the bomb went off. Like how the hell did it get there in the first place? You guys aren't telling us everything," he said, sounding almost angry.

This surprised Lauren even more, not what he was asking, but how. She wasn't used to seeing Jack be so assertive, almost aggressive. She liked it. Thing was, she could tell so did Sara. He continued while Lauren sat dumbfounded.

"I mean don't they check for that kind of stuff before the bags even get on the plane?" he said, sitting forward.

"Of course, they do, Jack. You know that," Sara said, still reeling from the tone.

"Well, what do you guys know?" he said, leaning back in his chair a little, realizing he was probably a little too heated but still staring at her waiting for an answer.

"Well, obviously the bomb wasn't on the plane," Sara said.

"You think?" Lauren said, not being able to keep herself from taking the opportunity to dog pile on Sara with Jack. This was fun, she thought, as she looked at Jack in a different way.

"So how did it get in Lofton's suitcase?" Jack asked her calmly but still firm.

Sara looked at them both, considering what she was about to tell them, wondering if she was allowed, but as she saw Jack's eyes she knew she didn't have a choice. Weren't the agencies supposed to be sharing information? she rationalized. Then after a slight hesitation, she was reminded of another reason. *Why should she listen to Todd, anyway?*

"The bomb wasn't in his suitcase," Sara said, almost knocking the two of them over.

"What?" they both said in unison, surprised.

"They found his suitcase underneath the baggage claim

area after the explosion. It had never made it up the convey-or to the carousel," she said as Jack remembered how it had stopped for a few minutes. "Someone took off his tag and placed on a similar looking suitcase," she said, waiting for their reaction.

"So someone switched the bags underneath the bag-gage claim," Lauren said.

"Looks that way," Sara said, nodding to Lauren.

"Okay great, speaking of the looks of things. Don't they have cameras down there? Let's just go to the tape and catch our guy," Jack said, excited but sensing from Sara it wasn't so simple.

"They don't."

"Don't what?" he asked.

"They don't have cameras."

"Why not?" Lauren asked.

"Unions don't allow it," she said.

"Are you kidding?" Jack said.

"Hey, these are airline unions, next to baseball and the Auto Workers Union, they are one of the best at getting what they want."

"Or in this case what they don't want," Jack said, sit-ting back as well.

"Yep, no cameras," Sara said, also leaning back in her chair, showing her shared frustration as she and Jack just stared at each other.

"Well, what do we know?" Lauren asked as if remind-ing them she was still in the room. She felt she was throw-ing out a guess at the intimate game of charades they seemed to be playing like some married couple reading each other's minds. She crossed her legs causing her skirt to rise as if a subtle reminder to Jack that she was in just as good of shape as Sara and deserving of his equal attention.

"We found the detonator, or what was left of it in the handle of the case. It was set to go off when it was picked up," Sara explained.

"And Jake was the one that set it off," Jack said.

"Yes. I'm so sorry, guys," Sara said clearly sincere, enough so that even Lauren had to ease up on her.

"Thanks," Lauren said, realizing that now wasn't the time to get into a competition for Jack's attention. The room became silent for a moment.

"Did you get another message?" Jack finally asked. "Another email?"

"I figured that would have been your first question. There was a message."

"Another email?" Lauren asked, sitting up anxious to hear.

"No, not an email it was in an envelope in Lofton's suitcase," Sara said, looking over at her.

"His suitcase? What did it say?" Jack asked.

"The authors of this plan have written their own fate," she said.

"Okay, so we need to talk to the guys that came up with TARP, clearly Lofton was one of them," Lauren said.

"Yeah, but he's not the main author. We might as well start at the top," Jack said reflecting on some of his studying.

"Okay. Who's that?" Lauren asked.

"Congressman Ray Childs."

CHAPTER 31

Jack parked outside Lauren's apartment and called her. "I'm downstairs."

"Be right down," she said.

He felt like he was picking her up for a first date in high school and, just like a teenager borrowing his dad's car, he still hadn't figured out all the controls. It was humid out and a little warmer than the previous couple of weeks since he'd been driving the car. The heat setting had been set fairly high from before this became his car and, until now it was where it needed to be, but not today. He watched as Lauren came out of her apartment and closed the door behind her. He took note of the form-fitting white blouse on the black slacks that hugged her curves as she turned. He watched her slowly come down the stairs as if one of the models at a Victoria's Secret show.

That was until the heat from the car started to fog the front window. He rolled down both windows half way, hoping it would clear up. It worked, just in time for him to see Lauren hop off the last step of the stairs and turn toward the car. He imagined her breasts without the blouse as he could see them move underneath. Then she was at the car, bending down to open the door. That's when his imagination was trumped by her reality. She hadn't buttoned her blouse fully. He caught himself staring as she climbed into the car and sat down, which was when he turned quickly away. He knew she had caught him.

"Are you all right?" she asked.

"What?" he said as he rolled up the windows, looking toward his door afraid his face was still flushed from the heat.

"It's like a sauna in here. You mind if I turn this down?" she said presumptively while leaning down in his direction and reaching for the controller. She rested her left arm on his leg as she turned the dial down to a cooler temperature. Of course, this all just made his go up.

"There, that's better," she said then slowly lifted herself back up by putting her hand on his thigh pushing herself up. Jack didn't say anything. "So do you know how to get there?"

"Yep, got the address plugged into the GPS."

"You're such a girl." She chuckled as she leaned toward him and turned, swinging her head around as she grabbed for her seat belt. Her hair brushed his cheek. All he could think was if she'd look down at that moment, she would see how wrong she was.

She had, that's why she smiled when she turned away from him. She bit her lip as she kept looking out to the right as she put her seat belt on. Her window fogged a little as she exhaled to calm herself from the impressive sight she'd just taken in.

Suit pants didn't conceal as well as the jeans that he was used to wearing. He'd have to remember not to wear boxers next time either. He started the car.

Lauren waited a minute, looking out her window until she felt like the extra blood had left her cheeks, even if still holding strong in other places. Time to talk work. That would help.

"So what are you going to ask him that you're not planning on telling me beforehand like you did with Sara?" Lauren asked.

"Nothing. I just want to ask him about the bailout plan and see if he has any ideas of who would have motive in all of this," he said as he entered the freeway, pushing down on the gas.

The thrust of the acceleration didn't help to calm either of them as the car vibrated.

*ↄ*ↄ*ↄ*

Ray Childs clearly wasn't hurting in his career as a public servant. His estate rivaled those of families who had taken generations to accumulate their wealth. Ray, though, had no family.

It was just him. There wasn't much written about Ray Childs from what Jack had tried to search online about him the night before. Only a small article in a political magazine about how he had grown up in the poor part of Queens and worked his way up. Got an academic scholarship to attend Columbia and then got his masters at Yale. Moved back to Queens and became a congressman. Now ten short years later, he was the senior member on the House Finance Committee. The only other news of note was that he had authored the plan that everyone hated. Apparently, some hated it even more than others and that's why they were there.

"Nice house," Lauren said as they walked up the stairs to the huge oak wood front doors.

Jack wasn't surprised at the wealth Ray had somehow accumulated. He knew that all politicians had their secret ways of becoming wealthy. What did surprise him was that Ray Childs answered the door himself.

"Hello, you must be agent Lauren Kurtz. Ray Childs," he said, offering his hand and gracefully shaking hers. Then he turned to Jack while still holding her hand. "Jack Shields," Ray said, pulling his hand gently from Lauren's grip to extend it toward Jack.

Jack took it and returned a firm but not crushing grip. This man looked younger than his thirty five years. He stood five nine but carried himself much taller. His warm politician's smile was made warmer by his brown, almond-shaped eyes that seemed to curve up at the edges, matching his mouth. It was as if his whole face was smiling.

"Come on in," he said as they entered and he closed the large door behind them. "Let's head down to my office."

He extended a hand forward next to Lauren, leading the way with the palm of his hand. The walk to his office seemed as far as a walk around his old block, Jack thought. They passed the royal-looking living room, the futuristic granite-overflowing kitchen, and then the library on the way.

"Nice library," Jack said, noticing all the books laid out so nicely, probably in alphabetical order by author.

Not simply stacked at random like at his old place. Of course, for him there was never a need to read a book a second time so no need to keep any of them where he could find it.

"Thank you, Jack. Are you a reader?" Ray said, turning toward him as they continued to walk.

"Mostly comic books," he joked with a smile "Although, I do love a good mystery every now and then as long as I'm surprised at the end."

"Oh, yes, we must have that surprise twist at the end don't we," Ray said.

"Yeah, although, I've read so many that I'm finding it hard to be surprised by much anymore."

"Oh, I'm sure I could find a story for you that you would find quite surprising."

"I'd appreciate that," Jack said.

"Oh, how cute," Lauren said all of sudden, bending down in front of both of them.

They each awkwardly caught the other admiring her as she bent down.

"Oh, that's just Lilly. Don't mind her. She won't hurt

you," Ray said quickly with a warm laugh, easing the discomfort between him and Jack.

Lauren stayed crouched down, petting the gray schnauzer. The two of them couldn't help but smile at each other admiring the beauty of her curves. She rivaled any of the impressive artwork displayed in the long hallway they had just traversed. They watched her body move from behind as she slowly stroked the dog's fur. They both took a swallow as she gracefully stood up, arching her back as she did so like a ballerina stretching. Then she turned, her hair swinging as if fearful of being left behind. She caught them both still lingering a little lower than eye level. She didn't mind and, although she clearly caught them, she let them off the hook.

"She seems like a nice dog," she said, smiling at Ray, then looked knowingly toward Jack and gave him a different kind of smile. He just shrugged.

"She is a nice dog. Come, here we are," Ray said as he opened the door to his large study.

A stark contrast to the rest of the home they had just traveled through, this had a more modern, agnostic feel. The wooden floors were covered by a large brown Egyptian rug. In the back by the large window was his desk. The bookshelves on each side of the room were black and had straight lines. Jack noted that on one side the books were finance related and on the other psychology. Ray noticed him looking at the shelves as they walked into the room.

"I majored in finance and minored in psychology."

"Interesting combination," Lauren said.

"Not really, I just wanted to know more about money and then also how it affected people," he said with a strange smile.

"How is that working out for you?" she asked.

"Well, the more time I've spent in Washington, the more I realized I don't know shit about either," he said with a loud laugh. His cussing threw both of them off, but then Jack remembered where Ray had grown up. "Here, have a seat," he said, gesturing to the two black leather chairs facing the desk. They both sat as he rounded the desk and sat down. "I'm so sorry for what happened to your coworker," he said, looking at them with an exaggerated somber expression.

"Thank you," Lauren said.

"Was he a friend of yours?" Ray asked them both.

"Yes he was," Jack said then turned to look at Lauren as if waiting for her confirmation. She saw this, looked at Ray, and nodded.

"Well, I truly am sorry. The FBI shared with me the message that was sent after the first bombing. I can't help but feel I had some part in these events unfolding since I am the one who drafted the plan that has brought whomever this person is to such extreme shows of dislike."

"That's actually why we're here. We thought you might help us find a motive beyond just the plan itself," Jack said.

"What do you mean?"

"Well, who do you feel the plan hurts the most or who has the most to lose?" Jack asked.

"Don't you have some leads?"

"Well, yes, but right now it's a big list. We figured you might be able to help us narrow it down."

"Who do you have on your list?"

"All the CEOs that took TARP funds," Lauren answered.

"Just all of them," he said, smiling.

"And the politicians that worked on the plan."

"Including me?" he asked, matter-of-fact.

"Well..." Lauren trailed off, not sure what to say.

"It's fine, Lauren. You have to start somewhere. Just like in chess you start with many pieces that get eliminated on your way to winning. I'll simply be one of those pieces that gets knocked out along your way. If I can be the pawn that takes out a rook to help you get to the queen, I'll be glad to help."

"Thanks," she said, sounding more like she meant for saving the awkward moment than offering to help. The consummate politician.

"So how can I help?" he asked more directly, looking over to Jack as well.

"We got another note after the incident at the airport," Lauren told him.

"What did it say?" Ray asked, turning back to her.

"The authors of this plan have written their own fate," Jack said, looking at him for any reaction.

"Another reference to TARP, I see," he said, steepling his hands in front of his face with his elbows on the desk.

"Lofton helped you write the plan," Jack stated.

"He did, yes, a little," Ray said, almost as if annoyed. He clearly would rather be known as its main author.

"Can I ask you a question?" Lauren said.

"Isn't that why you're here?" he said, smiling and leaning back in his chair.

"What do you think the first note was referring to? 'Tell America the Real Problem.' What is the real problem?" she asked, leaning forward.

Jack looked at her surprised. He liked the question, but what he liked more was how she asked it. Her voice had a confident, subtly accusatory tone to it. It reminded him of the cops that used to always catch him out late at night asking him what he was doing out and where he was headed. It made her look even sexier to him, the secure way she carried herself.

Where he grew up, there weren't any girls who had that kind of confidence. That was in short supply in the poor parts of town. Jack grew up seeing that insecurity keep people down all around him, even long after high school where everyone was insecure, even the jocks like him.

Lauren, on the other hand, must have left that insecurity back in high school where it belonged.

"Well, where should I start?" Ray said, sitting up in his chair noting her tone.

"Anywhere you'd like," she said still firm.

"Well, have you read the bill?" he asked them.

"Yes, it's not that long," Jack said.

"Well, we had to pass it quickly. The markets were about to collapse," he answered defensively, as if Jack were a literary agent's intern, not worthy of criticizing his masterful writing.

"Some would say too quickly," Jack responded.

"Yes, that is one of the common criticisms," Ray said as if pointing out the lack of originality in his comment. "But you have to understand, the best way to get a bill passed is to do it quickly. Like a boxer in the ring, the bill that hesitates and stands still too long will get knocked out. They all have flaws that can be exposed when looked over too long."

"So what flaws were in this plan that someone would be so upset about?"

"Well, for one we made them take it."

"What do you mean?"

"The banks, half of them didn't need it."

"Why?"

"Because it's all about perception. Americans, hell the world, were looking at us and they knew we were going to bail out the banks. They were waiting to see which ones so they knew which ones to run from. You can't have people running from the banks. We had to have all the big ones, the top twenty five, all take it," Ray explained.

"So you could hide the ones that needed it versus the ones that didn't," Jack said, considering this. "To avoid a run on the banks."

"Exactly."

"So the CEOs that didn't need it would obviously be more upset than the ones that did," Lauren added.

"Well, I would think so."

"Can you give us that list?"

"Sure darling," he said, smiling at her.

"You seem like you're not concerned about the news getting out now," Jack said curiously.

"Well, yeah, almost half of the ones that were in trouble have merged with the ones that weren't since then. What do you think the money was for?" he said, letting them think on it.

They just looked at each other. "I thought the money was for the banks to get back out there to help the economy by lending," Jack said, having read that in all the articles he studied about TARP the night before.

"Listen, you asked me what the real problem is. Let me tell you. Hopefully, you can handle the truth. There is no more money. It's all numbers and the numbers don't add up. We ran out ten years after Nixon took us off the gold standard."

"What about the FED?" Lauren asked.

"What about them? They're in on it too. Why do you think they build those large buildings? It's all perception. Build them big and make everyone think there's so much money in each one that they have to be huge. They're empty. Just like churches."

"Excuse me?" Lauren said, seemingly offended. Even though she grew up going to synagogues, she got the idea he meant those too and her dad was a rabbi.

"Well, look at them. Why do you think they build them so grand and big? To fool everyone into thinking the nicer they are and the bigger they are, the more likely they are to have God inside. Of course, they're empty too. Look, they all do it, every religion, so I don't mean to offend any particular one."

"No just all of them," Lauren said, clearly pissed off.

"I'm just using these as examples. Please don't be angry with me. My only point is that we needed to do something big to make it believable so it would work and calm the markets. Look, it worked. We avoided a total collapse."

"So that's the real problem the bomber is referring to?"

"Perhaps. I don't know. You have to ask him when you

catch him. If it is though, we obviously can't tell people. It would cause a global collapse," Ray said with a sigh.

"No we can't have that," Jack agreed.

"No, so how about you two catch this guy so we don't have to and preferably before he blows someone else up, especially me."

"Then let's start with that list. Here's my card. Email it to me," Lauren said.

CHAPTER 32

"Why are you exiting here?" Lauren asked as Jack exited the freeway.

"Just want to go see an old friend," Jack said, focusing on the road as he thought about his old El Camino.

"You couldn't just drop me off first."

"It's on the way. Don't worry I just want to drive by real quick," he said as he turned down the street entering the old neighborhood.

"Well, it looks old, all right."

After a couple more turns down the narrow lanes, he drove down the street to Charlie's place. He didn't see his El Camino. He did see two other cars parked out front. Something wasn't right. Most people on this street didn't own a car. Charlie had company. Jack parked the car on the other side of the street.

"I'm just gonna go say, 'Hi' real quick," he said, turning to Lauren as he was already opening his car door to get out. "Just wait here. I won't be long."

"Okay, at least I'm armed," she said, looking around the sketchy neighborhood.

"I'll be right back," he said as he closed the door and headed up to Charlie's house.

Lauren had already pulled out her iPhone and looked

like a teenage girl texting her friends. Jack passed one of the cars as he hopped onto the sidewalk. A black Cadillac about ten years old with those ridiculous oversized tires. He couldn't read the writing on the back window but he recognized it. "Serbs," he said followed by "Shit" as he quickened his pace. The door wasn't locked. It wasn't even closed.

"Hey, Charlie," Jack said casually but loud enough to get everyone's attention as he walked into the place.

The everyone, included Charlie, already severely beaten, bleeding from his nose, down on his knees. The other two larger men were Serbian gang members standing over him. Jack could tell which one did the holding and which the beating. The larger one was still wiping the blood from his hand with a handkerchief as they both turned toward Jack with a confused look on their faces.

"Jack Shields, Secret Service," he said as he held up his badge high enough for both of them to see. It only served to confuse the two even more.

"Secret Service?" the larger one said, putting the handkerchief in his coat pocket. "What are you doing here?" he said as he reached over to take the badge from Jack to have a closer look.

"Well, I was about to ask you two the same question but it looks pretty obvious," Jack said, taking a step closer toward them. As he did, he considered how he needed to make a better effort to remember he now had a gun he's actually allowed to carry. It wasn't going to do him any good sitting in the nightstand at home. Oh well, he'd have to handle this the old fashioned way. Too bad it didn't look like Charlie was going to be much help.

"Really, why are you here?" the second guy said, stepping up to the side of the other guy. He was shaking a bit, clearly still full of the adrenaline that aided in their handling of Charlie. Jack could feel his level start to rise as well, although there would be no shaking visible from him. He did clench his fist.

"Charlie here is helping us with an investigation and I need to talk to him. Are you guys done here?" he asked, still acting casual as if what he was seeing was no big deal, trying to calm the guys down versus giving them a reason to take up the violence a notch. He even unclenched his fist before they saw it.

The bigger one looked back at a dazed Charlie, then back at Jack, and said, "Actually no, we're not done yet. We were just getting started. Why don't you go grab some dinner and come back in about an hour Agent Shields?" he said, handing him the badge back.

"Look, guys, I'm kind of on a tight schedule and I really need to talk to him," Jack tried being polite again as he put the wallet back in his coat pocket.

"Look, you're just gonna have to wait your turn, and for now I think it's time for you to leave," the bigger guy said, putting his hands on his hips in a way that pushed his coat back, revealing the nine millimeter tucked in his pants.

Clearly being polite wasn't getting him anywhere.

"Okay, okay," Jack said, raising both his hands as if giving up. "I'll come back later. just don't make it so he can't talk when I come back," he said as he turned slowly.

He had a feeling the guy wouldn't just let him walk out. He'd dealt with the Serbs enough himself to know that their ego always won out in these situations. He figured he wouldn't make it out the door without a little shove on the way.

He was right. Jack felt a hand to his shoulder just as he made it to the doorway while clenching his right fist. He let the guy push him forward just enough so that when he turned his body around in that same direction it caused the guy to fall forward.

This added to the force of Jack's right hand flying forward toward the man's protruding chin. If the blow didn't succeed in breaking his jaw, perhaps the crash to the ground face first would. Jack took a second to admire his work. Unfortunately, like a baseball player admiring the homerun ball that turned out to just be a double, he was about to be reminded why you shouldn't make that mistake.

He went flying across the room as the other man crashed into him, hitting him directly in the gut with his shoulder. It knocked the wind out of him as his back crunched into the cheap sheet rock, putting a hole in it like a chalk outline of a corpse. The other guy got up of the ground quickly after they had both fallen down after hitting the wall. Jack was still trying to catch his breath. The kick to his gut from the guy didn't help matters. Jack leaned forward with both hands on the ground trying to find his breath as if it were a missing contact on the ground in front of him.

He hadn't found it yet when he did see another flash of the man's foot coming fast in his direction, since this time he was aiming for his face. Most men can't do the splits and when Jack grabbed the man's leg and pushed it out past him as he moved out of the way, it let the guy know why. He pulled his groin muscle as he fell to the ground after falling forward at the awkward motion of his leg being thrown farther than he intended to kick it. Jack got up and now could admire his work uninterrupted, at least briefly.

"John?" Charlie said barely legible from across the room, looking through swollen eyes. Luckily the two men were busy making their own noises that they didn't hear.

Jack walked over to Charlie and knelt down in front of him. "How much do you owe?" he asked him.

"Just two," Charlie said, coughing some blood from his mouth onto Jack's shirt.

The guys behind him were still rolling around making noises from the pain they were in so Jack didn't hear the person walking up behind him. Jack turned back only in time to meet a large fist across his face knocking him to the ground.

"What the fuck is going on here?" the guy said to Jack.

He placed the end of the barrel against the back of Jack's head as he stumbled his way back onto his feet.

Jack lifted his hands and began to stand up slowly, the

gun still pressed to his head. "Look, I'm Secret Service. My badge is in my coat pocket," he said as he stood up straight.

The man took a couple of short steps back, glancing quickly at his fallen partners on the ground as they were watching him, each with a look begging him to just pull the trigger on this asshole.

Jack turned and saw the man he recognized. Big Billy. He must have been in the bathroom when Jack came in. Problem was he was here now.

"John?" he said still holding the gun at his face.

"No, Jack Shields," he said reaching for his badge.

"Hold it right there."

"I was just going to show you my badge."

"Do it slow like in the movies, okay?" Billy said.

Jack reached for his wallet and pulled it out putting it in Billy's outstretched hand."

"Well, you sure look a lot like a guy we used to know." Then he tossed the badge over his shoulder. It landed next to the guy with the broken jaw. "Now you're going to look even more like him," he said, raising the gun toward him. Jack was out of moves. At least, he would die with his old friend Charlie.

"Freeze, don't fucking move!" Lauren shouted from the doorway, standing behind the two guys on the ground who hadn't seen her come in since they were watching Billy. She was standing with her knees bent holding the gun with both hands toward Billy.

Jack smiled. "Say hello to my partner, Lauren."

"Drop it," she said taking a step closer, her hands shaking just a bit.

Billy kneeled down as far as his knees would allow with that much weight and tossed the gun on the ground. Then he rose and slowly turned with his hands up. When he saw the person holding the gun in his direction, he didn't even notice it.

He couldn't believe how hot this girl was. He turned his head back toward Jack. "This is your partner?

Jack nodded and said, "Yeah," with a shrug of his shoulders.

"Man, I should have stayed in school," Billy said, turning back her way.

"What the hell is going on, Jack?" she said.

"Nothing much. They were just leaving. Right, Billy?"

"Yeah sure, *Jack*," Billy said with sarcasm.

Billy helped the two guys up off the ground and let them stumble through the doorway first. Then he turned to get another look at the surreal scene. As he did, Jack tossed him his gun, barley giving him time to catch it.

"How much does he owe you anyway?" Jack asked him.

"Three thousand," Billy said, tucking the gun into his pants.

"He told me just two," Jack said.

"He's never been good at math," Billy said with a smile.

"No he hasn't." Jack smiled back. "He'll have the money next week, okay?"

"Sure," Billy said, with doubt, as he turned and left.

Jack turned and went over to Charlie and helped him up onto the couch. Charlie was still dazed and about to pass out. Too dazed to follow up on questioning about whether Jack was John. Jack leaned down and whispered in his ear. "Where's Kristin?"

"School," he whispered back before fading to black.

Jack smiled and stood up, turning toward Lauren. "He'll be all right."

"*He'll* be all right?" she said, still holding her gun with both hands shaking. Her adrenaline level was still pushing eleven like the amplifier on *Spinal Tap*.

"Come on let's go," he said, walking over and picking up his wallet on the way out.

CHAPTER 33

"Go lie down on the couch. Let me get you some ice," Lauren said as she plopped her keys down on the island in the kitchen.

Jack let himself fall back on the couch. As soon as his banged up head hit the pillow his friend Tabby made his appearance on the coffee table next to his face. The cat hissed at him while arching its back. Jack rolled on his side to face the cat directly.

"Listen, dude, this wasn't my idea. I told her I was fine," he said, addressing Tabby.

The cat walked around in a circle, looking back and forth from Lauren to Jack.

"You two getting along?" Lauren said from the kitchen while putting some ice in a Ziploc bag.

The cat sat down and just stared at Jack, then it started to lick its paw and wipe its face. Jack took that as a cease fire for now and felt safe enough to turn onto his back. As he turned his head, he found Lauren looking down at him. Looking down would have still applied to the way she was looking at him even had he been standing. She felt his eyes on her and quickly shifted her gaze to his face, hers a little flush.

"Here, put this on your face," she said as if changing

the subject. She handed him the bag, the ice already beginning to melt in her warm grasp. He rested the bag on the
right side of his face.

"At least I got hit on the other side of my face this
time," Jack joked.

"Well, you couldn't have gotten any uglier," she said
as she walked around the couch.

"Ouch, hey, I'm already in pain, don't hurt my feelings," he said as he watched her slowly sit down on the end
of the couch by his feet. Jack could feel her back side on his
leg. She was warm and felt like an electric blanket on one of
his legs. He was warming all over.

"What's wrong?" he asked as she looked off into space,
clearly upset.

"We're not getting anywhere on this case," she said.

"We'll let Sara and the FBI figure it out," he said.

"Fuck the FBI!" she said turning to him in a slight rage.
He knew she meant to say Sara. "I don't want to wait
around for another one of our guys to get killed while we
wait around for the FBI to figure it out."

"So what do you want to do?"

"Let's go talk to his assistant."

"Whose assistant?"

"Mikal's."

"Fine, set it up, I'm in," he said. He had been holding
the bag of ice out to his side and Tabby was leaning from
the coffee table licking the condensation off of it. Lauren
saw it dripping.

"Here, put this back on your face," she said, leaning
over him and taking his hand with the bag of ice in hers.

She slowly guided the bag back. Her hair fell across his
face as she leaned over him. Her hair smelled like cotton
candy to him. It reminded him of the carnival he went to as
a kid. He never actually had enough money to spend on any
to try it but he remembered the smell. Here he was again,
with that sweet smell tempting him, but now he was left to
his own self-discipline to keep playing this game. He fig-

ured this charade wasn't going to last anyway. He was surprised he'd made it this long. He tried to be Jack in every way but he was not gay and, besides, he was never good at carnival games. When it came to women, this Jack still had a sweet tooth.

As she let go of the bag on his cheek, she stopped and hovered over him, looking down into his eyes. She started to move her hand from behind him but then he grabbed her wrist and squeezed. She moved her arm to his side, their eyes still locked as she began to back away.

He pulled her arm, bringing her slowly back down. She held herself above him, steady. No problem since she did fifty pushups after every work out, her triceps not even straining.

"What are you doing?" she asked him.

"Something, I've wanted to do since I first saw you," he said.

"Really? Well, that knock on your head must have given you amnesia so let me remind you. When you first saw me when we started working together, you were quick to tell me that you could never date your partner. You blew me off. So what's changed?" she asked, still hovering over him only a few inches of space between their bodies.

"Maybe that blow knocked some sense into me. Besides, you saved my life."

"You do kind of owe me," she said, smiling.

Jack pulled her down and kissed her. For six months when they first started working together she had imagined kissing his full lips. What it would feel like? She had an idea it would feel good. She didn't factor in the adrenaline of doing something she knew she shouldn't. It didn't feel good at all. It felt great.

Normally one to over think things and ruin the moment, she wasn't going to let this one go to waste. She had waited too long. In fact, she had given up waiting. She met someone else that had taken her mind off of Jack for once. It lasted a year, but now the engagement was off and she was free again. Free to long for Jack again and now here he was in her arms. She was done thinking and was ready for doing. Him.

They kissed each other with a lot of strength, almost as if in a workout. Each of them inhaling as the other exhaled breathing as one as if the other were their air tank underwater in some beautiful Caribbean sea. They forgot for a second that they weren't alone.

"Oww!" Jack yelled as Lauren bit his lip and not in a playful way.

Tabby had jumped onto Lauren's back, startling her. "Oh, I'm sorry," Lauren said as she sat up and turned to grab the cat.

Jack wiped his bleeding lip with his forearm, looking at her confused. She turned back to him, holding the cat up, and shrugged her shoulders.

"Guess he's jealous," she said as she got up to go put the cat in the bedroom and closed the door. Jack admired her movement along the way.

"That cat really doesn't like me," he said as she stood next to the couch. He lay there, looking up at her.

"I don't know what's going on. He used to love you as much I as did," she said.

She then took off her blouse and dropped her skirt as Jack just lay there in awe. Then she took off her bra and then pulled her panties down still standing right by his face. He couldn't move, frozen by her statuesque body but he felt his heart beating in his chest. He took in her scent and it beat faster.

"I already saved your life today. I'm not going to take off your clothes for you as well."

Jack quickly sat up, causing his head to spin. Small price to pay as he pulled his sweater over his head. He stood up next to her, undid his belt, and bent down, taking off his pants and boxers. Then he stood in front of her.

"Hey, did you just say you loved me?" he asked.

"Come on, Jack. It was a slip of the tongue. Now give

me yours," she said as she leaned in and kissed him, holding his body next to hers. It wasn't long before they fell back onto the couch. It would be a long time before Tabby would find freedom from the bedroom again.

CHAPTER 34

The jogging shoes he was wearing probably cost more than any of his old outfits. Some high-end Nikes that would have gotten him mugged in his old neighborhood had they been for playing basketball and not jogging. Saturday morning in Rock Creek Park should be safe either way. The only danger to his life would be the potential heart attack he'd have trying to keep up with Sara. He'd spent the last two weeks, trying to get in shape at the gym where he apparently had a lifetime membership. He didn't make any friends since he tried to avoid eye contact, especially in the showers after his workouts. He noticed more of those glances his way but pretended not to. He was there to get ready for Sara so he was focused. After eight days of working out over the past two weeks he was about to find out if it was enough. He noticed quickly how in shape she looked in her work out clothes so he wasn't sure he was ready. When he saw her stretching as he walked up he could see even better what great shape she was in.

"Hey, Sara," he said, walking up to her while she stretched out her legs against a park bench.

She was wearing those black stretch pants that so many women, probably many that shouldn't, were wearing these days. Apparently, those pants were designed for women like her. He could see every muscle on her toned legs as she bent and rocked back and forth with her back still to him. It was cool out and she had a long sleeve shirt on that hung a little long.

The way she was stretching it had crept up, revealing how toned her backside was while still holding its curves.

When she turned and looked at him, her large smile was almost all he saw.

He did see the eyes. They seemed to be smiling just as much as her mouth.

"I was worried you'd back out again," she said, still smiling and stretching, rocking back and forth one foot on the ground, the other on the bench.

"Nope, I'm here," he said just watching her. "Although, I'm still recovering."

"From what?" she said, putting her foot from the bench back on the ground and turned toward him. "Geesh, Jack, what happened this time?" she said, gesturing with her right hand toward his reinjured face.

"Oh this?" he said, pointing to his own face while shrugging his shoulders. "Broke up a fight this week."

"How, by putting your face between someone's fist and another guy's?" she asked. "You know, Jack you're not Superman."

"You don't know that. I have secrets," he said.

"Oh, I know you have secrets, Jack, but trust me I know that's not one of them, you're proof is in a mirror if you're wondering."

"Well, take it easy on me today then, okay?" he said.

"Don't worry. I can only do three miles today. I need to get to the office this morning," she said as she crossed her legs and bent down touching her toes. "Aren't you going to stretch?"

"Sure," he said, trying to remember how he had seen some of the guys doing it at the gym the past couple of weeks. He stretched his legs out and moved from foot to foot trying unsuccessfully to reach either. Luckily she was too busy finishing her own stretching to notice his lack of flexibility.

While she finished up, he stopped his futile efforts and asked her, "Is Todd trying to get back at you for breaking up with him?"

Sara looked up while still grabbing her crossed feet below and smiled, appreciating his concern. "No, I want to go in. Besides, Todd has actually never been nicer to me."

"Probably because he's scared of you."

"Scared of me how?"

"Well, you've seen how small his dick is, haven't you? He doesn't want you to share," he said.

Sara laughed, rising up quickly. "Really, Jack? Besides, he doesn't."

He smiled. "Oh, well, I just figured."

"We've been getting along great, actually. Breaking up has been great for our relationship, our working relationship," she said as she grabbed a foot and pulled up her leg behind her, leaning one hand on the bench in front of her. She looked like an elegant ballerina stretching before her performance. "Also I think with what happened to his dad has put things in perspective for him."

"What about your friend?" he asked. "Cynthia?"

"Hell, no! It's different with women."

"How so?"

"Well, she knows she's the bad guy, but girls have a harder time admitting it, so she acts like she's mad at me, instead."

"That's kind of backward isn't it?"

"That's women for you."

"I guess. So why are you going in to the office?"

"Come on. Let's get going and I'll tell you on the way," she said as she turned and began running.

In his mind, it was running and not jogging since she took off a lot faster than he had expected. *Shit*, he thought as he tried to catch up. At least while he worked his way catching up to her he could enjoy the view. He could see her muscles flex under that tight-fitting fabric on her butt. He wasn't sure why his brother thought these jogs were the thing to do every Saturday, but at least he had found one really good reason he would enjoy them. Unfortunately, Sara had slowed enough for him to draw even with her.

"Boy you are dragging today."

"Sorry," is all he could exhale out between the large gasps of air he was trying to refill his empty lungs with.

"So I found something?"

"What?"

"At FFB."

"Mikal's bank?" he barely got the words out that time.

"Yeah. Some of the trades don't make sense. Especially in the last six months," she said slowing down a little more seeing, that Jack was really struggling.

"What do you mean?" he said thankful that she slowed enough for him to actually say more than one word.

"I mean the timing is strange, well that and the amounts. It's strange because Mikal had always been conservative," she said as they began to round the turn into the woods.

"Hey, watch your mouth. We haven't run that far and we're still in DC so be careful where you throw around the C word," he said, laughing as much as he could as out of breath as he was.

"I think we're safe out here in the woods," she said, looking ahead as they ran into a tunnel of trees. The cool fall morning air cooled them both down as they went slightly uphill. "Listen, Mikal came up from the trading side. He knew what he was doing. And he had always done it safe."

"So let me guess, you found some trades that weren't so cautious," he said.

"Exactly."

"And they were large amounts?"

"Right again," she said just as they hit the top of the small hill and started to go down while also turning almost ninety degrees. She disappeared for a second on him until he could make the turn. At least now they were going slightly downhill.

"How big?" he asked when he caught up to her again.

"We're talking billions with a B," she said.

"Yeah but a bank that size, isn't that pretty common?"

"That's just it. They're not. That's what I've been researching. I've been doing spreadsheets, documenting all the trades over the last five years. They aren't anything like the trades that showed up in the last six months."

"What's wrong with them?"

"They're just really aggressive."

"Maybe they hired some new guy and he was doing them, plus it's a whole new world after the downturn."

"No, it was Mikal that signed off on these. And that's my other point, the timing is weird."

"Why?" he asked.

"Because, the OCC was already investigating their trade activity when these trades occurred."

"So?"

"So, the whole point of the OCC is to study this activity and to make sure the bank is making sound decisions. This flies right in the face of that and they were done while the OCC was there. It just doesn't make sense."

Just then there was a loud SNAP. Jack had not been watching where his feet were landing. He stepped on a fallen branch and twisted his ankle as the branch gave under his weight and snapped, causing him to lose his balance. Jack fell forward and, from instinct, reached out for the closest thing he could get his hands on to stop his fall. That was Sara's ass.

He couldn't help but squeeze as he did so, his face bouncing off just as he caught his balance.

"I'm sorry, I just twisted my ankle on that branch back there," he said more concerned with his embarrassment than the pain creeping up his leg.

Sara just smiled at him, said, "Okay, let's just walk the rest of the way," and began walking.

She could still feel where his large hands had grabbed her. One hand on each cheek, each side still warm from his strong grip.

As she stopped running and began to walk, she let the thought bubble up that perhaps he had done it on purpose even though she knew he hadn't. It still had her feeling moist in another area other than the sweat on her forehead.

She hadn't been touched anywhere near that part of her body since her break up with Todd and was still going through withdrawals. It was probably good that Jack continued on with the work conversation.

"Okay, but Mikal didn't look at all the trades going on at the time," he offered.

"That's just it. He usually didn't but the ones I'm talking about were all approved by him."

"So other than the size, what's wrong with the trades?"

"Well, I'm not exactly sure but I know they're derivatives. I don't fully understand them but all I know is that every bank in the world was trying to get out of them during that time."

"And what, Mikal wasn't?"

"No, he was buying them," she said, stopping for a second and looking at Jack as if to add emphasis.

"You're right. That doesn't make sense," he said.

"I know, right?" she asked excitedly as if her curiosity had just been validated. "That's why I need to go in and study these things some more."

"I think you're right. Sounds like you're on to something."

Jack was thinking at the same time about the email he had gotten from Mikal. There was something going on that last two weeks before he died. Jack would have to see if Richard could help him with more than just remembering names and faces.

He would have to have him use his other talents. He got a little excited at the idea of perhaps finding something that would help Sara.

This made him nervous since his heart was already racing from the jogging. Then as they rounded the turn he saw something that really scared him. It was a mile marker showing that they still had another mile to go.

CHAPTER 35

After taking a shower at his place, Jack decided he would head over to Richard's. As his car rolled past the gate of his complex he saw the young novelist walk out of the booth. He was wearing a coat that looked two sizes too big for him, making him look younger than normal. "Hey how's the novel going? You get past page one hundred?" Jack asked as he came to a stop.

"Hey, Jack," the guard said. "Great, I'm actually up to one hundred and forty pages. The story is really starting to pick up."

"That's great."

"Thanks. Hey, I'd still like to talk to you some time. You know, get some ideas about the real stuff that goes on in this town."

"The real stuff, huh? I'm still trying to figure that out myself. All I can tell you so far is that whatever fiction you come up with in that book of yours won't be as outrageous or as dangerous as what the assholes running this town are up to," Jack said.

"You think so?"

"Yeah, that much I do know. Gotta get going, keep working on it. I can't wait to read it."

"Bye, Jack."

❧❧❧

Jack used the key that Richard gave him and walked into his house. Something was off. Richard's house looked as if he had taken part in one of those reality shows letting some slob stay at his place. Newspapers were strewn about, outnumbered only by the empty pizza boxes and soda cans. The pleasant scent of his first visit was replaced by a pungent odor more like the gym locker room he had been visiting recently.

He saw shoes laying in the corner of the room looking as if they were knocked off a pedestrian trying to cross a freeway. Richard tended not to wear socks and he had very large feet. Of course, they had to be to hold up his large frame. At least Jack had a good idea as to the cause of the smell. The place looked as if the Brady Bunch had been canceled and they were now filming Rosanne. He quickly walked out of the living room, since breathing in anymore of the stale air in it would cause quite the opposite of its namesake.

Jack turned down the hallway and, taking in a breath of slightly fresher air, yelled for Richard.

"Richard, you here?" he said as he continued down the hallway.

Nothing. He continued down to his office. "Richard?" he yelled again.

He didn't get a response, but as he got close to the office he heard the muffled sounds of what sounded like Metallica. Sure enough, as he turned the corner he saw Richard sitting in front of his computer, pounding on the keyboard like Elton John on the piano. The large headsets covered his ears and were clearly cranked up to probably eleven. Jack walked up and patted him on the shoulder.

Richard reacted to the touch as if someone had hooked him up to a car battery to give him a jump, since that's exactly what he did. Richard jumped up while simultaneously turning and pushing Jack down before realizing who he was.

Jack fell to the ground, as if in slow motion, and locked in on Richards's scared face just like in a B-movie. But by the time his butt hit the ground, he saw recognition in that same face and it changed to that of an angel. Richard reached down with his right hand while sliding the headphones off with his left. The music now filled the room. "Enter Sandman" vibrated the walls.

"Hey, Jack. Didn't hear you come in," Richard said, still holding his hand out waiting for Jack to take it.

"No shit," Jack said, looking at the headsets still blaring.

Richard turned the volume dial down on the headsets. "Sorry, I was in the zone."

"Which one would that be, the *Twilight*?" Jack said.

"Yeah, probably so."

Jack let him take his hand. Richard pulled him up as if he didn't weigh the two hundred pounds that he did.

"So what are you working on, anyway?" Jack asked, looking around him at the computer.

Richard reached around Jack and turned off the monitor. "Let's just keep it anonymous, okay?"

Jack looked up from the black screen and smiled. "That joke never gets old for you, does it?"

"Made you smile, didn't I?"

"Yeah, well it must be something intense. Your place is a mess."

"I know, I've been locked down on this project. Got a deadline to meet."

"Deadline? You sound like a reporter. When is it?"

"Monday morning at nine a.m."

"And what if you don't meet the deadline, you don't get paid?"

"More like they drop the second syllable."

"What the hell are you up to, Richard? Are you in some kind of trouble?"

"No, not anymore. I'm almost in. Don't worry about it. Hey, I just noticed I'm hungry."

"More like you just finally heard that stomach growl now that the music is off," Jack said.

"Well, I say we go get something to eat. I'm still growing, you know," Richard said, smiling as he began to walk past him out of the office

"Maybe here," Jack said, patting Richard's belly as he passed by him.

୧୨୧୨

The two of them moved their trays down the metal bars at the cafeteria line. If their trays were a canvas, and the plates of food paint, Jack had only the earth tones of meat and potatoes.

Meanwhile, Richard's was a rainbow of colors, full of all varieties of food.

"You must think I'm paying," Jack said, looking back over Richards's overloaded tray.

"Relax, Jack, I got four words for you.

"What's that?" Jack asked as they moved the trays toward the person at the register.

"All you can eat," Richard said.

He looked at him and then leaned over him to grab a piece of pecan pie, fitting it somehow on his tray as if he was a puzzle master. "Oh, but you are paying, though."

Richard smiled and gestured with his head toward Jack for the checkout girl and walked off with his struggling-to-survive tray. Jack just shrugged at the checker and handed her his debit card.

"So how was it with her?"

"What? With who?" Jack said, wondering how he knew about Lauren.

"Sara, were you able to keep up?"

"Well, kind of, at least better than I will here with

you," he said, still admiring the massive ensemble of food on Richard's side of the table.

"Well, I know you're not in as good of shape as Jack was."

"Hey, you're not exactly training for a triathlon either over there."

"Well, I'm not trying to be someone I'm not."

"No you're trying to be anonymous," Jack said sarcastically.

"Exactly," Richard said as he stuffed a huge forkful of gravy-soaked mashed potatoes into his mouth. It looked like he'd just swallowed the whole mountain that Richard Dreyfuss made in *Close Encounters of the Third Kind*. "So she still thinks you're Jack? That's good. What about Lauren?" he asked. "How's it going with her?"

"It's going good," Jack said hesitantly, looking around nervously and feeling as if hooked to a lie detector that was running out of ink.

Richard put his fork down and looked at him. "Shit you fucked her, didn't you?"

"What?"

"Dude, don't deny it. I can see it on you," Richard said.

"Well, I don't want to talk about it, okay?"

"That's good. Make sure you don't around Sara," Richard said, picking up his fork again and moving on to the fried fish.

"Hey, I might not be as smart as my brother was, but I'm not stupid either." Jack picked up his own fork and took a bite of his chicken fried steak.

"I don't know. I think sleeping with your partner qualifies," Richard said then took a drink of his tea, eying his plate for his next victim.

"Look, I need something from you before I meet up with her Monday morning for something we're doing."

"What, a condom?" Richard said with a chuckle.

"Good one. No I need you to help me do something you're good at.

"Hey, I'm good with condoms."

"That might be so, and I don't need to know that, but I do know you're good with computers," Jack said with his regular-volumed tone.

"Hey, Jack, you don't need to make it public," Richard said, looking around the room.

"Don't worry. No one heard us talking."

"You clearly don't keep up with the latest in spy technology like I do. Who do you think invented the latest in hearing aids? Military design team used them first to listen to conversations from across the room.

"We're in a cafeteria. I think most of the hearing aids in here are just that since the average age in here is somewhere north of seventy. So even if they did work for the FBI or CIA, I think it's safe to say most of them are retired.

"Well, for my piece of mind, while I eat my piece of pie, just keep it down a little."

"Sure, Rich," Jack said, whispering.

"So what do you need?" Richard asked and shoveled a bite of pie into his mouth.

"Lauren and I are meeting with Ian Ginsberg at his dad's office Monday morning. I'd like to get into Mikal's computer," Jack said, waiting for him to swallow.

"Is that all?" Richard said as he finished swallowing and put his fork down.

"Yeah, I guess so."

"Here." Richard leaned back in his chair, pulling out a small device from his pocket about the size of a matchbox. "Take this."

He slid it across the table to Jack with his left hand while picking up his glass of tea with his right.

"What do I do with this?"

"Let me keep it simple for you. Just like you did with Lauren, you stick this in, but into Ginsberg's computer. It does the same thing," Richard said with an evil grin.

Baffled, Jack stared at him. "What?"

"It fucks them."

"What do you mean? Is it gonna mess up his computer?"

"No, but you plug this in and run it, you get information and there's no better way to fuck someone in this town than by getting information on them. Especially in this town, 'cause everyone's got something to hide. Isn't that right, Jack?" Richard said as he winked at him and stood up.

"Where are you going?" Jack asked.

"Get dessert."

"What was the pecan pie?" Jack asked, turning his head following Richard's walk back toward the buffet line.

"Appetizer?" Richard said with a shrug, "I just saw them put out some pumpkin pie."

CHAPTER 36

Jack walked into the bank, his shoes clicking on the marble like a tap dancer out of practice. He felt the urge to check his shoes for mud. Then he noticed the large columns made of oak seeming to go all the way up to where the giant from *Jack and the Beanstalk* lived. He could smell the wood as he walked by one while his steps echoed in the hall. This was different than any bank he had ever set foot in, and not just due to the lack of security glass in front of the tellers. This was a high quality bank, and so were the people working there. He noticed one of the girls working the teller line. He figured he had a few minutes before Lauren would show up and he needed to get some cash anyway. So why not get a closer look.

Jack worked his way through the maze of velvet rope, even though there was no one else waiting. *Do people even go to the bank for cash anymore with all the debit cards and ATM machines*, he wondered as he worked his way around. Fine with him. He could take his time with the red head.

"May I help you, sir?" she said to him, causing him to turn around looking for the *sir* she was addressing then realizing, when no one was behind him, that she meant him. She was young, probably a college girl working there part time while she finished school. He hoped the sir part just came with the training. It felt ruder to him than the "Next" he was used to hearing at banks on his side of town. He walked up to her window. "Hello," she said looking up at him with large green eyes.

"Hello, Nella," he said, noticing her name tag. He was trying to keep his eyes up but he had already noticed her low cut blouse. *So they like it that way in the city too.* He looked down despite himself and saw her typing away on her iPhone. That wasn't what caught his eye, it was the shiny bracelet she had on. These girls must get paid a lot better than the tellers he was used to seeing.

"Is that the new iPhone?" he asked.

"Yeah," she said, smacking some gum. It was as if she was doing everything she could to let him know how young she was.

"Was it a gift?" he asked, really wondering more about the bracelet.

"Yeah, I just got it a couple of weeks ago."

"Birthday?" he asked, figuring he could then follow up as to her age without being as rude.

"No, just a gift," she said, as she pushed send and then pushed it aside and looked back up.

"How can I help you?" she said again, keeping it formal.

"I need some cash," he said.

"Okay, do you have a check?" she asked.

"No."

"Okay, here fill this out," she said, handing him a withdrawal slip. "Do you know your account number?"

"No," he said.

"Do you have your driver's license?" she asked.

"Sure," he said, getting his wallet from his back pocket and flipping it open in front of her.

She noticed the badge before he pulled out the ID. She took the ID from him and swiped it in her machine. "Jack Shields," she said, looking at the screen, never once checking the picture on the card.

"That's me," he said.

"Here you go." She handed the card back to him. "How much do you want?" she asked, still smacking her gum, almost loud enough that it seemed to echo in the lobby.

"How much do I have?"

She looked back at the screen, got out another withdrawal slip, and wrote on the back.

Then she slid the paper across.

Jack picked it up and looked at it.

"Thirty two thousand?"

"Well that's just in the checking. Do you want the savings balance, too?" she asked him, still chewing.

"Sure." He chuckled at the idea that he had a savings account now. He handed the slip back to her to write on.

She wrote on the paper and slid it back over. "Here you go."

Jack looked at it and thought better of announcing that he had over eighty thousand in the savings account.

"So how much do you want?" she asked again.

"Just give me three thousand," he said, thinking that should be enough to get Charlie square with the Serbs.

"You want that any certain way."

"Just give me hundreds," he said. "Why don't you keep one for yourself?"

"Can't do that, sir," she said, smiling.

"Of course not."

She handed him the envelope and he touched her hand. It felt as if she grabbed on for a second as she smiled at him with her whole face. It was as if her attitude toward him had changed after seeing his balances. He didn't mind.

"So did you know Mr. Ginsberg?" he asked.

"Well, I saw him all the time. He said 'Hi' to me sometimes when he would come in. He seemed nice."

Jack stuck the envelope in the inside coat pocket and began to turn. "I'm sure he was."

"Oh, here you go," she said, offering him his ID back.

He turned back "Oh, I'll need that," he said as he got

his wallet back out and put the ID inside.

"Are you here to talk to Ian?" she asked.

It threw him off how casually she had thrown his name out as if she knew him. Perhaps he had said "Hi" to her also, the times he was in town. Perhaps he had been even nicer to her than his old man.

"Yes," was all he said, waiting to see her response.

She just smiled and looked back down at her phone. Before he could ask her anything about how well she knew him he heard Lauren from behind him.

"Jack," she said, her voice echoing from across the lobby.

"Thanks, Nella." He turned and headed toward the elevators where Lauren was waiting. He hadn't seen her since he'd left her place. They hadn't really spoken much other than to agree to meet at the bank.

The clicks of his shoes as he drew closer felt like a countdown to some kind of doom. It rivaled that first day at the Secret Service when he began his big lie. This seemed as though the consequences, if he said the wrong thing, could be much worse or at the very least more unpredictable.

"You ready to go up?"

"Sure," he said, watching her calmly turn and push the button.

They both got on the elevator and she hit the button to the sixtieth floor. Why did it have to be such a tall building? Jack just stood there watching the doors close slowly, trapping him.

Then she turned in his direction. "So?" was all she said.

"What?" He returned the one word response as if a volley in a tennis match.

"Seriously?" she hit it back, crossing her arms and staring him down.

"What?" He backhanded again.

"Uh, the other night?" she added, as if spiking the ball at his feet.

And there it was the elephant in the elevator. Had there been just one more person on the ride up then it would have felt a lot less crowded for Jack.

"What about the other night?" was all he could muster, after all the books he had read, all he could think to say sounded like a movie title.

"How about the part where you just left?" she said.

Jack looked up for a second, not only to avoid her glare but see what floor they were on, like a struggling boxer waiting for the bell to sound before he gets knocked out. *Fifteen only?* he thought, discouraged about his chances of surviving this round.

"Hey, I didn't want to wake you," he said sheepishly, turning back toward her.

"Oh so you were being polite, is that it?" she said, arms still crossed leaning a little forward like a prosecutor in front of the idiot defendant who had taken the witness stand against the advice of his counsel.

He looked up and saw they still had thirty floors to go. "Yeah,"

Lauren noticed him looking up and began laughing. Her arms fell to her stomach as if she couldn't help herself. "I'm just messing with you, Jack. You know me better than that. I'm not that pathetic. I'm glad you left. A girl needs her space too."

"What about Tabby?" he said, laughing as well, releasing some of that nervous energy he'd been holding in.

"He never wanted you there in the first place so what do you think? I can't believe how nervous you were just now. What are you so worried about?" she asked him.

They still had twenty floors to go. He grimaced. "Well, I just was wondering how that night was going to change things."

"Okay, let's see. I've seen you naked and I now know what your dick looks like. You've seen my tits. That about sum it up? Come on, Jack, we're both single right now. It was just fun. Let's just forget it and move on. Okay?"

"If you say so," he said, surprised but relieved.

"Besides, you're not my *bashert*," she said softly under her breath as she turned away from him toward the door.

"I'm not your bastard?" he said, a little confused at the comment, thrown off by the fact that he actually was one by the literal definition of the word. But she didn't know that, did she?

"I didn't say bastard," she said as she turned. "I said *bashert*."

"*Bashert*? What is that?"

"It means soul mate in Yiddish. And you are not mine," she said, looking at him with a slightly sad look.

"You sound sure of that."

"Well, my dad's a rabbi, and you're not Jewish, and I know you're good at math."

"Yeah, looks like I'm getting subtracted from that equation."

"Look, it was a fun night. Let's just leave it at that."

"Sure," he said, looking at her.

Then the bell dinged for the sixtieth floor, saving both of them.

"Hello, my name is Elena Shikov. I'm Mr. Ginsberg's executive assistant. I'm sorry I guess I should say former. I worked for Mikal, not for Ian," she said to them as they got out of the elevator.

She had a slight Russian accent when she spoke and Jack could tell she was sad. He wasn't sure if she was more sad about Mikal's death or the fact that she was losing her job. Jack figured she was in her late thirties, but she still looked like she could pass for twenty eight. Her big brown eyes and button nose added to the youthful appearance. It reminded Jack of the girl he had just spoken with downstairs.

"Hello, Elena. I'm Lauren Kurtz." She extended her hand, which Elena shook softly. Then she looked at Jack.

"Jack Shields," he said, extending his hand, which she shook a little more slowly.

"Nice to meet you. Let's head back to the conference room," she said, turning and walking them down the hall.

"Actually, could we meet in his office?" Jack said, surprising both Elena and Lauren.

"Mr. Ginsberg's?"

"Sure. Is that okay?" he asked.

"I guess it will be okay. I have water to drink for you in the conference room," she said.

"I'm not thirsty, are you?" he said, turning to Lauren who shook her head.

"Okay." Elena turned and began walking down the hall. Jack could tell she kept herself in good shape, the arch of her back made more prevalent by the high heels she walked in as comfortably as house slippers.

Jack didn't see the punch coming, perhaps because Lauren didn't even turn in his direction before throwing it into his shoulder. He was still rubbing it as they entered Mikal's old office, still full of his things. It felt like an old bedroom that a parent didn't want to change after an early unexpected death of their child.

"So how long have your worked for the bank?" Lauren asked her as she and Jack sat in the two seats across the desk while Elena sat in Mikal's old leather chair.

"Twenty years."

"Wow, did you start when you were twelve?" Lauren said, sounding sweeter than what Jack was used to.

"Eighteen, actually. I was a teller at Mikal's first bank. He used to say 'Hi' to me on his way up the elevators."

"When did you start working for Mikal as his assistant?" Jack asked.

"Well, after a couple of years I worked my way up to assistant manager at the branch in the building where he worked. He had come down one time to re-pin his debit card. He didn't use it much and would forget his pin quite often. I helped him with that. He didn't say much, but then the next day HR called me in to their office. HR only calls when you're in trouble so I thought I was in big trouble for chewing gum in front of him. I thought my banking career was over. Instead, I got a quick ride up to the top, kind of like landing on the ladder in that old board game."

Why not? Nothing moves you up the career ladder faster than a pretty face. He sat there imagining how pretty she must have been at that age, considering how good she looked now. With her short black hair, reminding him of Jackie Kennedy, he figured at twenty she must have looked like Natalie Wood. Shikov was clearly as Russian as Natalie Wood's real name, Natalia Zacharenko.

"So you worked for him for a long time. I guess his death really hit you hard," Lauren said which woke Jack from his gazing at her.

"Yes, it did," Elena said looking down and playing with a beautiful gold bracelet.

"That's a nice bracelet. Was it a gift?" Jack asked.

"Yes, Mikal gave it to me for our ten year anniversary."

"You mean your ten year anniversary working for him?"

"Yes," Elena said, looking down and moving her arm beside her almost behind her body as if hiding it from them. It was as if she were that young little Russian girl in the bad neighborhood she had grown up in again. Worried that they would try to steal it off her thin wrist. "So what did you want to ask me?"

"Well, we figured that, for as long as you worked with Mikal, you knew him better than anyone, maybe even better than his wife," Lauren said.

That comment got her a quick glance that didn't look as pleasant.

"What do you mean?" Elena asked defensively.

"I just mean I heard he was a work-a-holic and that you spent a lot of time with him."

"That's true," Elena said with a look of relief at the clarification.

"Did you go on trips with him as well?" Jack asked,

causing her to turn from Lauren back in his direction. This made her smile again.

Elena was still playing with her bracelet. "Well, not so much anymore. I used to. But I am married with kids of my own and the trips were not as convenient as when I was younger."

"We're trying to get an idea of his schedule the last few weeks, find out who he met with. Perhaps, can you help us with that?" Lauren said, drawing Elena's attention back to her

"Sure, I'm the one that made up his schedule."

"Who did he meet with that last week, did he travel anywhere?"

"Yes that was the week he went down to Florida to meet with the men from the German bank."

"Why Florida?" Jack asked.

"He didn't want anyone to know. If they flew into Washington, he figured it would draw too much attention. He asked where they wanted to meet and said he would go there and meet them. One of them wanted to go to Disney World."

"Really?" Jack said, sounding surprised.

"Why not? It's a fun place, not just for kids," she said, sounding like a Russian tourist.

"No, I guess you're right," Jack said. "I'd like to go myself sometime."

"So he went to Florida, and did anyone else go with him?" Lauren asked.

"No, just him," Elena said.

"Do you remember him meeting anyone else new that last week?"

"No, not really."

"Anything else out of the ordinary that you noticed?" Jack asked.

"Well, there is one thing," Elena said, becoming even more somber now as she considered what she was about to tell them.

"What's that?" Lauren asked

"Mikal had cancer. He was dying."

"What? We haven't heard that," Lauren said, sounding almost outraged at this new information as if she should have been told sooner.

"No one knows," Elena said.

"What do you mean no one knows?" Jack said.

"Well, his doctor knows I guess, but I don't think he's supposed to tell people that," she said.

"And how do you know?"

"Like I said, I set his schedule. He went to the doctor the week before he went to Florida. When he got the news from his doctor he told me."

"Did anyone else know?" Lauren asked.

"I don't think so. He didn't want anyone to know. He felt it would hurt his chances of fending off the merger if this news came out, so he told no one."

"What about his family, his wife?" Lauren continued.

"No, he didn't have a chance. He wanted to wait till after he killed the merger so he could share the good news with the bad."

"Yeah, that didn't work out too well, since someone killed him instead," Lauren said as she slumped back into her chair overwhelmed with this new knowledge.

"No, not at all," Elena said sadly.

"You said you had some water for us. I could use one now if you don't mind," Jack said.

"Certainly, I will bring each of you a bottle," Elena said and rose as gracefully as a Russian Ballerina.

As soon as she left the room, Jack was up out of his chair, making his way around the desk.

Lauren had turned to watch Elena head out, as if also admiring her beauty and grace that even women found entrancing.

She didn't see Jack pull the device that Richard had given him from his pocket as he sat behind the desk.

By the time she had turned back around, Jack had already plugged it in and turned the computer on. It was the beep of it turning on that caused her to turn.

"What are you doing?" Lauren asked him with a loud whisper.

"Not sure. I'm just looking," he said, his face covered by the screen.

She grimaced. "Ughh, don't say that!"

"Don't say what?" he said, still from behind the screen, waiting for the internet browser to come up.

"Just looking. It reminds me of when I worked at the Gap in High School," she said and shimmered, as if trying to shake off the bad memory.

This caused Jack to move his head to the side of the screen, revealing his face to her letting her see his big smile. "The Gap?" he said sarcastically. "How about just browsing."

"Shut up, Jack."

Jack just winked at her and slowly moved his head back behind the screen. He clicked on the browser and luckily it opened quickly. He saw the icon on the bottom pop up saying hardware detected. That was his cue to pull it out and shut it back down. As he reached down to grab it bending over he heard the door creek.

"Here you go," Elena said as she walked in, catching Jack at the computer.

"I was just checking on my stocks," he said nervously. "They're all down."

"Why should I care what you're doing back there? Soon I won't work here anymore," she said, smiling at them both then handing each of them their water of bottles.

Jack stood, putting the device in his pocket with his right hand as he grabbed the bottle with his left. They thanked Elena for her time and took their leave.

As the elevator doors closed behind them and Lauren took a sip of water, Jack said, "Time to go meet the family."

CHAPTER 37

I don't get it." Vice President Roberts said, sitting behind the desk in his office.

"What part don't you get?" Ray asked, standing on the other side of his desk.

"You want me to oppose the plan?"

"Adamantly," Ray said.

Roberts gave him a confused glare. "But it's your plan."

"I know it's my plan, but I've got bigger plans. Especially for you."

"And you think this will help me win?"

"This, my friend, is what will put you over the top," Ray said, sitting down in the chair in front of the desk.

Roberts rocked back and forth in his chair, making it squeak. "So you want your plan to fail, is that it?"

"By no means. It must pass, because it has to. I just want you to oppose it."

"Now I'm even more confused."

"Let me clear this up for you," Ray said, standing back up and taking the papers from Roberts's hands.

"I don't want you to be any part of this plan. Hastings will successfully pass it. Let me remind you, when he passed TARP the first time, how unpopular that was. You are already tarnished by that act since you were his vice president. Now Hastings is going to go against the will of the people and do it again. That, my friend, you would not survive, unless—"

"Unless I oppose it, adamantly, as you say," Roberts said, cutting him off.

"Exactly, now you got it," Ray said, folding the paper in his hands.

"Have you told Hastings?"

"No, of course not. It was my plan and I need him to be focused on passing it."

"It's not going to be easy. Selling that first one will feel like selling girl scout cookies, whereas this second round will be like trying to sell a funeral plot to someone that's already dead," Roberts said with a smile.

"And that's exactly what you'll be if you don't go against him on this and strongly."

"He's gonna be mad."

"Yeah, well he's had the job for almost eight years, and if you want it next this is what it's gonna take.

"And if I don't oppose it."

"Then your chances of becoming the next president will go down as fast as his popularity after he signs it into law," Ray said.

Roberts shrugged. "Which he will do?"

"Count on it," Ray said and then gave him a wink.

CHAPTER 38

Sara spent the morning reviewing her files. She wanted to make sure her notes made sense. If she was going to go talk to Todd she had to be clear there was a good reason. A good work reason. As she turned the corner outside his office with all those files in her arms she crashed right into Cynthia. Files went flying into the air but not for long as they all came crashing down.

They looked at each other at a standstill, each waiting for the other to apologize. That wasn't going to happen and they both knew it.

Cynthia looked down at the files, Sara's eyes following. She looked back up, just shrugged, and walked off with a huff.

Sara bent down to pick up the files but whispered loud enough for Cynthia to hear before she rounded the corner, "Bitch."

"Come on now, you used to be friends," Todd said, stepping out of his office and bending down to help Sara.

"Used to." Her glare reminded Todd of the reason for the change in their friendship. "Besides, do you see her helping me right now?"

"Yeah, well she's upset," Todd said as he pushed the files together.

"She's upset? What the hell is she upset about?"

"You," he said, sitting down himself.

"Me? Why is she upset with me? She got what she wanted."

"Had what she wanted."

"Oh," Sara said and then just sat silent. Todd looked down and began picking up files again. The awkwardness was too much. As she began picking up files she offered a comment with a smile to break the tension, "Really, Todd, already?"

"With my dad in the hospital, I can't really split my time anymore between work and checking on him right now."

"I'm sorry, Todd," she said, softening a little.

They both reached for the same file between them. Todd's hand grabbed around hers as she picked up the file. They froze, looking at each other as he held her hand.

"I made a mistake," he said, looking up into her eyes and causing her to pause for a second.

Then she yanked her hand away, along with the file. "So did I," she said with conviction, as if convincing herself that she wouldn't make the same mistake a second time. She cradled the files she had with both her arms against her chest as she stood up.

Todd followed her lead. He looked through some of the names on the files before handing them back to her. "What are you doing with these?" he said, flipping through them and looking back at her.

"I got the files from the other analysts."

"I didn't ask you where you got them. I asked why you have them. I thought I told you to work on Mikal's bank, so you can help Jack and Lauren," he said as he turned to carry the stack into his office, gesturing with his chin to let her know to follow him. "I wanted you to see if you could find anything strange," he said as he dumped the stack on the desk.

"I did!" she said excitedly as she dumped her stack

next to his and then stood next to him, waiting for his response.

"What did you find?" he asked, equally excited by her enthusiasm as well as her proximity to him. Out of the corner of his eye, he saw someone walk by his office so he took a step back and crossed his arms, playing the role of boss.

"Here, look." She bent over, searching through her stack and pulling out one of the files from the bottom. She flipped it open on top of the pile hitting him with a breeze. "Look at this trade," she said, pointing to a trade at Mikal's bank.

"What am I looking at here?"

"It's a derivative trade."

"Well, no wonder I didn't know. The guys that put those together don't even understand them."

"Yeah, but did you see the amount?" she asked, causing him to lean back down.

"Five billion? Shit, that's a lot," he said.

"Yeah, it is."

"Okay, so it's a big number, but FFB is a big bank. Isn't this common for a bank that size?" he said.

"That's not the strange part."

"So what is?"

"Look at the date," she said as he leaned back down.

"Hmm, that's just a month ago…" he said, trailing off thinking, one arm across his chest, the elbow of the other resting on it as his hand rested on his chin.

Sara was reminded of how she always thought how sexy he was when he showed he was thinking, since most men didn't seem to do that at all.

"A week before he was killed," he finished.

"Yes, it was, but it was also the week the OCC was digging through his bank's records."

"Okay?" Todd gestured for her to continue, rocking back on his heels as he backed away, now finally just focused on the job as he headed behind his desk.

"That's exactly the kind of trades they were looking for. So why would he do that trade the same time they were there? It doesn't make sense," she said, her eyes following his as he sat down behind his desk while she remained standing. She was too excited to sit and was just getting started.

"What do you mean, they were looking for? Besides the amount, what was wrong with it?"

"It wasn't normal. It was an anomaly, the size and type. This is the kind of trade that caused all the banks to collapse. I studied the files from the bank, went back three years, and one word describes all the trades I saw him authorize personally. Conservative. Then this," she said, beaming at him and allowing him a chance to respond as she caught her breath.

"Well, how did this trade play out?"

"It just about killed them and, even if it hadn't, just doing it would have given the OCC license to go in and put the clamps down on them. Why take the risk? Why then?"

"Well, I hate to burst your bubble, but isn't it obvious? Mikal was desperate. He was already ordered to raise his capital ratios under the new guidelines from Basel. He probably figured this was his last chance to raise it to where he could avoid the forced merger. He played a long shot and lost. That's what desperate gamblers do," Todd said as he rocked back in his chair convinced of his theory.

"I just find it hard to believe. Everything I've learned about Mikal is that he wouldn't do a trade like this."

"Maybe, he didn't. Maybe it was someone else at the bank who did the trade and he just approved it. Maybe, he didn't understand what he was signing."

"No, that was the first thing I checked, he initiated and approved it."

"Himself? He could do that?"

"When you're the CEO, you can," she said as she finally sat down. "I just can't believe that he did, especially knowing about the OCC looking over his shoulder."

"All I can think is he panicked," Todd said.

"I hate to say it, but it's hard not to agree," she said, leaning on the desk with both her arms. Then she looked at him and said, "Sounds familiar," the look clearly an accusatory one.

"I'm sorry. Maybe I did panic," Todd said as he grabbed one of her arms gently.

"Let's just focus on this, okay?" She jerked her arm from his grasp. Then she looked back at the stack, yanked another file out, and opened it in front of him. "Look at this," she said, pointing.

"Three billion?" he said, surprised. "Which bank is this?"

"First Federal of New York. The first bank to fail," she said.

"Oh yeah, FFNY, First Fucked, Now You," he said with a smile.

Sara didn't have time to laugh. She was digging through the pile, looking for the next file. When she found what she was looking for, she pulled it out and flipped it open so quickly the breeze it caused moved Todd's hair.

"Here, look at this one," she gasped, almost losing her breath from excitement.

"Four billion," he said and then gave her with a curious look.

"Fidelity Main Trust," she said.

"FMT, Fuck Me Too," he said.

"Yep."

"I'm sensing a trend"

"So you see it, too?" she said, getting even more excited.

"I'm not sure what I'm seeing. Look, everyone was trading those fucking derivatives. That's what caused the collapse in the first place. Everyone already knows that, so what's new here?" he said as he sat down.

"They all did these trades when they were already in trouble and knew these were risky trades."

"Goes to my first theory. They panicked, just like Mikal. And just like when someone is drowning, when they panic they just drown faster."

"Yeah, but so many of them making the same exact mistake. You'd think they would learn."

Todd shrugged. "That's another thing about someone who's drowning, sometimes they take others down with them."

Sara slumped in defeat. "I guess. I can understand some of these other banks taking the risk, but Mikal Ginsberg doing it just doesn't make sense."

"Well, if you think you've got something, keep looking. If anyone can find something, my money's always on you."

"Well, not always," she said sarcastically.

She stood up and he did the same.

"Look if you find anything else, maybe next time we talk about it, we can do it over dinner," he said, walking around this desk up to her.

Sara picked up the files from his desk and looked at him for a second, considering what she was about to say holding the stack like a barrier between them.

"Fuck you, Todd," she said, turned, and walked out of his office.

In a world where everyone only daydreams of saying that to their boss, she just had, and she knew there was nothing Todd was going to do about it. As she rounded the corner outside her office, she saw Cynthia look up at her from her cubicle. Finally, the first time since the breakup, a smile crossed Sara's face. Cynthia just looked away with another huff, misreading the reason for it.

CHAPTER 39

The tension inside the car was thicker than the traffic on the way to the Ginsberg estate. The short twenty minutes it took to drive there felt more like an hour for Jack and Lauren as they managed to not talk about the elephant in the back seat. Lauren had dressed conservatively for the meeting with the family, wearing a gray shirt and black skirt. Jack still couldn't help but notice her curves as she got into the car. As he put the car in park he decided to throw it out there one more time just to make sure they were okay.

"So the other night…" he said, trailing off as he took his seat belt off and looked over at her.

"You mean when I saved your life?" Lauren said, not looking at him yet.

"No the other thing."

"There was no other thing. I told you it was nothing."

"Nothing?"

"Look, our adrenaline levels were through the roof that night after that little stop over at your friend's place."

"So, it was just because of the adrenaline."

"It means we weren't thinking clearly and we were just releasing that energy. Look, I was so worked up that night I would have had sex with anyone at that moment."

"Anyone?"

"Well, you know what I mean. Come on let's go," she said, opening the door and getting out.

Jack did the same.

As they walked up to the house they had to make their way around a UPS truck parked in front of the entry way. As they were rounding the front of the truck, the delivery driver walked around the pair of them. Lauren didn't look back but Jack did, noticing the guy taking his time around the truck with his head turned back. He didn't even notice, or perhaps care, that Jack caught him checking out Lauren. Jack couldn't blame him.

"Are you still going to give your friend the rest of the money he needs?" Lauren asked, turning Jack's attention back toward the house.

"Yes, actually, I was planning on swinging by after I drop you off later."

"You sure that's a good idea."

"Why? You think I shouldn't help him out?"

"No, I mean going over there by yourself," she said, smiling at him as they made their way up the steps to the massive double doors.

As Jack looked up at the huge entryway he was reminded of the pathetic excuses for the same he grew up around as he bounced from home to home. This one had two large oak wood doors, whereas one of the places he stayed at didn't even have one after the home had been broken into. Of course, that one didn't have AC either so no one seemed to mind the extra opening.

He stared in awe as Lauren rang the doorbell. He could hear the chime from the inside as it played a classic melody from some old German symphony. The door was opened by a butler. That was the real reminder of how far removed he now was from his old world. People actually employed people to open the doors for them.

"Hello, welcome to the Ginsberg estate. You must be Jack Shields and Lauren Kurtz."

"We are," Lauren said.

"Please come in, I'll announce your arrival." He led them into the home and walked them to a living room area just off to the left of the entry way. "Please wait here while I let Ms. Ginsberg know that you have arrived."

"Thank you," they both said.

As they turned from the butler they found Sykes and Lopez sitting in the same room.

"I guess Ian is here, as well?" Lauren said, looking at the two of them.

"He is. What are you guys doing here?" Lopez asked.

"We're meeting with Mikal's wife," Jack said.

"She a suspect now?" Sykes asked, looking up from a newspaper he was reading from the other side of the large formally furnished room. He looked as if he was making himself quite at home.

"No, we just want to get her thoughts on what happened, see if she has any theories of her own," Lauren said.

"Well, don't count her out," Lopez said. "Wait till you meet her."

"Well, she is a *Jewish mother*. I know how they can be," Lauren said with a slight giggle. "They tend to major in being a bitch."

"Well this one has her masters," Lopez agreed.

"We'll keep that in mind," Jack said.

Just then the butler rounded the corner to come get the two of them. He walked them down the hall, their steps echoing under the high ceilings as if they were in a synagogue. As they rounded the corner, they found Mrs. Ginsberg sitting at one end of a couch, sipping a cup of tea. Next to her, a man in a suit wearing a yamaka bent over the coffee table with some paperwork spread out. Across the room in a love seat, sat Ian and his wife Lorena. Jack recognized her from the articles he had studied the night before. In her late forties, close to Ian's age, she looked ten years younger and was quite striking. The butler announced them to the Ginsbergs and excused himself from the room, after offering to get some tea which Jack and Lauren each accepted. They then made the rounds, shaking everyone's hand.

"Please have a seat," Mrs. Ginsberg said to them in a slightly raspy smoker's voice.

They both sat on the couch on the other side of the coffee table. Jack noticed Ian admiring Lauren as she sat down, crossing her legs, across from him. Jack found it awkward that he would do it so obviously while sitting, not only across from his mother, but next to his wife.

"Well, I hope we aren't interrupting anything by stopping by today," Jack offered, glancing over at the man in the yamaka.

"Oh, this is our family attorney Frank Hirsch. Nothing too important. Just going over Mikal's will," she said with a smile. "How is the investigation going, by the way?"

"We're still at the beginning stages, trying to find people with motive behind what happened," Lauren said.

"And you came to look here?" said a sarcastic, sultry and oddly familiar voice entering the room from behind Jack and Lauren, who both turned.

What they saw was a beautiful woman in her twenties, wearing jeans and a form-fitting long-sleeved shirt. The form it fit on was perfect. Jack recognized her right away from his research the days before. Mikal's daughter. And she looked even better in person than the pictures he had seen on the net.

There were a lot of them, since she was a former-model-turned-actress. She looked great in every picture he saw but now, seeing her in person made them seem average by comparison. She had just flown in for the funeral from LA.

"Sharla, please sit down. This is Agent Jack Shields and his partner Lauren Kurtz."

"Oh, another Jew. I feel like I'm still in Hollywood," Sharla said with a playful grin toward Lauren.

Jack glanced over at Ian and caught him rolling his eyes in a way that said he wasn't surprised. The way Lauren looked at her as they shook hands Jack could tell that even she was attracted to this perfect woman.

"Sharla, please!" her mother snapped.

"Oh, relax, Mother. I'm sure our guests can tell I'm joking," Sharla said then looked over at Jack who had stood to take his turn touching hands with this beauty.

"Were you?" Ian's wife piped in, which got a different kind of eye roll from Ian in her direction.

She also got a quick turn of the head from Sharla, staring her down, which she heeded and looked away. Sharla whipped her head back around, her long auburn hair flying behind, trying to keep up, as she turned back to Jack. She slowly wrapped her hand around his and squeezed while looking into his eyes.

She then turned and went to sit down next to her mother.

How can someone be so thin, yet have those kind of curves? Sitting next to her mother, Jack tried to find the similar characteristics that she had contributed to this attractive model. He could see the large blue eyes had come from the mother, but from pictures of Mikal it was clear that her tan skin and proportionate face came from him. She really got the best of both.

"What about you, Jack, Jewish, too?" she said with a seductive look as she picked up a glass of tea from the table in front of her and took a sip.

She kept those large eyes on him as she swallowed.

"I wish," he said, looking at Lauren with a grin.

"No, full Gentile here," Lauren said with a knowing smile.

Sharla looked at Lauren and then at Jack and nodded as if she knew they were more than just partners. This just peaked her interest in him that much more. "So don't let me interrupt. Go ahead and ask your questions," she said, taking another sip.

She then leaned over to put her drink on the table, still looking at Jack. Lauren noticed and had the same reaction, her own interest in Jack going up. She could see Sharla's interest in Jack in her eyes and her body language.

Aware that Sharla was making her self-conscious, Lauren pushed a lock of hair behind her ear. "Thanks, Sharla, I do have to say I liked you in *Murder in Third Person*."

"Well, thank you. I still think I was one person too many for that movie. It was okay," she said, moving her own hair and mirroring Lauren.

Lauren laughed. "I saw it just after my fiancé and I broke it off. Made me think back to some of the creative ways you killed some people in that movie."

"Oh, so you didn't get married?" Ian asked, clearly interested in the answer.

"No. It's for the best though," Lauren said as she broke from her trance and looked over at Ian.

"A beautiful girl like you, you'll find your *bashert* one day soon I'm sure," Mrs. Ginsberg said.

"I agree. I'm sure she will," Jack said, giving her a funny look.

"Thanks," Lauren said, turning to Mrs. Ginsberg.

"Well, we don't want to take up your whole day. You obviously have some important matters to attend to," Jack offered. "We just would like to get an idea, since you knew Mikal best, of who some of his enemies would be."

"He was a banker. The line starts to the left," Mrs. Ginsberg said.

"Well, anyone specific that was angry enough to kill him?" Lauren asked, looking from Mrs. Ginsberg over at Ian, prompting him to offer his opinion.

"Sure, he fired people. Well, too many to name," Ian said. "He also ruined some people along the way. He had some hostile takeovers himself back in the day. I mean they were always banks that were failing anyway, but people forget the reasons for their failings. They just want to blame someone. That's all public knowledge. You can look it up. Do I know if any particular one had the motive to actually do this? No, I don't. I do hope you can find him," Ian finished then grabbed his own glass of tea and took a drink.

"We understand. How is the merger going?" Lauren asked.

"Oh, that's as dead as my father."

"It is?" Jack asked a little surprised by the callous pun.

"Yes, my father's death put it on hold. The one good thing that came of this is that it gave us time to raise the capital we needed to get the FDIC to back off."

"The sale to the German bank?" Jack asked, thinking of what he had learned from his studying before the meeting.

"Exactly. Just like Greece, the fucking Germans are bailing us out, too," Ian said, clearly angry. He set his glass down hard on the table after standing from the love seat.

"You don't seem happy," Jack said, pressing him.

"Of course, I'm not happy. My father made that deal before he died. They are taking advantage for the price they paid for those assets."

"But it saved you father's bank, Ian," Mrs. Ginsberg said.

"I know, but I just hate that they got such a sweet deal," Ian said then began to head out of the room, after looking at his watch as if late for something. "I need to call someone, excuse me."

"He's under a lot of pressure, since he's taken over as CEO," Mrs. Ginsberg said with an apologetic look for her son's rude behavior.

"We understand," Lauren said. As she stood up, Jack did the same. "Here is my card if you want to call and talk anytime," Lauren said, handing it to Mrs. Ginsberg.

Jack followed suit, handing her one of his.

"Can I get one of those?" Sharla said, looking up at Jack. "In case I want to *talk*."

"Sure," Jack replied, walking over to her with a card in his hand.

She took his hand in hers then slowly slid her fingers across his palm until, clasping the card, she pulled it slowly from his grasp.

Just before they got in the car, Lauren stopped and looked over the car at Jack. "I think she likes you?"

"Who? Mrs. Ginsberg?" Jack said with a big smile as he put his sunglasses on.

"Yeah, right, Mrs. Ginsberg. Shut up and get in the car."

CHAPTER 40

Most people hated meetings. The one called at the Carlyle Hotel for all the bank CEOs in town was mandatory and equally disliked. In attendance were all the CEOs of the banks that had taken the first round of TARP. The only exceptions were Harris Lofton who was still in the hospital in a coma, and the deceased Mikal Ginsberg, replaced by his son Ian. As they all entered the conference room and sat down, they looked at each other, waiting impatiently for Ray Childs to address them.

The security detail of the Secret Service was asked to wait outside and, after the doors were closed, he began. "Thanks for coming, everyone," Ray said, looking around the room, still standing while they all sat around the large mahogany table.

In total, twenty-four CEOs. The men, as well as the two female CEOs, were still staring at each other. It wasn't until the CEO from Alabama First Bank spoke up that they all centered their attention to the front of the room.

"Not like we had a choice!" he said in a not so gentlemanly Southern voice.

"I thought it was a nice invitation," Ray said, not missing a beat.

"Felt more like a subpoena," the man said, almost as if

a joke but clearly not laughing.

"I'm sorry you felt that way Bob," Ray said using his first name, knowing how much he would probably be offended by this casualness around them. He didn't really care. "Nonetheless, I'm glad you made it. I'm glad all of you made it to this important meeting today. I wish that I had an update on the bomber. I do not. But I can assure you that the FBI is working around the clock on this case. I'm being briefed on the status daily."

"Speaking of clocks, can we get this going?" said one of the three CEOs from New York. "I've got more important things to do with my time, like running a bank."

"Well then, it's good that you are here because if you want to continue to have a bank to run, this meeting is important, even to you, Joseph," Ray said, taking a seat at the head of the table, while they all shuffled in their seats from his comment.

"First of all, I want to thank all of you for going along with TARP. It did a lot to settle the markets. You don't need me to remind you how dire the situation was at the time. For some more dire than others." He looked over at some of the smaller regional bank, CEOs who had sat close to one another like nerds at the high school prom all gathered together, sitting far from the Jocks, or in this case, the big National bank CEOs. "Let's just say that there'd be less of you in this room today. I realize some of you didn't need the funds but you took them anyway at our request and I want to say thanks to you again. It was the only way to keep from putting a spot light on your less fortunate peers who didn't have the asset strength on their own. It would have caused further damage by making it so obvious. The only way it was going to work was to spread it out evenly to all of you. So thanks to all of you. And so far it has worked," he said then went silent.

"You're welcome, now can we go?" said Joseph Randall from New York.

"Not yet, you see it wasn't enough," Ray said and went

silent again, steepling his hands in front of him as he let what he said sink to the bottom of their consciousness like the Titanic. It hit bottom with the Alabama CEO first, probably, Ray figured, because there was more space in his head for it to sink.

"What do ya mean not enough?" Alabama, said almost spitting out his chewing tobacco. He looked at Ray like a batter staring down a pitcher who tried to brush him back from home plate with an inside pitch.

"As you know, we are in a global economy now. Those of you who have business in Europe probably are more aware of what I'm going to say next," Ray said, eyeing a few of the National CEOs who were nodding their heads. "Europe is the domino that is about to fall next. They are just entering their recession and, unfortunately, it's going to come back to hit us hard. I guess it's only fair that they hit us back since we hit first. The problem is we are still fragile," Ray said, taking a breath which, in this room of large egos, would easily allow for another one to speak out at the slight pause.

"Are you going to make a point, or not?" Alabama demanded, sitting back and crossing his arms. "We don't have any business in Europe, so why am I here?"

"You're here for the same reason we all are here," Ray said, glaring at him. It was a look that always threw people off, such a pleasant face that one never expected confrontation from, so when it came, it always staggered his debate opponents. Then he relaxed again just as quickly and said rather casually, "You are here to save the global economy." Then he leaned back and smiled.

"And how are we going to do that?" the CEO from Minnesota asked.

"By fortifying our banks before the tsunami that's coming across the Atlantic hits."

"I second the gentleman from Minnesota's question, how exactly are we going to do that?" one of the CEOs from Texas asked.

"We need to raise the capital ratios," Ray said.

"They already did that in Basel," Richard said, referring to the Basel Accord—committee that meets in Basel, Switzerland, consisting of a group of international central bankers who meet to set the regulatory standards for banks within the G-20 nations.

"Well we need to raise them again," Ray said.

"How much?" three of the CEOs asked in unison.

"This won't be easy to hear, and even harder to actually accomplish, but the only number that works is three times the current level," Ray said, throwing it out there, almost as a dare.

"Are you fucking crazy?" one of the New Jersey CEOs yelled, followed by a few others who at least had the courtesy of cursing under their breath.

Ray was barely able to conceal his smile at this reaction. A room full of Ivy League educated bankers and they had quickly resorted to cursing, no different than the kids he'd grown up with. It had him feeling nostalgic for his old neighborhood.

"There's no way we could meet those ratios, we barely can meet the ones Basel set last time," said the CEO from Minnesota, standing up and pacing back and forth, looking at the others for support, successfully getting nods from most in the room.

"I said it would be hard."

"Riding a bull for eight seconds is hard, this is impossible," said the banker from Texas.

Ian Ginsberg finally commented, after spending most of the meeting looking around the room. He despised all these men and women, filled with anger at the thought that one of them was probably behind his father's death.

He did agree with their mutual reaction to the news, however, and joined in on the mutiny. "He's right. We just sold all our assets in Europe to get our ratio above the current requirement. We don't have enough assets left to sell."

"I admit for most of you in here it will be very difficult.

For some, too difficult. That's why we are meeting today,"
Ray said. "Please sit back down and hear me out." He
waved his hand at the four who had stood. "Look, I'm not
running for office, so I'm not going to bullshit you. Let me
cut to the chase."

"Please do," the CEO from Minnesota asked.

If calming the room down was his goal, then what he
was about to say would be a failure of epic proportions.
Luckily for him, that wasn't his goal.

Ray smiled. "Let me put it this way. Twenty-four bank
CEOs walked into this room. Only eight of you will leave
here as such."

"What the hell are you talking about?" Alabama said.

"Are you going to shut us down?" Minnesota demanded.

"Everyone just stay calm and sit back down," Ray said
in a surprisingly stern tone they had never heard before. He
felt like he was back in the convenience store with Brad but
this time he was telling the clerk what to do. It worked for
now, but he would have to get to his point quickly. They
were all on the verge of revolt. He continued quick before
one of them pulled a shotgun from under the register.
"Look, we've gone over the scenarios and this next wave of
bad economic news from Europe is going to wash over us
worse than the tsunami that hit Asia. We've already done all
the work and picked the eight remaining banks that we're
going to merge all of the rest of you under. In the packet in
front of you is an outline of the plan so you can see which
banks are acquiring which others."

"You can't do this!" the Alabama banker yelled out as
he saw his bank's name underneath one of the New York
banks and felt as if he'd lost the civil war all over again.

"Is the president behind this?" asked one of the New
York bankers who wasn't so upset since he had a surviving
bank that was about to absorb two other large banks. It
would be a merger never approved by the same government
asking for this to happen now, under normal circumstances.

It was as unbelievable to him as a snake swallowing a cow.

"He is aware of the plan and it has his approval."

"Of course it does," said Alabama.

"If it makes you feel any better, Vice President Cullen Roberts is opposed to this plan. However, if you want to risk waiting to see if he'll win election this November, I can't guarantee your bank will survive long enough to find out. We have directed the FDIC, with the help of the OCC, to move quickly with Cease and Desist Letters at the first sign of trouble. Then not only will you be without a bank, anyway, but you will also miss out on this one time offer we have for you today for following through on this plan," Ray pulled out envelopes from a briefcase on the table in front of him. Each letter had a CEO's name on it. He walked around the table, placing an envelope in front of each of them.

"What's this?" Alabama asked.

"An envelope. Now, what you'll find inside is a payment made out to each of you individually. Please go ahead and open it, and before you get curious and start peeking at the other's I assure you the offer is the same for each of you," Ray watched each of them tear the letters open with the same curiosity as a child on Christmas morning. For some a Hanukkah present, in this case, all eight days wrapped into one.

As they each stared in silence at the check inside, Ray continued explaining. "These funds will be placed in a secret Swiss bank account under your name. Oh, and before you start doing the math, this is tax free," he said as he looked around the now silent room.

Some began to lift their heads and look at each other, a few with their jaws agape.

Ray chuckled to himself. *Funny how a number can change the mood of a room, especially when that number starts with a B.*

"I don't get it," said one the CEOs from another Southern state with a drawl and a dumbfounded look on his face.

Figures. "Really, sir, you're the head of a bank and you can't understand what you have in your hand?" Ray said, surprised.

"What I mean is, if you can just hand out this kind of money so easily why not just give us the money we need to get to those ratios, just like the last time," the man said, grasping the check tightly as if not trusting the other men not to take it from him.

"Oh, now you really have me worried. Good thing yours is one of the banks being acquired today, Arthur," Ray said to the Georgia bank CEO. Now most of the others also lowered their hands holding their checks and looked at Ray. "It's not about the money it's about perception," he said. "If we were to do as you say and just give you the money, it would shatter the value of our currency. The world is watching now and a move like that would jeopardize the dollar as the world currency, and if that were to happen, that check you hold in your hand would maybe buy you a big screen TV, but not HD. We are already dangerously close to that happening. One false move and it's over for all of us, or I should say for the US."

"If things are so dire, how will this help?" asked the banker from Chicago.

"Like I said, perception. Let me use an analogy. We all like baseball, right? Doesn't get any more American than that. I think it's also a good analogy because just like banking, baseball is a numbers game. And why is that? It's because most true baseball fans love numbers, so the sport is filled with numbers. ERAs, batting averages, on base percentage, etcetera. Why do they promote this activity? The main reason is to keep you interested, more interested than in any other sport. Look, not every team can be like the Yankees and pay the biggest salaries to get the best players and so compete for a World Series championship every year. Heck most teams never even make the playoffs, so why do people go every year? Because they get caught up in the numbers. Fans get so focused on all the various numbers they don't think about one of the key ones."

"Wins and Losses," Alabama shouted out.

"Exactly. And you know the best number baseball ever came up with?

"What?" the banker from Texas asked.

"One hundred sixty two. The number of games played. And why? Because at the start of each season everyone has hope, even though, if they were realistic, most fans know their team doesn't stand a chance. Most people are optimistic at heart, though, and with one hundred and sixty two games, it takes half a season before you know for sure your team is out of it. By then, they've made their money."

He paused and looked around the room. "That's what we're trying to do here. We're just trying to distract everyone with the ratio's, long enough to get us through to the next season. In other words, this economic downturn," Ray said, ending quietly, with quite the dramatic pause.

Most were now nodding their heads. Although it didn't really matter how good the analogy, the home run he hit was with the billion dollars he had handed each of them in the ninth inning of this meeting. He reminded them before they left the building to act upset at what would transpire in the next few weeks and, more obviously, to keep their mouths shut. Otherwise, he would place a stop pay on their check. That was language they each understood.

As they stood up to head out of the room, Ray felt the need to offer up one more baseball analogy. "You know, guys? Baseball is also a game of failure. Where else can someone with a three hundred batting average, which equals failure seventy percent of the time, be celebrated as a great player? Well, banking has now become a game of failure as well, and I commend you for making the right move to keep the right three hundred average of banks afloat so that the game can go on."

They all just shrugged and continued out of the room. While most of them headed out to the lobby to meet up with their security detail, a few had too much of the coffee or water provided and needed to make a quick pit stop.

"Can you believe this, one billion dollars?" said the banker from Minnesota.

"Hey, he didn't want us talking about it remember," the CEO of the Alabama bank said, laughing as they both entered the bathroom.

"Hey, no danger there," the Minnesota banker said. They both walked up the urinals and started to pee. "You know who I'm not telling? My wife," he said, laughing so hard at his own joke that he got some piss on his shoes.

As he looked down he thought of how many new pairs of shoes he was going to be able to buy soon so he didn't even get upset.

"Great idea," Alabama said.

While the CEO from Alabama was still peeing the other man went to wash his hands. "See you on the ski slopes in Switzerland, buddy," he said as he was exiting the door.

The banker from Alabama turned slightly to say goodbye before flushing and didn't notice the small wire protruding from the handle. Before the man from Minnesota could make it out of the doorway, the blast lifted him off his feet and flung his body as if a throw pillow. He landed on his back across a couch in the lobby. He would soon be grateful for his wife who would take care of him, at least until he got used to using a wheel chair. The Alabama CEO's wife just became a very wealthy widow.

ↄ〜ↄ

Claus Steinherz was ushered to his room in the hotel, the same as all the other CEOs, to keep him safe while the various agencies huddled around the scene of the latest bombing. The rooms had been swept and deemed clear, so they just posted a man outside each room. What they forgot to consider was that the door to the room wasn't the only way in.

Claus being the oldest at the meeting, the killer had assumed he would be the first to go to the bathroom after the meeting. Claus, however, had to do more than stand to go to the bathroom and he wasn't one to do that in a public restroom. He had headed back to his room and was safe from the blast.

The killer was persistent and made sure to finish the job. There was a smirk on the killer's face behind the shower curtain as Steinherz grumbled at the realization there was no toilet paper on the roll next to him.

As the killer reached out and slit his throat with the blade, there was an appreciation of the irony of a man so wealthy longing for a ninety-nine cent roll of toilet paper. Claus had been a fan of all those Elvis movies they showed over and over in Germany when he was younger. He often wondered what it would be like to be him. Now, at least, he had the location of his death in common.

CHAPTER 41

"Who all knew about this meeting?" Todd asked Ray as they walked into his office at the FBI building.

Sara was standing behind the desk with a stack of files in her arms. Lauren and Jack were both sitting on the couch across the room.

"Well, obviously everyone that was there, the CEOs of the top twenty five banks," Ray answered as he took in everyone in the room and stopped in the middle as Todd walked around his desk.

"The TARP recipients. Go ahead and have a seat." Todd gestured at Ray to take the chair across from his desk. "You too, Sara," he said, gesturing at the other chair with one hand while placing another on the small of her back.

Seeing that, Jack felt the green devil of jealousy stirring inside.

Sara gracefully walked around the desk and sat next to Ray, laying the files in her lap. Jack watched as she crossed her toned legs and leaned back in the chair but still sat straight. He admired her posture.

"So what was this meeting about?" Todd asked.

"I was letting them know that they were still in trouble," Ray said.

"And what does that mean, exactly?" Todd said, leaning forward and speaking in a deep authoritative voice, after catching Jack and Lauren's eyes on him, trying to impress them both.

"We are raising the capital requirements again, and—"

"I bet they weren't too happy about that," Jack interrupted, thinking about his reading the night before about the Basel Accord where they came up with the original set of capital ratios and how most banks were already complaining about those levels. They brought about the first flurry of mergers and the markets seemed to have settled down after TARP.

"No you're right, Jack. Most of them weren't," Ray agreed.

"So what did you discuss after telling them this?" Todd asked.

"Well, it was obvious that some, actually most, of the banks in that room were not going to be able to meet the new requirement."

"So what was the point? Are you trying to force the banks to fail?" Lauren asked.

"No, of course not. That was the point of the meeting— to come up with a way to avoid that," Ray said, looking intently at Lauren, making Jack's jealousy stir again.

"And did you come up with something?" Todd asked.

"A lot of smart guys in that room, so you know what? We did," Ray said.

"Well, what did they come up with?"

"They decided to merge."

"Who?" Todd asked.

"All of them. They came in as twenty-five banks and they left as eight."

"Eight? What happened to ending too big to fail?" Sara blurted out, almost knocking her files to the floor but catching them just before they slipped from her lap.

Jack was already on the edge of his seat ready to help catch them, had they fallen. Lauren saw his eagerness and rolled her eyes just as he scooted back in his seat catching her look. Sara reddened in the face from blurting out her comment.

Todd saw it and bailed her out. "Yeah, what about too big to fail?"

"Well, plans change," Ray said.

"Yeah, but what about the president?" Jack asked. "He's the one who said when he was re-elected that he wasn't going to let the banks get too big. Does he know about this plan?"

"Of course, he does and, before you ask, yes, he supports it, and it's because he has no choice."

"I don't understand," Lauren said. "Why is this happening exactly, the ratios going up?"

"It's all about debt. Put simply the damn is about to burst. When this whole mess started with the subprime market, the damn sprang a leak. When we passed TARP, we put our finger in it to slow it down. Then China passed their stimulus plan and they put their finger in the damn. The problem is with Europe. The water is about to come crashing over the top of the damn. So we need to build a new damn and raising the ratios is the first step. Consider that the life preserver to keep people from drowning while we build the new damn."

"And how are your building this new damn?" Todd asked, all in the room waiting intently for the answer.

"We're passing a second round of TARP."

"You're countering the world's debt with more of our own?" Sara asked, totally confused.

Ray chuckled. "Fight fire with fire I always say."

"Yeah, but in your analogy, a damn bursting with water would usually put out a fire, so I don't see how this will work."

"The same as it always has. Our nation is built on debt and the world is used to it. It's just another number to them, so that number goes up a little bit more."

"A little bit more? How much more?" Sara asked.

"Two trillion."

"What? There is no way you'll get that passed. Where are they gonna come up with that?"

"Where else? The Fed, like always," he said with a smile.

They all shook their heads at the same time in utter disbelief at what they had just been told.

Todd refocused them on the original reason they were there. "Look, did you notice anyone leaving the room early that would have had access to the bathroom, perhaps one of the bank CEOs who was being asked to allow his bank to be swallowed up by the others?"

"No one left early. They all exited at the same time," Ray said. "Besides, someone would have had to plan this ahead of time, anyway, and they wouldn't have known the agenda of the meeting before that day. This had to have other motivations behind it. Am I right?" Ray asked, looking at Todd then at Lauren, with that silly flirty grin again that made Jack's back stiffen.

"What about Claus? Were there any arguments with him in the room, any one of the other CEOs seem angry with him, as if they didn't like him?"

"I'm sorry to say that these men are competitors with tremendous egos. None of them like each other. For that reason, it would be hard to notice anyone's particular anger, more so than normal," Ray explained.

"I agree, clearly someone has their own agenda here," Todd said. "That's actually why I asked Sara to talk about something she's stumbled upon."

Ray frowned. "Really, what is that?"

"Well, it's just something that seems strange." Sara shuffled through her files, pulling one out. "You are aware that the OCC had been going over the books at Ginsberg's bank prior to his death?"

"Quite aware, especially since there was a pending merger," Ray said, listening intently.

"Well I found a trade transaction during that time they

were there, and I just find it odd—the timing and type of trade."

"What are you suggesting?" Ray asked, stiffening his jaw as he asked, his pulse quickening a bit.

"I'm not really sure, exactly. It's just strange. What's really weird is that I saw the same kind of trade in other banks that failed prior to Ginsberg's becoming a takeover target."

"Interesting. Any theories?" he said, trying his best to sound mildly amused.

"Not yet. I just thought it was strange and since you review the OCC findings in your committee that you could perhaps check on this, too."

"I'll be sure to talk to my guy at the OCC about your findings, Sara. You can count on that," Ray said, then looked at his watch. "I actually have to get to that committee you were just referring to if you don't mind."

As they all stood, Sara looked at Jack and asked if they were still on for jogging Saturday.

"You two jog together?" Ray asked.

"Every Saturday morning at Rock Creek Park," Sara said to him. She noticed a grimace on Lauren's face at the comment.

As Ray stood up and was saying his goodbyes, Jack's phone rang. He excused himself and stepped out into the hall to take the call. It was Richard.

"Hey, Jack, I got into Ginsberg's computer."

"Okay, great. What did you find? Did you see Mikal's calendar for the week before? Give me some names of who he met with."

"Well, Jack, I did get in Ginsberg's computer, but the thing is it's not Mikal's computer. It's Ian's computer."

"Shit, he must have switched it over already."

"Yeah, well you wanted me to look at the calendar and see if Mikal met anyone in Florida. Did you know that Ian went with him?"

"No, he didn't say anything about it. You see anything else on there?"

"Actually no, just that he was in Florida at the same time as Mikal."

"Okay, well that's something. Thanks for checking."

"Anytime, now back to the real hacking. Maybe if I get done before my deadline I can go on a little fishing trip to Florida myself. Hell, maybe I'll just take my laptop and work from the boat."

As Jack was hanging up he got a head nod from Ray who walked past him toward the elevator. Jack just nodded back.

It struck him as something people from his old part of town would do, not a ranking congressman. When Jack went back into the room, they were starting to kick theories around to motives behind the bombings.

"I still think we need to go back to the beginning and look at where this started with Ginsberg," Lauren said.

"I would agree, but my father and Ginsberg were anything but close. My dad ousted Mikal from his bank years before, so he wouldn't have had any ties to Ginsberg and he was the second target," Todd said.

That's when Jack had a thought since he was still thinking about Florida. "Lauren's right we need to go back to the beginning. Not Ginsberg's death, but the email sent the week before. The IT guys traced it back to Florida, right?"

"Yes, but it was some single mom's laptop that she got for her daughter," Todd said. "They checked out. No ties to Ginsberg, or any bank, for that matter. The email got read-dressed somehow to just look like it came from that computer."

"Did anyone ever ask when she got that computer?" Jack said. They all just looked at him and stood as still as Medusa's victims. "You mind if I call that single mom?" A few minutes later Jack hung up the phone and smiled before looking up. "Best Buy."

"What?" Todd asked, Lauren and Sara's faces asking the same question.

"That's where she bought the computer just that weekend for her daughter's birthday, got a display model on discount," Jack said.

"Okay, so now we know it was at Best Buy when the email was sent."

"And what I know is that Ian was in Florida when that email was sent."

"How do you know that?" Lauren asked him.

"And how do we put Ian at Best Buy sending that message anyway? They would have purged their security tapes by now. It's been a few weeks."

"Let's just say I have a feeling Ian bought a certain someone a phone from there and that person might just still have a gift receipt," Jack said. "Lauren, you want to go with me to the bank?"

She took his lead and nodded.

"Sara, I'll see you Saturday morning," he said, giving her a quick hug just to rile up Todd, oblivious to the fact that it did the same to Lauren.

CHAPTER 42

Jack parked the car on the street in front of the bank and put a couple of quarters in the meter while Lauren got out. He had explained to Lauren on the way over the conversation he had with the cute teller the week before and her new gifts. Lauren shared his excitement in feeling like some of the puzzle pieces were starting to fit together. She went inside first as he held the door.

"What are you doing?" she asked as he stopped at a table by the door.

"Filling out a withdrawal form," he said, grabbing a pen from the table along with a withdrawal slip. He filled it out for three thousand, even though he still had the money he'd withdrawn before.

"Didn't you already get money for your friend?" Lauren asked.

"Yep. But I have a feeling he may need more. Come on," he said, walking past her as he looked over the girls at the windows, searching for one in particular.

"May I help you, sir," said the blonde on the end of the row of windows.

Lauren noticed how anxious the girl was to get Jack to her window.

Jack just noticed the politeness, which threw him still,

compared with the "Next" to which he was more accustomed.

He gave Lauren a look of "Wait here," while he stepped forward.

"Sure," he said to the teller and handed her the slip.

"Do you have your ID, sir?" she asked with a big smile.

"Yes, here," he said, grabbing his wallet from his back pocket and flipping it open.

"How would you like that, Agent Shields? she said, a little more nervous than flirtatious after seeing his badge.

"Hundreds would be fine," he said.

She opened her drawer and pulled out the bills to count out in front of him. While she counted he asked, "Is Nella not working today?"

"She is."

"Oh, I didn't see her," Jack said. He leaned back a little and looked at the other teller windows on each side of the blonde.

"She doesn't work down here, anymore," she said with a certain disdain in her voice while she continued to count out the hundred dollar bills.

"Where does she work now?"

"She works for Mr. Ginsberg," she said, cramming the hundreds in an envelope as if she were taking out her anger on the money itself.

"Mikal?" Jack asked, confused.

She handed over the envelope with a sarcastic grin on her face, accompanied by an eye roll "Ian Ginsberg, she's his assistant now."

"Oh, I see, and she's up there now?" Jack said, pointing up with his left hand while grabbing the envelope with his right.

"Yes, don't tell her I said 'Hi,' because I don't," she said.

"No, of course not. Thanks for getting this for me," he said, with a smile while wiggling the envelope, which actually worked to distract her from her jealousy long enough to smile back.

Jack walked back up to Lauren and took her by the arm with a big grin.

"What is it, Jack?" she said, looking sideways at him as he had her walking toward the elevator. "Where are we going?"

As the doors opened and they got in, he pressed the button for the top floor. Lauren continued to give Jack a curious stare to which, when the doors closed, he finally turned and acknowledged her. "We're going to talk to Ian's new assistant."

"Are you kidding? Already?" Lauren said, surprised.

"Yep," he said, watching the numbers go by on the elevator.

"Boy, can you say, 'like father like son'?"

"Quickest way from the bottom to the top floor is a pretty face," he said giving her a sarcastic grin.

"Shut up, Jack."

"Hello, Nella." Jack said as he walked into her new office.

She looked different than just a week earlier. Her hair was a little more professional and the outfit a lot more expensive. She was already playing the part, addressing Jack in a more business-like manner, sans the gum.

"Hello, Agent Shields. Did you have an appointment to see Mr. Ginsberg? I'm afraid he isn't scheduled to be in this morning," she explained as she looked at his calendar on the computer.

"Actually, that's okay, Nella. I just wanted to come up and ask you a quick question," he said, feeling pretty confident in his theory now.

"Okay, what would that be?" she said, glancing at Lauren and then back at him.

"Did you keep the receipt from the phone that Ian got you?" he said and then peered down at her, trying to look the part of Secret Service agent Shields.

"Yes," was all she could muster.

"Good, I just want to make sure you hold on to that, okay? We may need it sometime soon."

"All right," she said and grabbed her purse. "I have it here."

Jack grinned at Lauren as Nella dug through her purse, then he turned back to her with his serious face again. "Thanks, Nella," he said as she handed it to him. "Credit Card number," he said, glancing over at Lauren. "Here you go," he said, handing it back to Nella.

"Do you want to keep it?" she asked, eager to please.

"No, you hold on to that, Nella. Just don't lose it," Jack said as he gestured with a look toward the door at Lauren, to which she just nodded. "Thanks for your help, Nella."

"Is that all you needed?" Nella asked as they exited her office.

"Yes, Nella, that's it," he said, waving as he made the turn down the hall.

As the elevator started back down, Lauren began, "You know it's just circumstantial, right? It places Ian at the Best Buy when the computer that sent the email was there, but that's all. You can't prove that he sent the email, what's the motive?"

"Killing his dad to take over the bank, how about that one?"

"Okay, but what about the other bombings?"

"I don't know. Maybe, to distract from it being just about his dad. Bad guys in a lot of books I've read try to throw you off by covering up the true crime with other crimes."

"Books you've read? Are you kidding me?" she said, rolling her eyes.

"Yeah, I'm just messing around," he said, catching himself. "Look, it's leverage, that's all. Set up another meeting with Ian. I'm going to turn up the heat on this guy and see if he sweats."

"What about her phone? Do you want to order a warrant to get the receipt?"

"I guess either that or his credit card records. Either way, he was there."

❧❦❧

After dropping Lauren at her place, he figured it was time to get back home and do some more reading on the Ginsberg family and Ian. As he pulled up to the gate, he swore at himself for still not knowing the name of the kid who worked the booth.

"How's the novel coming along?" he asked as he rolled his window down since the kid hadn't opened the gate, yet.

"Oh hey, Jack. Sorry about that. I'm actually working on it right now. Sorry I didn't see you pull up. Let me get the gate," he said as he got up out of this chair and hit the button for the gate to open. It squeaked as it opened, clearly needing some oil.

"So how far are you?" Jack asked.

"Just passed two hundred pages. The story just turned a corner and now all the shit is going to hit the fan," the kid said enthusiastically.

"So you have the ending figured out?" Jack asked.

"Well, almost. You know there always needs to be that big twist at the end."

"Yeah, of course, that's what makes mystery novels so great. Real life is never that exciting. Usually it's pretty obvious who the bad guy is," Jack said with a grin, thinking of his meeting with Nella.

"How's your current case going?"

"Let's just say I've turned the corner and, for a certain someone, the shit is about to hit their fan."

"So you got the guy?"

"About to, yep, no surprise ending here," Jack said.

"Be careful, Jack, that's usually about the time the

twist comes in," the kid said, laughing a youthful laugh that just made Jack smile.

"Hey, if I'm wrong on this, I'll buy a hundred copies of your book when you're done."

"Maybe, I should self-publish then," the kid said, still laughing.

They were then both lit up by the lights of a car approaching behind them.

"Okay, see you. Let me know when the book is done," Jack said, driving off while the window went back up.

ↄ

The phone was ringing as Jack got inside. He ran to pick it up, not sure what ring it was on.

"Hello," he said, slightly out of breath from running for the phone.

"Hey, Jack, it's Richard. You okay? You sound out of breath."

"Yeah, I'm fine, just got in and ran for the phone."

"Really? Out of breath, from that? Are you planning on going jogging with Sara tomorrow morning?"

"Yes," Jack said almost reluctantly.

"Better think of another excuse for not keeping up with her," Richard said with a smile that Jack could imagine on the other end.

"Got one, don't worry. How are you doing? How's your *project* going?" Jack asked, the sarcasm trailing his voice through the line like a fishing bob.

"Actually just finished. That's why I was calling. Figured we could go out and celebrate tomorrow night if you don't have any plans with Lauren."

"Funny, Richard, no plans with Lauren tomorrow night."

"Sorry, couldn't resist. How's your *project* going by the way?" Richard asked in return.

"Actually, you know what? Since you're done with your deal, maybe you can help me out with mine some more."

"Sure. What do you need?"

"Are you still able to get into Ian Ginsberg's computer?"

"Of course."

"Can you get me access to his email?"

"Ha, Jack, if you only knew what I just worked on you would realize how silly that question is. Give me a second." There was a brief pause. "There you go. I just downloaded all his email from the last six months to a zip file and sent it to your email."

"Thanks, Richard, six months, huh? Well, I better get reading. See you tomorrow night, just text me tomorrow to let me know when and where to meet you."

❧❧❧

Two hours and three hundred emails later, there was nothing revealing Ian as anything other than an adulterer in those emails. The only thought Jack had when he was done was that he felt like he just read one of those mommy porn books that were so popular now instead of one of his mystery novels. He got to see the whole relationship between Ian and Nella develop over email conversations that started out innocent and quickly changed to much more. Oh, what Mrs. Ginsberg's divorce attorney could do with these emails.

Not what Jack was looking for but now he had enough leverage to tip over a dump truck. He'd have to wait till his meeting with Ian that Lauren had set up for Monday.

❧❧❧

Back to studying more about the Ginsberg's. He forced

down another gulp of coffee, still not used to the taste. Jack started with Ian, figuring the most telling information was his background in the Israeli military. Definitely made painting him as a bomber more realistic. No surprise there, though, since with conscription in Israel everyone had to serve at some point during their youth. Even Sharla had served. This proved a distraction when he clicked on some links about her. They opened up a whole cache full of pictures on the web about her acting and modeling career. He found himself wandering farther down that path as he marveled at her beauty. Unlike most men, he did actually read some of the articles interviewing her.

He noted how in one she contributed her athletic build to her time in the military albeit only for the minimum two-year requirement. Some of the pictures were quite revealing. He thought back to meeting her at the Ginsberg estate imagining this body he was now seeing on the web with even less clothing.

It was time to turn off the screen or he would find himself doing what he caught Charlie doing one time when he walked into his place. That image cooled him off quickly. Then he remembered the six thousand dollars in his coat. He made a mental note to swing by Charlie's place after his jog with Sara.

CHAPTER 43

Y ou going to be able to keep up this time?" Sara asked as Jack got out of his car and walked over to where she was already stretching.

He was glad he got there when he did so he didn't miss the view. She smiled at him then turned away and bent down. "I'm gonna try," he said, turning away and trying not to stare.

"Well, hurry up and stretch so we can get going," she said as she turned back with a smile catching his lingering eyes.

"What's your hurry? It's Saturday," Jack said as he lazily spread out his legs and began to slowly stretch down toward his right foot.

"I wanna go into the office and look over some stuff," she said, standing upright.

"Like I said, it's Saturday, you can take a break, Sara."

"This is my break, now hurry up," she said, starting to bounce in place anxious to get going.

"You really think those trades have something to do with the bombings?" he asked as he placed one foot on the bench and leaned forward stretching a hamstring.

"Well, to be honest, I don't know if there is a connection to them, but I just can't understand the timing of them.

There's something there, I'm just not sure what," she said still bouncing.

"Okay, let's get going since you're so anxious," he said, lifting his foot off the bench and twisting his back to the right and left.

"Aren't you going to the stretch your other leg," she said with a quick hand gesture to his left side.

"Nah, one's fine, I'll get the other one next time," he said with a grin.

She just gave him a strange look and shrugged her shoulders. Then she turned and was off in what looked to Jack like a sprint. He was going to have to hurry to keep an eye on what he wanted.

It didn't take long for Sara to see that Jack wasn't keeping up again so she slowed her pace to let him catch up. "You're getting old," she said as he caught up and was jogging beside her, while trying not to breathe as hard as he really wanted, or felt like he needed to.

"We're the same age," he said, looking forward as they rounded a turn on the path between the trees as they entered the wooded area. The early fall breeze had picked up and wasn't making things any easier on him. At least it would be to his back on the way down.

"You're six months older than me, and always will be," she said with a chuckle as she patted him on the butt and sped up ahead of him again. Jack looked on for a second before trying to keep up and whispered to himself, "Not if I die first."

As the path straightened, she let him catch up again. He noticed that she wasn't even breathing hard.

"Seriously, Jack, are you okay? You've never had this hard a time keeping up before. Is your ankle still bothering you?" she said, looking down toward his foot.

"Yeah a little, but I've also been staying up late the last few nights doing some of my own research," he said, thinking that at least this excuse was actually true.

"You do look a little more worn out than normal," she

said, leaving him wondering what normal really was any-more. She sighed. "I guess I should be glad you even showed up."

After a few hundred yards of silence, she asked him something that made his already straining heart beat even faster. "So, how's Lauren?"

She didn't look at him. He couldn't tell for sure through his trying to breathe, while he kept to Sara's slower pace, but it sounded as if there was some meaning behind the way she asked the question.

"She's fine, why?" was all he could muster, physically and emotionally, since he wasn't sure what she was really asking.

"Well, I can kind of relate with what she's going through."

"What do you mean?" he asked, rather nervous about where this was going.

"Well, I just broke up with Todd after a year, but she was engaged, so obviously that's a lot worse. I was just wondering how she was doing, that's all," she said still be-side him and still looking forward.

Jack decided he'd better be careful with his replies since this might be some FBI interrogation technique he wasn't aware of. "She seems okay."

"Just watch out for the rebound. After the depression stage, comes anger, where you think you can write off men forever," she said as they reached an incline in the path.

"Lauren's definitely in the anger stage. I've got some bruises to prove it," he said, which got a funny glance from Sara. "What's the next stage?"

"Then come the withdrawals," she said as she turned toward him, looking down as she ran up the hill backward in front of him. Her hair swung back and forth as she smiled at him. "Women have needs too, you know," she said as her smile widened, accompanied by a knowing look. Then she quickly turned her head swinging her hair around and run-ning faster.

Is she flirting with me? he asked himself and grew concerned about how much more his heart could take. He decided to find out even at the risk of giving himself a heart attack. He couldn't let her out run the conclusion to this conversation. He tried to speed up the hill, but it was more like a ten speed bike slipping a gear as he jerked forward.

"So are you speaking from experience," he asked as he was finally able to catch up, fueled by a more familiar form of hormonal energy to which he was more accustomed.

"Hey, I'm human too, but this is about Lauren," she said with a smile and continued on, not looking at him now.

"You know Lauren doesn't even like you," Jack said after an awkward pause.

"I know," she said rather casually, surprising him while still looking forward.

"You do?" he asked, genuinely not sure as he looked over at her to try and gage her.

"Yep, and I know why?"

"Why?"

"You," she said as she sped up. "Come on, Jack, enough talk. I need to burn off some of this energy I've got pent up. I'll meet you in the parking lot if you can't keep up." She started to leave him behind easily, like so many of the horses he had lost money on. Now he finally knew what it felt like, especially since her first kick, as she took off, threw some dirt up toward his face. She was literally leaving him in the dust. As she reached the top of the hill and started back down around a curve at the top, she was quickly out of sight. Jack took the opportunity to finally stop and catch his breath. He figured, at that point, catching the bomber would be an easier proposition. He hadn't even had a chance to tell Sara his theory about Ian.

Sara had found her more natural stride. She figured she probably had put about a mile between her and the strangely-out-of-shape Jack. She figured the extra distance between them would give her more time to decide how much further to take the flirting. She had to be careful that this was something she really wanted and not the runner's high of added endorphins bouncing around in her head. Maybe it was the withdrawals she was talking about, but Jack looked so good to her this morning—the way the long-sleeved polyester Under Armour shirt wrapped around his body from his large pecs to his muscular arms. While she ran, she imagined him grabbing her and holding her in those strong arms. And not the way he used to when they were younger, but to ravage her, instead, more like Todd. If she could just combine a little of each of them, she would have the perfect guy. She actually laughed out loud at the silliness of that thought. Maybe she should keep running and find a new guy.

Whatever type of guy she imagined, it more than likely wasn't anything close to the one waiting for her behind some bushes as she came down the hill. With the wind to her back, it carried her laugh up ahead, alerting him that she was almost in range. As he saw her coming at such a great speed, he readied himself, bending down like a sprinter in the starting block. This man was anything but a sprinter, but for the distance he was going to cover, he was in shape enough. He had watched her enter the woods with Jack and figured he would have to take him out first. Sara taking off from Jack had just made his job easier. He got ready to jump.

At the last second, Sara thought she saw something move from behind the bush, thinking it was an animal. In some ways, she was right. The man leapt out of nowhere and hit her as unexpectedly as an NFL linebacker taking out someone at Wimbledon. She didn't even feel her body scrape on the gravel of the path as he slammed her to the ground then rolled with her into the forest a few feet from the view of the trail.

Before she could even comprehend what was going on, he sat his two hundred forty pounds on top of her. His legs straddled her waist as he held down, both her hands above her head captured in just one of his large hands. As her vision cleared, her eyes focused on the sunlight breaking through the trees, shimmering off the knife he held in his other hand. She was about to scream when he lifted the blade to her lips and made a "Shh" sound as he pressed hard enough on the blade that she felt the skin start to give. Then he just sat there, taking her in.

As he evaluated her, she did the same. This was not a guy she had ever seen on the trail. He clearly wasn't your typical jogger. If so, he skipped the trail and ran through the woods, tree branches beating up his face along the way. Perhaps, a boxer? That part she had correct, but didn't guess that he had honed those skills in prison.

He'd served twenty years. Spent eighteen of them boxing. He was the prison champ up until the last two years. Father time finally beat him where many others who had tried to prove themselves could not. But he wasn't too old to take out a female. He knew how to fight, that was for sure. What he didn't know was his way around a woman. And now he found himself on top of one of the most beautiful he had ever seen or forgotten how to even imagine after twenty years.

He couldn't just kill her as he was paid to do. Not at least without satisfying his long pent up needs. *She's so pretty.* Then he lifted the knife, causing her to curl as much as she could underneath his weight. He thrust it down but turned the blade up as he did. He cut through her top and the sports bra both, with one quick motion upward.

Sara struggled as she felt the cool morning breeze on her exposed breasts. She watched him just staring at them as if she wasn't even there. She had to try and scream out for Jack.

Just as she let out a brief but loud "Jack!" he threw the knife to his side and quickly placed his other hand over her mouth. She could taste the gravel and sweat from his hand. He still held her hands, struggling uselessly above her head, with his other hand.

At least he had dropped the knife. She hoped that Jack had heard her, but resigned herself to the thought that he had not. She braced herself as she watched the man lower his damaged face toward her right breast while opening his mouth. She closed her eyes after seeing that he was missing a few teeth. She squinted harder as if that would help distract her from the warm breath and rough tongue she felt on her nipple. She kept squirming so he couldn't find purchase on her with his mouth, to the point that he finally grew frustrated with her. He sat up and took her in one last time.

"What a waste," he said as he moved his hand quickly from her mouth to pick up the knife.

As he raised the knife up above her she resigned herself to the fact that she was about to die. At least she'd spent her last moments with Jack. As she saw the sunlight gleam off the blade, she realized her last thought would be the revelation that she still loved him.

Sara closed her eyes as the man began to lower the blade. Then the ground shook.

Jack had dived into the man. He hit with such force that the two men flew ten feet before either hit the ground. When they did, they both tumbled downhill through the brush for another twenty. The blade flew through the air as Jack hit him.

Sara opened her eyes to the sun shining off the spinning airborne blade like a disco ball lighting up the trees around her. It took her a few seconds to realize what had just happened and where the two men had gone. Their tumbling had come to an abrupt end with a thud as they crashed into an old oak with a trunk thicker than the two of them. Even with the force of their impact, it merely dropped a few leaves, as if unimpressed. Unfortunately for Jack, his back took the brunt of the hit against the immovable tree. It had knocked out the little bit of wind he had left in him from all the running. His face landed on a rock. Luckily, the man was also in a daze, made dizzy not just from the intense blow delivered by Jack's shoulder into his side while he held the knife high, but also from the turning of his roll down the hill with Jack.

He was able to clear his head faster than Jack could gain his footing. He looked over at his attacker and saw the tell tales signs of someone too tired to last much longer. This was usually followed by a knockout. He had forty-five of them out of fifty-one bouts in prison. He eyed Jack while slowly standing. He knew this would be number forty-six. With Jack clutching at his side, leaning on one elbow, the man felt no need to hurry. He steadied himself and spread his feet while lifting his fists.

Jack had seen the stance a few times in the bars he worked, and he knew he was dealing with a boxer. '*Don't worry about the jabs, it's the knockout punch you have to watch out for,*' his mentor at the first bar he worked at had told him. He had a pretty good idea this guy wasn't in it to score points with the judges. From the size of the man, Jack realized that it would only take one punch. Lucky for Jack, the man couldn't help but follow old habits. Just as Jack finally righted himself on his feet, the man took two quick steps and hit him with a jab to the body. Fortunately it was on his left side, not the right where he felt he already had broken a rib. The guy definitely knew what he was doing and hit him hard, knocking Jack right back to the ground. Jack realized quickly that this wasn't going to last long. He had to end it quick. If he were in a ring with this guy, he'd have no chance, but fortunately he wasn't in a ring. The difference between being a boxer and a bouncer was that Jack was used to not having any rules. He grabbed that same rock his face had landed on with his left hand as he began to push himself up. The man grabbed Jack's shoulder to set up his next, and probably, last blow. Jack continued turning, as the man lifted him by the shoulder, and swung the one pound rock right into the man's jaw.

Sara, who had made her way toward the noises she had heard, got close enough just in time to hear the very unpleasant crunch of the man's jaw being broken. She also saw some of his few remaining teeth fly from his mouth. As the man stumbled and began to fall over, Jack saw Sara still shaken standing behind the man. This just added rage to Jack's initial instinct of survival. Before the man could topple over, Jack swung his body the other direction and hit him as hard as he had ever hit anyone right in his already-bent boxer's nose.

This would be the last time it was broken. The man looked to Sara like one of those blow up dolls that kids try to knock over that swing in one direction then pop up the other way. Except this time, he was never bouncing back up. Sara was fine with that.

CHAPTER 44

After about an hour of questioning from police and refusing medical attention Jack insisted on following Sara home. As banged up as he was physically he knew she was much worse off emotionally. He didn't want her to be alone and she felt the same. Jack followed her in to her apartment. As they walked in through the kitchen, Sara grabbed a large Ziploc bag from a drawer and went over to the freezer. He was taking in the place when he heard her hand shuffling through the ice. He watched her grab a handful and put it in the bag. Then she wrapped the bag in a small towel.

"Here put this on your face," she said after closing the freezer door. She held it up as she gestured to his bruised cheek with a nod.

"You think this will help?" he said as he took the ice-pack from her, holding on to her hand for a few seconds.

"Can't hurt, but yeah I don't see the point. Every time one of your bruises start to clear up, you find a new creative way to get an even bigger one," she said with a slight smile.

"Hey, the rock that did this really helped me out. Reminds me of when I grew up. Some of my best friends were guys I fought with when I first met them," he said, smiling back but grimacing as he felt the swelling start.

"Some friends," she said, leaning in to look at the swelling "Better put this on it."

She took his hand with the bag of ice from his side and lifted it up, pressing on his hand gently to put it to his face. Then she just held it there for a second while he stood still staring at her with his uncovered eye.

"Well, better this bruise than the alternative."

"Yeah," was all she said.

She let go of his hand on his face and turned to walk away. Jack cursed himself silently for saying what he'd said and ruining the moment.

"I'm going to take a shower and change, go lay yourself down on the couch. If you want, you can take one after I'm done," she said as she rounded the corner to the hallway toward her bedroom.

"I don't have a change of clothes," he yelled after her as he headed toward the couch.

"I've got some of Todd's stuff here," she said from the bedroom. "He didn't bother picking them up after we broke up. I think they will fit."

"Okay, just wake me up if I doze off while you're in there."

Jack plopped himself on the couch, thankful that Sara didn't have any jealous pets. In his current state, even Lauren's cat would have been too much to handle. He lay down, placing the icepack gently on his face. Although thinking of Sara taking a shower so close by made him think he could use the ice somewhere else. He couldn't believe he was thinking that after what had just happened to her. He punished himself by lifting the pack and smacked it down hard on his already swollen cheek.

Sara took her time in the shower, trying to wash off the dirt she felt more on the inside than out. What she wanted to wash off most of all was the shame of having felt so helpless in the situation. No matter how much she lathered and rinsed, it would be a long time before she could wash away those feelings. In the time that she took to shower, dry off, and put on her robe, Jack had indeed fallen asleep on the couch. Watching him lay there as she walked into the living room made her feel at ease. It reminded her of better, more innocent times. Well, as innocent as you could be away from home for the first time in college. As she walked closer, she could see that the icepack had fallen from his cheek to the floor with his arm hanging close by. He was laying on his side, which left some space on the front of the couch. She sat down in that space, being as careful as she could as not to wake him or so she thought.

Jack felt her next to him. He could feel her warmth on his stomach through her robe. Her weight had caused his body to shift toward her. He kept his eyes closed.

Sara, after gently brushing back a few loose hairs from his forehead, remembered the icepack on the floor. She placed her left hand on the couch next to his chest and leaned down to pick it up. As she did, Jack felt her hair fall onto his face. If it wasn't the soft feel of her hair that got him excited. It had to be the smell of it. He caught himself breathing it in heavily. Her hair was still just a little wet and it left a drop of water on his cheek, making it hard for him not to twitch or rub it off with his hand. As she grabbed the bag on the ground, he opened his eyes. He could see the robe hanging open revealing one of her breasts underneath. He thought about how they probably saved her life and wasn't surprised. They clearly distracted the guy long enough for Jack to reach them. Now, he too was entranced.

Sara straightened up after placing the icepack on the coffee table. As she leaned back upright, she turned and saw that Jack was awake. She also noticed where his gaze had landed. She felt herself blush as she quickly grabbed her robe and closed it with her left hand. She then leaned over to grab the icepack with her right hand in an attempt to hide her embarrassment. She wasn't sure why she felt that way. Jack had seen her naked many times when they were together. Of course, that was many years ago and, no matter how in shape she knew she was, no woman thought they looked better with age, especially compared to when in college. She saw how the young interns at the office always caught all the men's eyes, not just Todd's.

"You dropped this," she said, holding the icepack above his face. "It isn't going to do you much good lying on the floor."

"No, I guess not. Here." He reached up and grabbed the pack in her hand, holding onto both for a few seconds, the condensation slipping between their fingers. Neither of them noticed the cold temperature. Sara feared her warmth would melt the rest of the ice if she didn't let go soon. She did, reluctantly.

Jack took the pack at the same time he shifted himself onto his back. After laying it on his cheek he looked up at her and asked, "How are you doing?"

She pushed some of the hair that had fallen onto her face out of the way. "I'm fine. I didn't get hurt as bad as you."

"That's not what I meant," he said, reaching up with his free hand pushing some strands of her hair with two of his fingers.

"I know," she mumbled and quickly turned her head. With his hand still up as she turned, it fell between her hair and the back of her neck. He decided to leave it there and gently rub her under her hair. He could feel the tension in her neck release as he gently squeezed.

Sara turned her head even more so that Jack wouldn't see the tears that had started to form in her eyes. She turned back toward him to let him know to stop massaging her so he laid his arm down at his side. When she did turn one of the tears broke free from her eyelashes and dripped down onto his other unbruised cheek.

This drop of water didn't make him want to twitch or rub it away. He could have left it there till it evaporated on its own. She slowly reached down and rubbed it softly off his face with her fingers.

"Sorry," she said quietly.

"For what?" he said, causing her to pause.

"I miss you," she finally said but then slowly stood up from the couch.

"I'm here, Sara," he said.

Then there was just silence as they were both unsure what to do next.

"I'm gonna take that shower now," he said to at least end the awkwardness.

Jack placed the icepack on the table, as he stood up and headed to her bedroom.

The hot water felt good on his back as he lingered longer than normal. The bathroom was as foggy as the San Francisco Bay under the bridge on a humid morning. The mirror was completely covered from the steam. When he finally stepped out, he grabbed the towel that she had left on the railing for him. He wrapped it tightly around his waist then leaned over the sink to wipe a streak from the mirror so he could assess the damage. His cheek on one side did look a bit larger as if he had stuck some cotton in his mouth like Brando in The Godfather.

"I'm gonna make him an offer he can't refuse," he whispered to his reflection in his best Brando. Then he fixed his hair.

Jack walked into the bedroom, after drying off, with the towel again cinched around his waist. He saw the clothes she had laid out for him on the end of her bed. He looked down at them as he walked over. A pair of black jeans, some designer brand he'd never heard of and a blue polo shirt. He didn't see any underwear, which was fine since he wouldn't' have put it on anyway. Another man's pants and shirt was bad enough.

As he reached for the jeans leaning over the towel loosened and then dropped to the floor. He bent down quickly picking it up feeling as though he had littered. He stood there for a moment holding the towel with one hand by his side. The idea of standing in her bedroom, naked next to her bed got him more than just a little excited. He wished he was undressing for her versus doing the opposite and definitely not in her old boyfriend's clothes. Not wanting to lay the water soaked towel on her bed, he turned and went to hang it back in the bathroom first. As he hung it on the hook on the back of the door he noticed that the steam had cleared from the mirror. Now he could see for the first time the big bruise on his back from where he had hit the tree. It looked like it must have hit back. The purple and black mark covered a third of his back as he bent in front of the mirror to try to see how wide it had spread.

While still standing there twisting in front of the mirror he could see in the reflection Sara come into the bedroom. He didn't even consider that he was still not dressed.

"You doing okay in there?" she asked loudly, expecting him to either still be in the shower or at the very least have the door closed. What she got, instead, as she turned in that direction was a good look at Jack. The bruise on his back was the last thing she noticed. It wasn't until her eyes made it up his backside and a little front side as well, that her eyes met his in the reflection.

"Oh, I'm sorry, I thought you'd be dressed by now," she said as she turned, looking down at Todd's clothes still on the bed. She stood there motionless not sure what to do. For as still as her body was, her heart was more than making up for it. It beat so hard in her chest she was afraid he could hear it.

Jack walked out of the bathroom, emboldened by the look of admiration he saw on Sara's face, before realizing she had been caught. He stepped up right behind her as she kept looking down at the clothes. She could feel his warmth behind her only a few inches away. A few thoughts raced through her head. She wanted to turn, even more so she wanted him to just grab her from behind and hold her tight. Instead of waiting for what she figured wasn't going to happen anyway, she decided to bend down and pick up the jeans on the bed to hand to him. She did bend a little more than necessary and felt him on her backside.

The softness of her robe did nothing to settle his own elevated heart rate as something else was now in danger of elevating whether he wanted it to or not.

Sara fought every urge to turn. Impressed with her own willpower, she smiled as she swung the jeans over her shoulder at him. "Here you go," she said simply, not turning, smiling, and almost giggling like a schoolgirl.

Jack grabbed them from her, but also still held her hand. He then began to pull her hand around, causing her to turn. She didn't put up any resistance. She felt the anticipation building in all parts of her body as he kept pulling her hand slowly causing her to turn all the way around. She felt more excited than an eight year old waiting to see her first one.

When he was done, he let go of her hand and just stood there holding the jeans next to his side. She looked him up and down.

Feeling her eyes on every part of him quickly gave her more to see. "I'd really rather not put these on," he said, lifting the jeans up so her eyes would do the same.

"Well, I already put your clothes in the washer so it's gonna be a while," she said, biting her lip as she looked into his blue eyes only a few inches from hers.

"I'm not in a hurry," he said as he tossed them onto the bed next to her.

She turned, watching them land, then turned back, her hair hitting him in the face. That was the final straw that made the camel forget its probably broken back. As she turned back to face him, he grabbed her arms at her sides and leaned in to kiss her. She just thought to herself, *Finally*.

After about thirty seconds, of them giving in to each other with their mouths, she stepped back to catch her breath. "Like I said, I just put your clothes in the washer so it's going to be a while," she said, smiling while Jack looked at her, unsure of which direction she was heading. "And I only have the one robe, but—" She paused as she undid the rope in front, "—if you want to wear it you're welcome to."

She let it fall off her shoulders onto the floor. She stood there now and let him take her in with his eyes. As he did, she felt like he was doing so for his first time. She just reminded herself it had been a while. She could tell that he definitely liked what he saw and now she was emboldened. She grabbed onto him between his legs.

"It's been a while since I've seen it," she said as she gently squeezed.

Jack was speechless. Then she reached around his shoulders and pulled him toward her, her other hand still wrapped a little tighter around him. It pulsed as if undergoing a blood pressure test. That was a test he surely would not score well on if taken at that exact moment. Then all of a sudden his feet left the ground the same time her lips met his.

She had pulled him down on top of her onto the bed—more accurately on top of Todd's now-soon-to-be-wrinkled clothes that would later find their way into the trash.

The two of them grabbed at each other's bodies as if ravished. Then he moved from kissing her lips down to her neck. On his way down to his final destination, he got sidetracked at her breasts. She felt like the impatient child on the traditional family cross country drive to Disney World. Her body was ready for him to just get there already. She pushed down subtly with both hands on his broad shoulders, guiding him back on his original path.

He didn't mind the encouragement. After a brief stop at her navel, he obliged.

She felt his hair on her inner thighs before he dove in. When he did, she just laid back and let herself enjoy. This was better than any roller coaster.

At some point, he had to come up for air. When he did, he moved back up, hovering over her. She didn't mind tasting herself when he started kissing her again. She only had one urge left that needed to be filled. Then he did.

Maybe because it had been so long, but this felt really different to her.

Jack *was* different, definitely more aggressive than she remembered, and women didn't forget those kinds of details. He wasn't as rough as Todd, but was now that guy somewhere in between, and she loved every second of it. Not too soft not too hard, but just right.

They didn't speak when they each finished the first time. They just lay there on their sides, looking into each other's eyes while catching their collective breaths. After a few minutes, Sara saw Jack's eyes evaluate her body and she saw the excitement return to them. When his eyes shifted back up to hers, she knew the question she saw in them. She gave her answer by not so gently pushing him from his side back onto his back.

"Ouch," he whispered with a bit of agony on his face.

"Oh, I'm sorry, I forgot. Here, I know what will make the pain go away," she said as she lowered herself over him.

If this was how morphine worked, he finally realized how so many of his friends had gotten hooked on the drugs he'd never tried growing up. He knew he was going to be addicted to Sara after this.

Before he could reach that ultimate high for a second time she stopped, moved back up, and started kissing him again.

The two of them tasting each other and themselves as they kissed excited them both at a whole other level. They grabbed each other harder as Sara guided Jack into her with her hand. She then sat up and looked down at him.

Jack couldn't imagine a better image. No painting that any great artist in history could have painted could match Sara's beauty in that moment. That moment was then soon followed by an earthquake-like tremor as her body shook on top. They both simultaneously felt that plunge from the highest point of the roller coaster ride they had been on for the past hour.

As their bodies settled back into the station, she collapsed next to him. She just lay there, silent, and stared at him for a few seconds. Then she spoke one simple shocking sentence.

"You're not Jack."

CHAPTER 45

Brad answered his cell phone on the first ring. It wasn't the call he was expecting.

This was the person he was *supposed* to call after the other guy called him. Things were happening out of order, and just like *that* sign on the restroom door when you really gotta go, this was not good. The way the call started had even given him the same feeling, of almost shitting his pants.

"What the *fuck*?" Ray screamed on the other end.

"What?" Brad answered back in confusion.

"You're guy fucked up!"

"Why, what happened?"

"Let's start with what didn't happen," Ray said then had to catch his breath. "Sara didn't die, that's what didn't happen."

"What happened with Nick?"

"That's the only good thing. He did," Ray said, starting to calm down but not much.

"Oh," was all Brad said.

"All you can say is 'oh'? You said this was the perfect guy for this and he blew it. Look, I just want to know one thing now."

"What?"

"Can this guy in anyway be connected to you?" Ray asked.

"I doubt it. We were in prison together five years ago right before I got out. He just got out a few months ago. And obviously he's not gonna talk," Brad said with a smirk.

"No, he's not," Ray said, calming down even more. "So you don't think anyone's gonna connect the dots on this one?" he asked as if hearing him deny it again would help.

"Not even Monet on his best day," Brad said confidently.

"Studied some art while in prison, did we?" Ray said on the other end with a smile.

"Among other things," Brad said.

"Let's just hope you're right or you'll be going back long enough to get your masters in fine arts," Ray said then abruptly hung up.

CHAPTER 46

W hat are you talking about?" Jack asked, trying his best to smile like he had just heard a joke.

"You're just so different.

"I guess," he said, blowing it off as he got off the bed and headed toward the bathroom.

"I mean it, Jack, you're so different." She paused and watched him turn in the bathroom to grab the towel he hung on the back of the door. "It was so different."

"It's been a long time since we'd done that," he said as he wrapped the towel around his waist and cinched it while walking back out. "I've learned a few things."

"I don't know. I think it would take a lifetime to change like you have, Jack," she said resting her head on her hand as she lay on her side, admiring him.

"I'm a fast learner," he said with a shrug. "You think my clothes are done drying? I really don't want to get dressed in 'asshole's' clothes."

I don't want you to get dressed at all. "Probably, let me go get them," she said as she lifted the sheet off herself got up.

Now it was his turn to do the admiring. He really hadn't had a chance to truly take in the beauty of her shape since they were so close together in bed. From across the room, as she stood up, he could truly appreciate the results of her consistent workout schedule. She knew he was watching and arched her back as she stood, taking her time as she stretched, then turned her head just to be sure she was correct in her assumption. She was, and that excited her. She turned and walked by Jack, touching his forearm as she reached down to pick up the robe on the floor next to him. As she started back up from her crouched position her eyes met his and she slowed her rise and smiled. She put the robe on slowly and went to get his clothes.

Jack walked back to the bathroom to take another quick shower, but not before Sara got another glimpse of his backside and smiled to herself.

"Here you go," she said, tossing his clothes on the bed next to where he was sitting with the towel wrapped around himself. She picked up Todd's clothes from the floor. "I'm going to go throw these out while you get dressed."

Jack put on his boxers and his jeans but left the shirt lying on the bed. He went into the bathroom to wash off his face. As he did, he noticed his disheveled hair and tried to fix it best he could with the water. He figured he got it the best he could under the circumstances without any hair gel.

"Wow, that looks horrible," Sara said as she walked back into the bedroom and looked over at him in the bathroom.

Jack looked up and saw her in the mirror standing behind him. "Hey, I'm doing the best I can here," he said, gesturing with both hands toward his hair.

"Not that. I'm talking about the bruise on your back. I didn't really see it till now. You really should go get that looked at. We should have at least put some ice on it. I think your face is a lost cause anyway."

"I'm okay," he said, checking his hair one last time before turning the water off. As he walked by her to get his shirt off the bed he said, "Besides, I read somewhere that sex is good for your back."

"Sure you did," she said as she headed into her closet

to get an outfit to put on. From the closet she yelled back at him, "Where do you want to go eat? I'm starving and I don't have anything here."

Jack was so thrown by her question that when he pulled the shirt over his head he didn't even notice that he messed up his hair again. Things were definitely working out of order here. He wasn't sure what they would talk about now, especially after the last couple of hours. The last thing he was going to do after what had happened to her earlier on top of what they just did was leave her. It was going to be a challenge to keep the conversation going over dinner. As of yet, they actually hadn't done much talking.

"You pick," he finally said just as she came out of the closet.

She had on some jeans and a bra but was still working her shirt before pulling it over her head. He just watched as if she were a Victoria's Secret model. In slow motion, she arched her back while putting it on.

When she finished pulling the form-fitting shirt down to her waist she looked up to catch him staring at her. "What happened to your hair?" As she walked by she raised a hand and ruffled it up some more on her way to the bathroom to fix her own and laughed.

"I'm going to call Richard. We were supposed to meet up at five for an early dinner. I'll tell him I'm not gonna make it."

"What are you guys, senior citizens?" she said, still laughing as she ran a brush through her hair.

"I feel like a senior citizen," he said and reached for his aching back as he picked up his shoes in the corner of the bedroom. He headed out into the living room to get his phone.

"Hey, Richard, it's Jack."

"I know, Jack, I can see the number on my phone. Don't even need to be a hacker to figure that out. So what's up? We still on for tonight?"

"Actually no, I'm with Sara. Something happened today and I need to be with her. We're getting ready to go eat now."

"I understand, you got a better offer. You guys are eating dinner pretty early."

"It's more of a late lunch. Thanks, Richard, we'll grab dinner soon," Jack said as he was about to hang up.

"Oh, Jack," Richard just caught him.

"Yeah?" he said stopping and waiting to see what Richard wanted.

"If something more happens after dinner I wouldn't tell—" he was saying when Jack cut him off.

"It already happened," he said quickly.

"Wow, you know you're usually supposed to buy them dinner first. We really need to work on your manners during our next learning how to be Jack session."

"Sure, Richard, among other things," he said smiling.

"Well, either way definitely don't tell—" he was saying when Jack cut him off again.

"I won't tell Lauren," he yelled at him jokingly. "Goodbye, Richard."

"Tell Lauren what?" Sara asked as she walked from the hallway into the living room. Although she already had a pretty good idea of about what.

"Huh?" was all Jack could say as he turned to see Sara coming toward him.

"Yeah, if what you say about her not liking me is true, I really don't see how telling her what just happened would help. Better just keep it between us," she said as she just walked right past him to go pick up her purse from the kitchen.

He stood motionless not sure what to say.

"Come on let's go, I'm hungry," she said, turning back toward him.

Jack finally began to move and walked forward, meeting her at the front door.

"Oh, and about what happened here today," she said as he stopped next to her. "Just to be clear, that was just something I needed, and just that, nothing more. Okay?" she said, her eyebrows curling up like question marks awaiting a confirmation.

"Sure, just something you needed, nothing more," he said then stepped out the doorway in front of her. Before she could turn to lock the door behind them, he continued, "Well, next time you need something again, I'm your man."

She looked at him funny, turned back, and locked the door "Right now, I just need some food. Let's go."

$$\text{\textcyrillic{e}\textcyrillic{ce}\textcyrillic{ce}}$$

Jack drove home, after dropping off Sara at her place. They had agreed that him coming back inside would have just confused matters worse between them. What had happened earlier could easily be accepted by each of them as a reaction to the days heightened emotions. To do it again would carry no such convenient excuse.

In his happier mood, he smiled as he pulled up the young writer at the security booth. "You're still here?"

"Yeah, I took Julio's shift so I could make some more money, plus it helps me with my writing anyway," the guard said.

Jack laughed inside, considering that now he knew Julio's name but still not the kid's.

"I'm really getting close to finishing now."

"Really?"

"Yep, the big twist is coming soon and then I'm done."

"That's great. Let me ask you one thing. Does the guy get the girl in the end?"

"What girl?" the kid asked, looking confused as only someone youthful as him could.

"What do you mean, what girl? There's always a girl," Jack said with a concerned look.

"Shit," the young author groused. "You think I need to go back and add one?"

"Definitely," Jack said as the gate finished opening in front of his car. "Like I said, there's always a girl." He turned and starting driving the car forward. As the car rolled away, he offered one more comment. "Sometimes there's more than one."

CHAPTER 47

"How's Sara?" Lauren asked as she got into Jack's car.

He felt his face flush with guilt, hoping she wouldn't notice as she put her seat belt on, and wondered if she knew. If so, how did she find out?

"She's fine," he said as he turned quickly away from her and started the car.

"Fine? That's all you got?" she said, sounding surprised.

Uh oh, sounds like she knows. Jack hesitated with an answer.

"I know what happened," she said.

"You do?" he said, glancing over briefly then turning back to check his window for traffic as he exited her parking lot onto the street. He stepped on the gas a little too anxiously, as if it would help him get away from this situation. Lauren fell back into her seat but it didn't stop her from talking.

"I heard about the attack at the park," she said, to which Jack eased up on the gas pedal.

The engine sighed in relief at the same time as Jack. Jack pretended to be really focused on the Monday morning traffic as he entered the freeway. "Oh, yeah, she's doing okay."

"Were you with her that morning? Don't you guys still go jogging every Saturday?" she asked as he merged into the middle lane.

"Yeah, I was there," he said more calmly now as he settled into the flow of the traffic.

"So what happened?" she asked with a hint of concern.

"Sara ran ahead of me—" Jack started by turning toward her and then back to keep an eye on the traffic "—through the woods."

"And you couldn't keep up?" she said, almost laughing, but then remembering the plot of this story he was telling she stopped herself.

"Well, my ankle still isn't one hundred percent."

"Okay, so what happened?" she said, taking the more solemn tone again.

"Well, I came around a turn and didn't see her anymore. I just figured she had really left me behind and already made it out of the park back to her car. So I slowed down a little."

Lauren stopped herself from saying, "You were able to go even slower?"

"Then I heard a muffled scream. I looked through the bushes and saw the guy on top of Sara."

"And..." she prompted.

"Well, I dove into him and knocked him off of her. We fought, and then I—" He paused.

"What?" she asked.

"I killed him," he said, looking at her intently, then he slammed the brakes as he just barely caught the traffic stopping ahead out of the corner of his eye.

Both of them jerked forward against their seatbelts. Their hearts raced from the near collision.

"Good," she said after a pause and they both settled themselves again. "One less rapist in the world. There really is only one bad thing about you doing that, Jack."

"What's that?" he asked, glancing back and forth again as to not almost have an accident again.

"The paperwork," she said, smiling at him.

"Oh, yeah," he said as if he knew. "I'll have to drop you off after this meeting with Ian so I can meet with the DC police at the station to sign a statement."

"Have fun. Hope you had a good breakfast," She said, rolling her eyes "'Cause you'll probably miss lunch."

"I don't really eat breakfast," he said.

This got more of a reaction out of her than when he mentioned that he killed Sara's attacker.

"Since when? You're the one that gave me a lecture on the importance of eating breakfast after I told you Starbucks was my breakfast place. How you learned that during your brief time in Medical school. Now you 'don't really eat breakfast'?" she said, doing hand quotes on the last part.

"Sorry, I meant to say didn't really. I just had a banana," he said, trying to fix the mistake.

"Did the doctors check you out afterward?"

"Yeah, I'm fine," he said.

"Well, I wouldn't use that word, but you do look handsome with that bruise on your face," she said sarcastically.

"Well, at least it's not on my good side."

"You have a good side? Huh, I've never really noticed," she said, laughing this time.

"You're really funny in the morning, you know that?"

He leaned forward to look past her so he could get in the right lane to exit. He smiled as he changed lanes and put on his blinker to exit.

∽∾∽

Jack and Lauren were greeted by Nella again as they got off the elevator on Ian's floor. After a simple polite greeting between the three of them, she took them back to Ian's office.

Jack smiled as she walked passed him, walking nervously back to her desk.

She hoped what they had talked about last time wouldn't cost her this new job.

Ian stood up and came around his desk to shake Lauren and Jack's hand and then gestured to the two chairs. "Agents Shields and Kurtz, please have a seat."

As they sat, Jack hinted as to which direction he wanted this conversation to turn "I see that you replaced your father's assistant for one of your own."

This brought a look from Lauren, signaling him to play it cool. Jack just looked back with a quick show of apology on his face and a shrug of his broad shoulders. Lauren always marveled at how such a rugged looking man could so easily make himself look humble. She had to admit it was part of the attraction. Such a Jewish trait, she thought to herself as she signed. *If only.*

"Actually, that was mother's idea," Ian said. "She asked me to fire her. Look. I liked Elena, but my mother was grieving and I wanted to do what any son would do to try and make her happy. So when she asked, I couldn't say no. I gave Elena a good severance and letter of recommendation."

"Firing her made your mother happy?" Lauren asked.

"There was a history there, and I'm sure you can understand, Lauren, forgiveness isn't a strong suit in Jewish women," Ian said with a smile.

"No, it's not and they don't forget either," she said returning the smile.

Then she turned to Jack and gave him a strange look. The comment and the look had him worried again that she knew more than she let on earlier.

"No, they don't. But let's not be sexist. That might just be an overall Jewish thing. We didn't forget to go home to Israel after two thousand years," Ian said, testing the strength of their common bond as if Jack weren't even in the room.

"You didn't take long finding a replacement, I see," Jack said.

After a few seconds, Ian looked over and stared at Jack. He could feel the man's eyes on his bruise.

"No, Nella is a good girl. She is going to be great." Ian said. "What happened to you Agent Shields?" he asked, lifting a hand toward his own face.

"Rough weekend," Jack said casually back to him. Out of the corner of his eye, he saw Lauren frown, as if insulted. He wondered again if she knew.

"That's too bad," Ian said then turned to the much prettier face in the room. "So what brings you by this morning? I'm guessing you've got some news about my father's case?"

"Actually we do," Jack said. "But we had some questions for you first."

"Sure, what do you want to ask me about?"

"Florida," Jack said.

"Okay. Well, I'm not a travel agent, but I imagine it's warmer down there this time of year," Ian said with a chuckle, looking immediately at Lauren to see if he had made her smile. He had used humor to flirt with Nella and it had worked as it had on so many other women before.

"You were there recently," Jack said in a formal voice, trying to keep himself from being jealous of the vibe he was getting between Ian and Lauren, even if it was just his own overactive imagination.

"Yes, I was there with my father. We went together to close the Europe transaction."

"But you weren't scheduled to go," Jack said as more of a statement then a question. One which got just as surprised a look from Lauren as it did from Ian.

"Yes," Ian continued after a pause. "My father hadn't told me about the transaction until the day before. He was trying to keep it secret, which is hard to do in this day and age. Especially with the spot light on our bank. I was still in New York and he didn't want to send an email or even tell me over the phone. He didn't trust any form of communication, a carryover from his days in Israeli Intelligence. He just called and told me to meet him down there. It was one thing for him to go down there by himself, but if it had been made public that we both went down there it would have gotten even more attention. Too much attention would have potentially revealed the reason for our trip and blown up the deal," he said.

His statement got a shrug of discomfort from Lauren.

"Sorry, poor choice of words," he said.

"That makes sense but I do have one more question for you," Jack said, glancing briefly at Lauren and giving her a look of "Here goes."

"Okay?" Ian said.

"Did you go to Best Buy while you were down there?"

"What?" he asked, more confused than anything else.

"You know the electronics store?" Jack continued.

"Yes, I know it, so what?"

"Look, let me just tell you, we already know you were there."

"And how is that?" Ian asked.

"Because your new assistant told me about the phone you got her for a present and it was purchased at Best Buy in Florida. The one in Orlando to be more specific. At least that's what the receipt showed." Jack said.

"So I bought Nella a gift. What does that have to do with anything? That's not a big deal," Ian said, clearly agitated.

Jack sensed the man's anger getting worse at his line of questioning and innuendos and figured he might be more likely to slip up if Jack kept his foot on the gas. It was time to go for the checkered flag, even while Lauren's face looked to be waiving the yellow caution flag.

"No, I guess cheating on your wife with someone and then promoting that person runs in the family. Like father like son. No big deal, as you say." Jack paused and braced himself for the explosion.

"That's a hell of an accusation and I don't see how it has anything to do with the case. You better get to the point or I'll have you escorted out of here!" Ian yelled.

"You know what? You're right, that's not the point. There is something more interesting that happened at that Best Buy while you were there buying the phone that day."

Ian had both his fists clenched on top of his desk. "Yeah, and what is that?"

"That also happened to be the same place where the computer that sent a particular threatening email originated from. Strange that you were there at that time. Who do you think could have sent that email?" Jack said in a strangely calm voice as he sat back and prepared himself to gage Ian's reaction, as did Lauren.

The one they got was more surprising than what either of them had expected. Ian sat completely still for a minute with a look of horror on his face. Then he simply whispered, "My Father," then lifted his hands to his face, and slumped over.

Jack gave Lauren a "What the hell?' look. She just turned her head back toward Ian as if pointing for Jack to follow up, reminding him this was his doing.

"What do you mean your father?" Jack asked.

"It was his idea for us to stop by there after he picked me up at the airport. He was acting strange that whole trip. He picked me up in his own car which surprised me that he had driven instead of flying. It was his idea to stop at the Best Buy on the way to the hotel. When I told him I was going to go look at the phones, he said he would be in the computer aisle," Ian said quietly.

"So you're saying your dad sent that email?" Lauren asked before Jack could, both of them sitting at the edge of their seats and not because they could barely hear his whispering.

"He must have, because it wasn't me," Ian said in a way that they both felt they could believe based on his reaction. They all sat in silence for a few seconds.

"That means he killed himself. Why would he do that?" Jack asked.

"Time," Ian said, after a moment. He removed his hands from his face, tears still flowing from his eyes. "He knew he needed time for the Europe transaction to close before our deadline to raise the bank's ratios. His death would do that for sure." Then he shook his head as if to disagree with himself. "But he could have found another way to stall, I don't get why he would do it this way."

"There was one reason why he chose this way," Jack said.

Ian lifted his head again, wiping the tears from his cheeks with one of his hands.

"Your dad was dying," Jack said.

"What?" Ian asked in disbelief. He looked at Lauren for confirmation, to which she just nodded.

"He would have told me," Ian said. His emotions swung back to anger.

"Like you said, your dad would have wanted it to be a secret so as to not kill the transaction. He would have kept it secret from anyone. Even you, even your mother."

"So how do you know? Who told you?" Ian asked.

"The one person who he couldn't keep a secret from, the one who set his schedules. Set his schedule for the many doctor visits. The one your mother asked you to fire."

"Elena," Ian whispered.

"Yes."

"Why didn't she tell me?" Ian said, looking almost helpless at this revelation.

Jack shrugged. "She thought he did, during your Florida trip. He didn't really need you to close that deal. He had told her he was going to tell you while you were down there. I guess he changed his mind."

"He didn't," Ian said angrily.

"I hate to ask, but any idea how he got the bomb?" Lauren asked.

"That's easy," Ian responded rather quickly without

thinking. "He would have had it shipped from one of his military friends from Israel. Rudolf Hirsch."

"Wouldn't they pick that up during shipment?"

"No, he would have had the components shipped in separate packages. He could easily reassemble them when they got here."

Then Jack did something really unexpected, he stopped and got up out of his seat. "Obviously this news has been quite upsetting. I think Lauren and I need to regroup at our office and figure out what this means to the case. You should probably go ahead and let your mother and sister know. Thanks for your time, Ian, and I'm sorry."

"Yes, I'm sorry, Ian," Lauren said as she stood, still unsure of Jack's retreat.

Ian just nodded, his head in his hands. Jack noticed the puddle of water that threatened to warp the wood of the desk.

As the elevator door closed behind them, Lauren immediately addressed Jack. "So you believe him? That his dad sent the email, meaning he probably killed himself, and that Ian didn't do it?"

"I do," he said simply, pondering something.

"Yeah, so do I. Unfortunately. This really confuses things. What about the bombings afterward? Mikal couldn't have done all of those after he was dead. And Steinherz?"

"No, of course not," Jack muttered under his breath, still thinking.

"That was a pretty low blow in there especially when you said, 'like father like son.'"

There it was. That comment went off like the elevator ding that rang at the same time.

"That's it," Jack yelled, just as the doors opened, startling the people crowding the outside of the elevator, waiting to get on.

"What's it?" she asked as they shuffled themselves between the people.

Jack grabbed her arm and pulled her to quiet space in

the lobby. "Just because he didn't kill his dad, doesn't change the fact that he's still our number one suspect," Jack said, grinning ear to ear as if a child revealing a secret he's not supposed to share.

"It doesn't?" Lauren said, still confused.

"No, it just changes his motive. Instead of wanting to take over the bank from his dad, it's the most traditional of all motivations."

"And that is?" Lauren asked.

"Revenge. You saw him in there. Up until ten minutes ago he thought someone had killed his father. You heard him say it himself, Jews never forget. Well, he never forgot his dad's enemies. Look at all the people that have died or he's tried to kill since. All enemies of his father."

"Okay," she said, still not convinced.

"Look, he even knows how to build bombs and get the materials to do it," Jack said, almost shaking with his own enthusiasm, knowing he'd cracked the case.

"Why would he have shared that with us?" Lauren asked, playing devil's advocate.

"Because, like we both do believe him about not knowing his dad killed himself, he was thrown and he wasn't thinking clearly. Let's go. I've got to get to the police to give my statement and I need to drop you off," he said, walking toward the exit, beckoning for her to follow.

"What actual evidence do we have, though?" Lauren said loudly, more out of curiosity this time than trying to just go counter point again.

"I've got an idea."

CHAPTER 48

Richard just sat there in there chair across from Jack, staring at him.

"What? You can't do it?" Jack asked him, surprised by his silence as well as the curious look he was giving him.

"No it's not that," Richard said, still slumped back in his chair.

"Don't tell me you won't," Jack said, getting a little frustrated with him.

"Are you kidding? Of course, I'll do it," Richard said and sat back up.

"Then what is it, why the strange look?" Jack asked him.

"I just can't believe it."

"Believe what?"

"That you actually solved this thing. I mean shit, you're a fucking bouncer," Richard said as he stood up out of the chair.

"No, John was a bouncer, I'm Jack," he said, standing up as well.

"Well, it's pretty damn impressive," Richard said.

"So you'll do it?"

Richard stopped halfway down the hallway and turned

back. "Wait, how do you know the packages came by UPS?"

"That part was just dumb luck. There was a UPS truck outside the Ginsberg estate the same day Lauren and I stopped by and Ian was there," Jack explained.

"Okay, but why do you want me to do this?"

"I already explained it all to you. What part do you not understand?"

"I get it. I understand about tracking the packages from Israel. What I don't get is why you want me to do it. The FBI can do all that pretty easily."

"I know they can, but I've got two reasons. Number one, they'll take too fucking long. Getting a warrant and whatever other rules they have to follow."

"I probably can do it faster, no rule following here. And reason number two?" Richard asked.

"Because I want to bust this guy myself."

"Of course, that is the Jack I know. So how quick do you want this info?" Richard asked, looking forward to the challenge.

"How quick can you get it?"

"Actually, I know a guy that got into their system before. I just got to get a hold of him and he'll get me in," Richard said with a grin.

"You know a guy, huh? I guess you guys aren't that anonymous after all," Jack said with a chuckle.

"I didn't say I knew his name. I just know how to get in touch with him, or her," Richard said, smiling back.

"Well, don't let me keep you. Reach out and touch that someone."

"Grab yourself a beer and sit back down, this shouldn't take long," Richard said and headed down the hall to his office.

Jack cracked open a can of Heineken and headed back to the sofa to sit down. Just as he sat down he felt his phone vibrating in his pocket. He put down the beer on the coffee table. As he grabbed the phone from his pants pocket, he noticed out of the corner of his eye that he hadn't used a coaster. Before answering the phone he reached over and grabbed one placing his beer on top. He realized as he did this that he was changing, after all.

He turned his attention back to the phone, wondering if it would be Lauren or Sara, not sure which he would prefer at that moment. As he answered and realized it was neither, he felt like a contestant on that old game show *Let's Make a Deal*, and wondered what was behind door number three. It was Sharla Ginsberg.

"Hello, Agent Shields?" Sharla said, as if she was interrupting something.

"Hello, Sharla," he said, recognizing her voice.

"Are you busy?" she asked.

Just before he could answer, Metallica started to blare from Richard's office.

"Can you hold on a second?" he asked.

It was hard to hear anything else but Jack figured she said "Sure." He stepped outside of the house and closed the door behind him.

"Okay, how can I help you?" he asked, then immediately mentally kicked himself. He sounded like a worker at the Gap like Lauren back in the day. His worry didn't linger long, after what Sharla said next.

"I'd really like to see you."

"Okay, sure, when?" he asked, while pondering her choice of words.

"Tonight." She said it in a way that the short two syllable word sounded more like a short story with a very happy ending.

"Okay," he replied.

He immediately began convincing himself that this was a good idea. He could ask her questions about Ian. It was work related. Then the truth hit him just before the last of the blood in his head flowed to the other part of his body. He just shrugged, considering he wouldn't have this chance after he busted her brother for the bombings. "Where?"

"I'm staying at the Carlyle hotel, room five-twenty-five," she said and then hung up.

Never had there been a hang up that was more welcome. The implication wasn't lost on him. It was anything but rude. Quite the opposite. He rushed back into the house and down to the hall to Richard, who was swinging his head up and down to some other heavy metal song Jack didn't recognize.

"Hey, Richard, I gotta go," he yelled.

"What? Are you sure? Look, I already gotta hold of the guy and he already sent me the back door. I'm almost in. Just give me ten more minutes to get through the fire wall," he said as he turned back to the keyboard.

"Sorry, I really gotta go. Just call me when you find the packages," he said then headed down the hall.

"Okay," Richard said, turning back in his direction but seeing that he was already gone.

CHAPTER 49

Jack got out of the elevator on the fifth floor of the hotel and made his way down the lushly carpeted hallway. He stopped when he reached room five-twenty-five. He held his breath and then rapped on the door with his knuckles.

"If that's you, Jack, come on in," Sharla said from inside.

Jack lowered his hand and grabbed the door knob. When he did, he got a shock from the static electricity picked up along the walk down the hallway. He jerked his hand back. After clenching his fist then shaking his hand, he went at it again. As he opened the door, he was shocked a second time but in a much more pleasurable way. As he looked across the room he found Sharla sitting at the table across the room. She was nude.

"Ahh, hello?" Jack just stood there, this shock having more current than the static kind.

"You wanna close the door behind you, Jack?" Sharla said looking beyond him at the open door.

"Sure," he said awkwardly as he turned and closed the door, taking a deep breath and telling himself to calm down before turning back in her direction.

It was an unsuccessful command since, when he

turned, he saw that Sharla had stood up. Jack had seen many naked women before, and many would qualify as beautiful. Lauren and Sara definitely fit that category. But Sharla deserved a category all her own with a word he couldn't come up with. For that matter, he couldn't come up with any words as he just stood there taking in her picturesque beauty. She stood five foot eight, tanned and toned. Her muscles seemed to all be flexed at the same time, as if every one of them were slowly lifting a weight at the gym. As much as his eyes and other parts of his body wanted to focus on hers, he couldn't help from also looking at her face. Those large eyes and full lips.

They both stood there for a few seconds, as if in a standoff on some small town main street in a western movie at high noon. She drew first.

"You look surprised to see me," she said with a slow smile.

"Well—to see you like that," Jack said, returning his own awkward grin and a slowly lifted point of his right hand in her direction.

"Oh, Jack. I'm a model. You know how many people have seen me naked?"

"I guess a lot," he said with a laugh, releasing some of the nervous energy.

"Yes, and many of whom I didn't even like."

"No?"

"Jack, you I like, so relax. If you want me to put something on I can."

"Hey, as long as you're comfortable."

"I am. Why don't you make yourself more comfortable?" she said as she began to walk toward him.

He struggled to swallow with what little saliva he had in his mouth as she came closer.

"Here, hand me your coat," she said as she stopped right in front of him with her arm out next to him.

He took off his coat and draped it over her outstretched arm. She caressed it down over her arm with her other hand as she turned. She walked back over to the table and laid the coat over the back of the chair. She bent over slightly. As she did, her muscles flexed in that part of Jack's favorite body part on any woman. Sharla stood, turned, and looked at him. She tilted her head and smiled.

"That's better." Then she slowly walked up to him, but kept going, and walked past him toward the bedroom. "That coat sure seems lonely lying there all by itself. Why don't you leave it some company and then come into the bedroom with me?"

If getting undressed was an Olympic event, he would have at least qualified as he kicked off his shoes then began unbuttoning his shirt, almost losing a button or two in the process. He laid the shirt and then his pants over the chair. He heard something buzzing in his coat as he laid his boxers over the chair. He took out the phone and saw that Richard had called him. He shrugged and put the phone on silent. *It can wait.*

He put it back in his coat and turned to go meet Sharla in the bedroom. He wondered how he would look to her as he entered the bedroom since she had left the lights on. This was a woman that was used to other movie stars who kept themselves in good shape. Even some star athletes. Thank god, he'd been working out a little bit for those jogs with Sara. He had a feeling keeping up with Sharla was going to burn just as many calories, but at least in a much more pleasurable, if not less exhausting, way.

Jack found her lying on the bed. "You want me to turn off the lights?"

She was stretched on her side, facing the doorway. Her B-cup breasts were hanging slightly to the side, enough to let him know they were real, but still firm like a teenager's. "No, I'm kind of like a guy in that way. I'm very visual, so I want to see you," she said then she leaned back on her elbows. "Stay there for a second let me get a look at you."

He could tell her eyes were going over his body as he stood up straight and sucked in the little bit of a gut he still had left, even after all the exercise the last few weeks. Damn, Richard and that cafeteria he always wanted to eat at. Jack realized buffets were not for him. Just like with women, he had no will power to hold back. As he followed her gaze, feeling her eyes on him he noticed them being pulled down by something other than gravity. He could tell by the reaction he saw in her eyes that she was impressed. The excitement expressed within the widening of those eyes made him get even larger in return. She bit her lip in anticipation and then pulled the covers over from the side of the bed.

"Come over here," she said curling her finger at him.

After thirty minutes she did, twice.

ഏഏ

Sharla was lying on her back, still catching her breath. It made Jack feel good to find a form of exercise he was better at than his partner. As she breathed in and out Jack watched her stomach move up and down. With each breath, he watched the muscles ripple as if a rock had been thrown into a still pond. He couldn't help but put his hand on them to feel the waves rock under the pressure of his hand. This didn't help her breathing slow. She grabbed his hand and turned onto her side, facing him.

"Jack."

"Yeah?" he said as he lifted his eyes from her body to her face.

"How is the case going?" she asked, causing his own body to shift with a jerk into neutral as if a teenager was at the clutch for the first time.

"Actually, it's going well," he said, hoping she wouldn't press the issue. He put his hand on her hip hoping that would distract her onto other things.

"So you know who killed my father?" she asked excitedly.

Jack rolled away from her onto his back—the car stalled—and stared at the ceiling as he answered her, "Actually, yeah, I think so."

"Was it Steinherz?" she asked, looking down at him.

"You know, he was one of the other victims right?" he asked, confused by her question.

"Oh, yeah, so any other leads? Who's your number one suspect?"

"Do you really want to talk about this right now?" he asked.

"Why not now?"

"I feel like you're some Israeli spy, pumping me for information right now," he said with a chuckle as he leaned back onto his side, took his right hand, and ran it through her curly long hair.

"Well, it's only fair since you've been pumping me all night," she said, laughing and falling onto her back.

"Well, you didn't seem to have any complaints."

"No, I don't. But I will if you don't start talking," she said, propping herself up again.

"Okay, but this will change the mood a bit," he said as he propped himself up on both elbows as well.

She sat up. "I'm a big girl, Jack, spill it."

Jack did the same. He knew after he told her there wouldn't be a round three.

"We know who killed your dad," he said then paused, waiting for her reaction.

"Who?" she said, leaning in.

"It was him."

"I'm confused. Who do you mean?"

"I'm saying it was your dad. He killed himself."

"What? How did you figure that out?" she asked, then she sat straight up, looking at him in shock.

His attention drawn only to the intense stare coming from those blue eyes. "Well, our first clue was that he was in Florida and had access to the computer that sent the first threat. Ian was with him," Jack began, explaining.

"Wait a minute. Ian knew about this?" she asked, putting a hand on his arm.

Her hand felt like a tourniquet on his bicep as she leaned down on him. "Actually, no he didn't know about your dad. He just found out himself," he said as he grabbed her hand and pulled it loose from his arm before he lost all feeling in it.

"What did Ian say about it?" she asked.

"He didn't believe us at first."

"Well, that I can understand, because what I don't understand is why my father would kill himself. It doesn't make sense why he would do that. He was in the middle of saving his bank. In fact, he just did with that deal he closed in Florida," she said as she began breathing hard again.

"Well, it actually makes perfect sense when you know that he was dying, anyway," he said, waiting for her reaction.

"What do you mean, anyway?"

"He had cancer and he was told by his doctor he was dying. Probably only had a month or two left, anyway. He couldn't save himself but he could save his legacy, his bank. He just needed time. It seems he figured his death, if it caused an investigation in this way, would give him the time he needed."

"It worked," she said softly staring up as if looking for her dad watching down on her.

"Yes, it did. I'm surprised your familiar with all this. I didn't think the family business interested you," Jack said looking at her with concern now.

"Not the business, but my family always interests me."

"Well, I do have a bit of other family news to share with you, but it's going to upset you," Jack said as he pondered for a second if he really should tell her now.

"Worse than what you already shared about my father?" she asked.

"Yes, I'm afraid so."

"What?" she asked.

"We think it's your brother Ian who is the one behind the other bombings," Jack said, bracing himself for her response and wishing he were in a bomb shelter.

She bolted upright and crossed her legs. "Ian? Are you crazy? What makes you say that?"

"Well, to be honest, we first thought he was the one who killed your dad, until we found out he killed himself."

"Why would you think that? He adored our father," she said with more than a hint of anger.

"Well, he had the motive, taking over after his death. He also had the knowledge in making bombs, with his training in the Israeli military."

"Okay, but you just said that he didn't kill our dad, that he killed himself. So how do you know that he killed the other CEOs,"

"Well, we don't know for sure but we are looking into something that will let us know." Jack was regretting his decision to tell her.

"What is that?" she said as she started to slide to the edge of the bed and put her feet on the floor.

"Well, when we asked how his dad would have got the bomb making materials, he explained rather easily how he would have had them shipped from a friend of his in Israel," Jack explained as he too sat up, putting one leg on the floor taking her cue.

"Rudolf Hirsch," she said rather casually.

"Yes, that's the name he gave us," Jack said.

"What does that prove?"

"Well, nothing, unless—" he started.

"Unless what?" she snapped.

"Unless the shipments were still coming after Mikal's death. We are looking for those shipments now. I'm sorry," Jack said as she turned away, clearly upset, walking to the bathroom.

"I think you should leave now," she said and closed the door.

Jack had to pick up his coat that he had laid on top of

the rest of his clothes on the chair. As he did, the phone fell out and landed on the floor. He bent down and picked it up with his right hand as his left was still holding his coat. He glanced at it not intending to check messages until he saw that he had thirteen missed calls, all from Richard. He saw there was a voice mail and the high number of calls had him too curious to resist.

He typed in his code when prompted.

"Jack, it's Richard. You were right there were more shipments, from the same guy in Israel going to the Ginsberg estate. But they weren't addressed to Ian. They were being shipped to Sharla Ginsberg!"

Jack was too into what he had just learned that he didn't hear the gun being cocked behind him. He didn't have time to hear the shot go off, either, like he had imagined when at the race track a few weeks back. Everything just went black...

CHAPTER 50

Jack stirred and slowly awoke at the sound of the beeping alarm clock. He was still tired and didn't want to wake up. He couldn't shut out the noise, but he kept his eyes shut. He reflected back to the crazy dream he had. A twin brother, the Secret Service, beautiful women. At least it was one of *those* kind of dreams, he thought as he started to fully awaken. He realized even before opening his eyes that it was bright out. He must have slept a little long since the sun was clearly shining brightly into his room.

As he slowly lifted his eyelids, his vision was blurred. Even so, he could still see the light shining down at him from above.

That doesn't look right. He stared at it, confused as his eyes adjusted to the light and the pain it caused. He lifted his arms to rub his eyes.

Jack didn't notice the IV cord hanging from his arm until it hit him in the cheek as he rubbed his eyes with his fists. He backed his hands from his face using them to block the light above and saw the cord. He grabbed at the cord attached to his right arm and held it with his left hand. Then he turned onto his side and saw that the beeping wasn't, in fact, coming from an alarm clock but from his own heartbeat.

He watched as the light bounced up and down on the screen. He hadn't gone to med school like his brother, but he knew that was a good sign.

It wasn't a dream. He smiled. *Good, I hate stories that end like that.* Of course, he wasn't exactly sure how this one had ended. Like how he got here for that matter. As he looked from the heart monitor toward the door, he heard a noise like a dog growling, which couldn't be the case in a hospital room. Jack turned his head in the direction of the noise and found Richard slumped in a chair. He was asleep—Jack could tell by the snoring—with a book in his lap.

"Hey, Richard!" he yelled, as best he could with his dry throat.

"What?" Richard said as he shook himself awake and looked toward the door, thinking one of the nurses or doctors had walked into the room. When he realized no one was standing there and the door was closed, he adjusted himself in the chair and reached for the book in his lap. After opening the book, he felt the spittle on the edge of his mouth and wiped it off with the back of his hand.

He started reading.

"Must not be that good of a book if it keeps putting you to sleep," Jack said to him from the bed.

"It's actually really good—" Richard started to answer before even looking up. Then he recognized even that severely dehydrated scratchy version of Jack's voice. He jumped up out of the chair, letting the hard cover book slam loudly on the floor.

"Oh my god, you're awake!" Richard yelled.

"What else you got, master of the obvious?" Jack asked with a grin, even though it hurt as he said it.

Richard just stared at him as if still in disbelief of his own eyes and ears. "I gotta tell the nurse," he said out loud as if Jack wasn't in the room. He looked for the call button next to the bed.

"Hey, I'm not going anywhere for a while," Jack said,

gesturing to the IV stuck in his arm. "What's the rush?"

Richard stopped reaching for the button. "Jack, you don't understand."

"You are right about that. I have no idea how I got here. Why don't we start there? Let the nurse wait till after you fill me in."

"Okay, I gotta sit down." Richard sat back in the chair, his eyes not leaving Jack as if worried if he took his eyes off of him he would be gone again. "What's the last thing you remember?"

"Oh, you're going to ask me questions? Well, if that's the case, can you get me a cup of water?"

"Sure." Richard quickly, and somewhat nervously, jumped back to his feet. He walked to the sink by the door and filled a paper cup with water. He placed it on the tray next to Jack's bed. "Here you go," he said then went back to his chair and sat down.

Jack picked up the cup and took a sip. It hurt as if swallowing razor blades but he was too thirsty to stop. "Ugh, my throat's killing me," he said as he put the cup back on the tray.

"Okay, speaking of killing you, let's just start there. Sharla tried to kill you," Richard said, a tinge of anger in his voice.

Jack's eyes widened as they darted toward Richard from the cup he just put down. "You asked me what the last thing I remembered was and now you're kind of ruining that memory for me. I was with Sharla, that's the last thing I remember, but when I say with her I mean—"

"I know what you mean, Jack, you were naked when we found you," Richard said cutting him off, still excited by his being awake.

"We?" Jack asked.

"Yes, Lauren and me."

"Great," Jack said and rolled his eyes.

"Yeah, but you weren't in the bedroom, you were in the living area. Do you remember what you were doing or what she said to you?" Richard asked, as he leaned forward in his chair.

"She didn't say anything, I was getting ready to leave. I had just told her about her brother. That we suspected him. She got upset and asked me to leave."

"That's it?" Richard said, falling back in his chair.

"Well, yeah. I was going to get dressed after she went in the bathroom. Then I saw that you had called, a bunch. So I listened to the voicemail," Jack explained then paused as his memory came in more clearly. "You said you had found the shipments. That we were right. They *were* coming from Israel." Another pause, then he continued, "But they weren't for Ian, they were for Sharla."

Richard just sat there nodding at him.

"Sharla did it," Jack said, the realization showing on his face. "She was the one getting revenge for her father. She didn't know that he was dying. I remember when I told her she had the same reaction as Ian. Then I mentioned that we were looking into the shipments. She knew we would find them going to her. So it wasn't Ian."

"Nope," Richard said. "She served in the Israeli militarily too, conscription they call it. They all have to serve. Of course, she's the one that studied explosives."

"So it wasn't like father like son, it was like father like daughter," Jack said. "So what happened?"

"She shot you, Jack."

"Where?"

"Nowhere important, just the back of your head. I always say, beauty over brains, and you still have your looks," Richard said and smiled.

"Shit, Richard." Jack just stared at him, contemplating his good fortune. "So how many times?"

"Just once. Lauren and I were just outside the room when we heard the shot. I kicked in the door and Lauren was right behind me with her gun drawn already."

"Lauren shot her?" Jack said, surprised.

"Multiple times."

"Is she dead?"

"No, but she won't be doing any more modeling or acting anytime soon. Well, unless they put on a production in the Federal prison she's in. She recovered quicker than you."

"How long have I been under?" Jack asked with a fear common in coma patients of the answer.

"It's been four months, Jack," Richard said as calmly as he could, hoping he wouldn't upset him to the point that his heart rate would go up. If it did, he wouldn't have to push the button to call the nurse.

"Four *months*?" Jack yelled, then grabbed at his throat that felt as if it had just split open.

"Easy, Jack, do you need me to call the nurse?" Richard said as he got up from his chair, leaning toward the call button.

"No," Jack said, gesturing with one hand at Richard to stop, as he grabbed the cup of water with the other. He took another sip, but swallowed slowly this time. "So I've been in a coma."

"Yep."

"Just like Lofton."

"Yeah, he's just down the hall," Richard said, pointing toward the door.

"Still?" Jack said, surprised.

"Yep, Todd comes to see him all the time."

"He ever stop in here?" Jack asked with a grimace, not sure which answer would piss him off more.

"Every once in a while, more often early on, especially when Sara was in here."

"Figures," Jack said, while Richard gave him a frustrated look as if he didn't want to tell him something.

"What?" Jack asked pressing him.

"Well, I don't want to upset you."

"Don't tell me, really," Jack said, already figuring it out.

"Yes, they're back together. You were in this coma. She was sad and vulnerable, and look, so was he, about his dad. It's your fault when you think about it. Finding you that way didn't help her feel any loyalty to you," Richard tried to explain, as if that would help.

"No, I guess not. So how did you find me?"

"Lopez. He saw you go into the hotel. He was standing outside Ian's room and saw you go into Sharla's across the hall. He knew she was staying there since they picked both of them up from the airport when they flew into town. I guess he's not that fond of Lauren and sent her a text earlier that night that you were with Sharla, just to rub it in," Richard said with a shrug.

"No, they're not friends," Jack said, thinking back to the last time they ran into Lopez together at Mikal's home.

"Well, when I couldn't reach you I called Lauren to give her a heads up on what I had found and asked if she knew where you were. Luckily, it was right after she got that text. Lopez saved your life."

"So was Lauren upset about me being there like that?"

"Well, yeah, at first. She comes to see you quite often. She told me about how she had pushed you away and you didn't owe her anything."

"I guess me almost dying kind of softened her up a bit," Jack said with a sigh.

"Well, I wouldn't bet on it. Half the time she curses at you to wake up. Say's it's so she can punch you as soon as you do," Richard said with a chuckle.

"Shit! Speaking of bets. I have a feeling me almost dying probably cost Charlie his life. He needed that money I was going to get him," Jack said, sitting up.

"Hey, relax, calm down. Lauren took care of that. She picked up your coat that night after the ambulance took you to the hospital. She saw the envelope with the money and told me she had to deliver it to a friend of yours, I imagine that was Charlie," Richard said.

"Boy, she saved two people's lives that night. I'm really in her debt now. Good thing I'm not Jewish or I'd have to marry that girl."

"Ah, Jack, about that."

"What?"

"Well, since I finished my last project and this case I was helping you with was over, I've had some time to go back to researching your history."

"Yeah, so?" Jack said.

"I did some more digging about your mom and well— You're Jewish, Jack."

"I am?"

"Yep, your mom's real name was Josephine Weinstein. I still haven't found your dad, so you're technically still a bastard, but you might very well be Lauren's *bashert* after all," Richard said with a big grin on his face.

"Great, now I've got another secret I've got to keep from her, at least for now. Okay, Richard?"

Richard nodded. After a minute of silence, he realized the book was still lying on the floor. He bent down from his chair and picked it up.

"So what's that book you're reading?" Jack asked him, gesturing toward it.

"Oh, yeah, this," he said, holding it up next to himself to show Jack." Some kid came by here about a month ago and dropped this off for you. He said he wrote it. It's actually pretty good," Richard said, handing it to him.

"Holy shit, the kid actually got published," Jack said as he took the book and looked at the cover. "*Gridlock*," he said, reading the cover aloud. He opened it up and read the inscription made out to him. Jack then flipped to the back cover since the signature the kid signed with was impossible to read.

"So that's his name."

EPILOGUE

After three weeks of rehab, Jack was ready to leave the hospital. Richard came to pick him up. He figured he'd do so in Jack's car which he had parked outside.

"Do you think you can handle driving home?" Richard asked as they exited the hospital and walked up to the black Lincoln.

"Yeah, I think so," Jack said.

Richard tossed him the keys which he caught with ease.

"Okay, you look ready. If you had missed, I would have taken a cab home instead of riding with you, just in case. I've spent enough time in this hospital, although it has been good for my diet," Richard said as he grabbed his now-less-protruding belly.

Jack hit the unlock button on the keys and opened his door. "You do look like you've lost a few pounds."

About a minute after they had gotten buckled in, Jack was still sitting in the driver's seat just staring forward. Then he started to laugh.

"What's so funny?" Richard asked him smiling since Jack's laugh had spread his emotion to him even though he wasn't sure why he was laughing.

"Well, I'm no brain surgeon and I didn't go to med

school like my brother but I think I know what part of the brain that bullet was lodged in.

"Oh please do tell. I gotta hear this quick before I give you a few guesses. You're making this one too hard for me not to mess with you and I promised myself I'd go easy on you for a while," Richard said, struggling to keep his mouth quiet.

"Memory," Jack said while still looking forward with his hands on the wheel and the car idling.

"What makes you say that?" Richard asked, looking at him.

"Because I don't remember how to get home," he said and looked at Richard with a grin.

"Oh, that's okay, you've got GPS. Here," Richard said as he turned it on. "She'll remember how to get you home." He began to scroll down the list of preset destinations while Jack watched. Then he abruptly stopped and took his hand away. They both looked at each other.

"Does that say Dad?" Jack asked.

"Yes it does," Richard said, looking up from the screen at Jack.

Then they both turned back to the screen.

Jack's hand came up and pushed the button on the screen, selecting it. The sultry woman's voice came on, "Calculating."

⌒⌒⌒

Jack had followed the directions she gave. The whole time neither he or Richard spoke a word as if not wanting to interrupt her.

"Turn left. Destination two hundred yards ahead."

They entered a plush neighborhood and made their way slowly down the street lined with huge multi-million dollar homes. Jack and Richard shared a few glances at each other between ogling the large magnificent-looking homes.

"You have reached your destination," she said.

Jack pulled up to the curb. He sat and stared for a minute with his foot on the brake as if unsure what to do next. Then he put the car in park and turned the key and let the engine die. There was a *For Sale* sign out front. Mazyck Realty, one of the top guys in DC. The guy wouldn't be caught dead with one of his signs planted in front of a house not worth at least two million. This just piqued their interest even more. They both continued to stare, not saying anything for a minute.

"Wait here," Richard said as he got out and closed the door behind him.

He looked around as he walked up to the sign. He fixed his shirt as he walked toward it as if trying better to look like he belonged in this neighborhood. The sign had one of those tubes underneath with fliers describing the home. Richard looked around nervously, first when he reached it and then quickly grabbed one of the fliers from the tube. He uncurled it and looked at it. Jack watched as he did it.

He saw Richard's face turn into a picture of surprise. That look reminded Jack of how he must have looked when he read the ending to one of his favorite books. *Primal Fear* by William Diehl. Richard curled it back up and looked around again, glancing toward the home. Then he came back to the car. He opened the door and got in. He closed the door and just sat there, shaking his head.

"What?" Jack asked, boiling over with anticipation.

Richard looked at him and then back at the house through his window.

"Well, do you know who's house it is or not?" Jack asked, almost angry this time.

Richard looked down at the curled up flier in his hand then over at Jack.

"Well, the guy that owns it doesn't live here anymore. He's already moved out," Richard said, nervously turning back to look back at the house.

"How do you know he's already moved out?" Jack

asked still put off by Richard's dragging this out.

"Because I know where the guy moved to," Richard said, still looking at the house.

"And where is that?" Jack asked, at the same time that Richard turned back again and handed him the flier. Jack uncurled it and looked down at the name on the flier as Richard answered him.

"The White House."

About the Author

Mark Petry lives in Texas. He writes mystery & suspense thrillers. He's a member of International Thriller Writers. *Secret Service* is his second novel.

His website is www.markpetry.com

21147261R00183

Made in the USA
San Bernardino, CA
10 May 2015